ALMOST AMISH

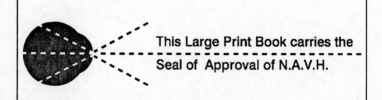

This Large Print Book carries the
Seal of Approval of N.A.V.H.

ALMOST AMISH

KATHRYN CUSHMAN

THORNDIKE PRESS
A part of Gale, Cengage Learning

Detroit • New York • San Francisco • New Haven, Conn • Waterville, Maine • London

GALE
CENGAGE Learning

Thorndike Press, a part of Gale, Cengage Learning.

LIBRARY OF CONGRESS CATALOGING-IN-PUBLICATION DATA

Cushman, Kathryn.
  Almost Amish / by Kathryn Cushman.
     pages ; cm. — (Thorndike Press large print Christian fiction)
  ISBN-13: 978-1-4104-5324-2 (hardcover)
  ISBN-10: 1-4104-5324-3 (hardcover)
  1. Self-realization in women—Fiction. 2. Amish—Fiction. 3.
Tennessee—Fiction. 4. Large type books. I. Title.
PS3603.U825A76 2013
813'.6—dc23   2012036550

Published in 2013 by arrangement with Bethany House Publishers, a
division of Baker Publishing Group

Printed in Mexico
1 2 3 4 5 6 7 17 16 15 14 13

Kristyn Krutenat

You are the heart and soul
of so many wonderful things,
yet you are never out front,
never in the limelight,
always behind the scenes.
It is to you, and women like you,
that I dedicate this book.

Grace Griffin

Mama Griffin, you exemplified
simple living. Holidays at your home
were never full of gourmet food, fine
china, or gleaming silver. Still, sitting on
the floor in your tiny living room,
surrounded by love, is among the
happiest memories of my childhood.

Melanie Cushman

Watching you battle through
so much illness with a smile on
your face causes me to grieve for
families who live in misery because
of the pressure to keep up and outdo.
Goals like "live through this" and
"find relief from constant pain"
have a way of putting these things
in perspective. You are my hero.

PROLOGUE

The cupcakes drooped like wilted daisies. Instead of the nice rounded tops shown in the recipe book, they leaned left. Or right. And a few managed to sag both ways at once.

Julie Charlton carried the tray into the junior high's multipurpose room, purposely keeping her eyes averted from her frosted nightmare. She had put so much time and effort into these. Why did her baking never turn out right, especially when she was under pressure? Especially now, with the semiformal eighth-grade parent-child dance only hours away?

Scores of balloons hovered at the ceiling, dangling red, black, and white ribbons in festive chaos. Streamers formed graceful arches against the walls; glitter sparkled on the windowsills. Everything looked festive, and intentional, and flawless. Everything except for Julie's cupcakes. She looked

7

around the room to see who might be there, but saw no one. "Hello?"

Nothing but silence.

What luck. Julie could at least drop these off and escape without having to acknowledge the debacle of flour, sugar, and eggs that had taken hours of her morning. She carried her load over to the food table, which was draped in a black tablecloth with a gold lamé runner, and placed the cupcakes as far away as possible from the crystal pedestal at the end of the table. She knew that Colleen's famous chocolate cake would be highlighted there before the beginning of this evening's soiree. Not one single inch of fondant would be out of place, and it would be displayed in all its splendor for the eighth graders and their parents to admire and devour. Meanwhile, her misshapen little cupcakes would hide at the far end of the table, hoping no one noticed them.

She hurried back to her car, thankful that at least one thing had gone right this morning. Now, she needed to get over to the high school for the meeting of the financial committee and could only hope no one would notice the chocolate frosting stain on her spreadsheet. She'd known it was a bad idea to balance the volleyball team's bank account and bake at the same time, but both things were due this morning. What other choice was there?

She glanced down at her watch. 10:30 A.M. Forty-five minutes until the meeting. Maybe she could run home for just a few minutes. She'd left the kitchen a complete wreck. By now, cupcake batter and frosting were likely dried onto every available counter, cupboard, and backsplash. She needed to get started on the cleanup.

No. There wasn't time.

Yet if she drove straight to the school now, she'd be there half an hour early. A wave of exhaustion flowed over her, making her wish for a pillow and a blanket. How was she going to make it through today?

As she drove past the movie theater, she saw the answer in all of its green and white glory.

Starbucks.

Minutes later, Julie sat at a small window table, enjoying her tall fat-free double-shot latte. By the sixth sip, she could feel the caffeine start to slowly filter energy into her body. She leaned back and simply savored one of her favorite pastimes: people watching. How long had it been since she'd taken the time to do this?

A couple of women entered, talking back and forth at a rapid pace, complaining about a coworker who apparently messed up a report. Julie recognized them both as mothers from the junior high that Brian attended. Would they be at The Soiree this evening, eating ugly cupcakes and wondering what kind of terrible mother could possibly have the lack of pride to bring these things? No, these women would definitely go for Colleen's sculpture of a cake — or perhaps broccoli and carrots with fat-free ranch.

Both women were bone thin, sleeveless silk blouses showing off their toned arms. Tailored pants and heels, perfect accessories. It must be so nice to wear pretty clothes like that every day. Julie looked down at her jeans, T-shirt, and sneakers and sighed. Still, she was truly thankful for the gift of being able to stay home with her family.

She took another sip and looked at her watch. Time to go. The financial meeting would last an hour; then she needed to stop by Thomas's office to help his secretary plan the company barbeque, make a quick stop at the grocery and the pharmacy, then home to a kitchen that would be covered in something like chocolate cement. Hopefully she could get it scrubbed off before picking up Brian from chess club. After that it would be time to cook dinner and fight with Whitney about homework.

Julie walked past the businesswomen, now standing at the counter getting napkins. As she passed by, she heard one of them say to the other, "Wouldn't it be nice if we got to wear comfy clothes and lounge around Starbucks all day?"

That's when the thought that had been residing in pieces throughout Julie's mind finally came together and crystallized into one cohesive and indelible truth. She made it to her car and simply sat for a moment, trying to get the energy, or desire, to keep moving.

She pulled a tube of lipstick out of her purse, then looked at the tired, middle-aged woman staring back at her in the rearview mirror. It was more than obvious that the haggard reflection felt the same way she did, so there was no reason not to give it voice. "I hate my life."

There, she'd said it. The words hung heavy in the air, each syllable clogging her lungs with the toxic truth.

Hate.

My life.

Likely, it had been true for longer than she'd even realized. For just one fraction of a second, Julie turned the key and considered driving in the opposite direction — leaving behind all she'd known and starting fresh in some new, exciting location. Somewhere with fewer demands and less under-appreciated drudgery.

The thought lasted only until a flash vision of her family pulled her back — Whitney's brows knit together as she waded through her own heavy load of school and activities . . . Brian's earnest face as he explained the newest asteroid discovery in deep space and puzzled over bullies at school . . . the lines of exhaustion on Thomas's face after a hard day at work. They needed her. They needed her support. Who was she to whine about being unhappy? She drove toward the high school, ashamed for even having the thought.

Still, those were the words that echoed through her head, giving her the courage to act, when later that evening her sister-in-law Susan rushed over with an unbelievable request.

"Julie, I've got this *amazing* opportunity, but you've got to help me. . . ."

Was it love for Susan or her own need to escape that made her answer yes? Even in the aftermath, Julie would never be completely certain.

CHAPTER 1

"We're going live in five, four, three, two, one." As the countdown culminated, the audience did as they were instructed and began to clap wildly, as if this moment was the greatest in their lives. An overhead camera swooped forward, and two camera-men walked through the aisles, pausing at anyone who caught their interest.

"Welcome back, everyone." Lisa Lee stood in the middle of the set, smiling and nodding her appreciation of the applause. The curls in her long black hair bounced with every move she made, framing her face with the same perkiness that permeated every-thing about her. "I've got some people I'd like for you all to meet, but first, there is exciting news to share." She gestured toward a large video screen behind her. "Last year we did a three-month segment called *Going Almost Blue Blood.* Do y'all remember that? Did you enjoy it?" The audience went wild with their cheers as the video screens behind Lisa Lee lit up with snippets from last year showing a middle-class family being placed amid some of New York society's elite destinations, hideaways, and social events.

The host nodded, her perfect smile welcoming and friendly as always. "We enjoyed doing that, so we thought we'd try again, but this time, we're going to try something just a little different. Everyone on our staff, myself included, is always talking about how busy our lives are, how we don't have time to do the things that are really important to us. Can anyone out there relate?" She held out both arms, hands upturned, gesturing toward her audience. Applause, vigorous head nods, and all-out whooping came from the mostly female audience.

"Well, here's the deal." Lisa took a seat on a high stool just in front of her cooktop. "We were trying to think of a series we could do on simplification, and how it might work. One of the hairstylists on the show is a big fan of Amish fiction — and she was talking one morning about how wonderful that lifestyle sounded to her. And it got me think-*ing* . . ." She almost sang the last word, as she was known to do when excited about something. She looked toward the backstage and motioned with her hands. "Okay, y'all come on out here."

Julie's knees shook as she took each step onto the stage . . . onto national television. She'd been watching everything unfold on a monitor and now followed her sister-in-law out into the lights, taking her exact place on stage, just as she'd been instructed. Her kids came to stand in front of her, as they'd rehearsed, and she put a hand on each of their shoulders, per plan.

It was really happening.

Lisa Lee moved closer and put her hand on Susan's shoulder. "This is Susan Reynolds. I'm sure you all remember her from the occasional cooking features she has done on my show, and this is her daughter, Angie. How old are you, Angie?"

"Seventeen."

Lisa Lee then moved over to Julie. "This is Susan's sister-in-law, Julie, and her daughter, Whitney, and son, Brian. And you two are how old?"

"Sixteen." Whitney's voice projected loud and strong, showing not a bit of fear.

"Thirteen." Brian's voice was barely audible.

Lisa continued. "We're using some extended family for this scenario, because extended family is very important in the

Amish culture." She smiled again. "So we're sending this lovely family to spend the summer in Tennessee, near an actual Amish community. They will live without cars, television, or even — can you imagine? — *cell phones,* for the entire time." The audience began to "ooh" and "aah" over this. "They're not completely roughing it. They'll have a few modern conveniences *most* of the time, like air-conditioning and a refrigerator — and they will also have indoor bathrooms." She held up a hand beside her mouth and pretended to be whispering a secret to her audience. "That one was their main condition before agreeing to do this."

The studio audience laughed appreciatively. Lisa covered her mouth and giggled, in a display of cuteness that had made audiences around the world love her. "Each week they'll have a different challenge — to accomplish a task or work through an issue that the Amish face on a daily basis. By the end of this season, we'll just see if the Amish way of life is really all that simpler than our lives today, or whether it's just complicated in a different way. What do you think?" She smiled broadly. "Who thinks this might be our best idea yet?"

The audience went wild with applause.

Julie thought she might throw up.

16

■ ■ ■ ■

Julie sat numbly in the green room, her mind going over and over the last hour. She thought they'd done well enough, not that any of them had done anything but stand there and smile.

"Wow, look at all this hardware." Whitney stood next to a shelf full of awards and plaques. "If the Lisa Lee show is really this good, how is it I've never even heard of it before?" She picked up a crystal trophy and turned it over in her hands. "This thing is heavy."

"Whitney, put that down." Susan, who had been pacing back and forth, rushed over. "The last thing we need is for you to break something." Then, as if suddenly realizing she might have sounded too harsh, she offered a not-quite-believable smile. "And I'm guessing most girls your age don't watch too many lifestyle shows. That's why you've never heard of it."

"I guess." Whitney set the trophy back on the shelf and shrugged.

The door to the green room opened and Lisa Lee walked in, followed by one of her assistants — a pretty young blonde. Lisa hurried over to Susan, arms outstretched, and drew her into a hug. "Great job." She looked around the room. "Great job, everyone. The audience was just eating you up. I think this is going to be our most interesting segment yet, don't you, Jane?"

The blonde looked up from the clipboard in her hands. "I do."

"Now, kids" — Lisa looked around — "how would you like a tour of the studio? I'm pretty sure Taylor Swift is making a guest appearance on the talk show filming next door. You want to go watch?"

"Yes!" Angie and Whitney hugged each other and jumped up and down.

"Sounds interesting." Brian's words were controlled and even, but Julie suspected that even he was considering joining the girls in their Snoopy dance.

"Great. We've got a little bit of behind-the-scenes interviewing to do with your mother and aunt. Jane is going to take you around the studio. It shouldn't take us terribly long."

"Don't hurry on our account." Whitney skipped her way to the door, before returning to grab her younger brother by the arm. "Hurry up. We're going to see Taylor Swift."

The kids all made a collective squealing sound as they disappeared out the door. Jane giggled and followed them out.

18

"All right." Lisa's dimples seemed to glow in her ever-smiling face. "Now that the kids are gone, I'll take you to your next assignment, your first sit-down interview. Follow me."

She led them down a long hall, stopping about halfway to open a door. Lisa tilted her head toward the small conference room inside. "Julie, this is your stop."

"We're not doing this together?" She looked toward Susan, silently begging her to do something.

"For now, you'll be separate," Lisa said quite casually. "Have a seat right here, and the producer will be in shortly. Would you like some coffee, water, anything?"

"No, thank you."

The door shut with a click, but to Julie it sounded more like the clanging lock of a prison holding cell. She stared at the door, awaiting the arrival of the executioner. How many ways were there to say something stupid on national television? "Get a grip, Julie." She ran her fingers through her hair. "Stop being so melodramatic. It will be fine." Speaking the words aloud helped, if only a little.

The door opened and a tall man entered the room. His head was shaved smooth, and he wore an obviously expensive golf shirt and khaki pants on his wiry frame. Every step he took exuded a quiet confidence that most people would envy. "Hello. I'm Jim Waters, one of the producers." He smiled in a relaxed, friendly way, and soon they were making small talk.

Julie was thankful that he'd decided to warm up without cameras or other people in the room. It did help relax her quite a bit. By the time they were ready to get down to business, perhaps she would be able to think straight.

"What do you hope to gain from your time on the farm?" he asked, shifting the conversation a bit. It was a question Julie had been asking herself all throughout the prior days.

"I'm here to help Susan. So I'm just hoping to avoid messing things up for her." She tried to smile but was too nervous to completely pull it off.

"I know you're here because of her. But surely, there must be something you are hoping to get from this experience?"

Julie thought for a moment. What did she hope to gain?

What she most hoped was to find a reason to believe that something about her life was worthwhile — or more correctly, a reason that she might want to return home when it was over. *Perhaps there's more truth than necessary in that answer.* "I'm mostly looking forward to slowing down and enjoying my kids. Our lives are so fast-paced that we often do little more than pass each other on the way in or out."

He nodded. "My wife says the same thing about our family. Especially with kids in sports."

"Exactly." Julie could feel the tension melting from her body. She was so thankful to have a producer who at least understood what she was saying.

"What do you most hope your sister-in-law will gain from this experience?"

"I'm hoping it will help launch her career to the next level. It means so much to her, and she really does deserve it."

"That's what we're all hoping." He smiled and nodded as he leaned forward on his elbows. "But I mean, other than that, what do you hope she learns from the experience?"

Julie thought about that one for a moment, then decided to stick with the safest, and most obvious, answer. "Well . . . I guess I'm hoping that she learns to relax a little."

"Type A, huh?"

"Definitely." Julie thought about the last couple of years. "Honestly, I don't know how she does all that she does. She's pretty amazing."

"Why is it I feel like there's a 'but' to that statement?" He grinned in a conspiratorial manner.

"She can be a bit uptight." Julie supposed there was no reason to deny the obvious. "She pushes her daughter pretty hard, too."

Jim laughed. "Gotcha. My sister is just like that." He started a story about her that sounded exactly like Susan when the door opened. Julie looked up, expecting to see a film crew. Instead, she saw Susan and another woman. Thank goodness! They had decided to let them do this together, after all.

Jim offered his hand across the table. "It was really nice talking with you, Julie."

"You too." She shook his hand.

"Okay, ladies, now that we're all done, we'll see if we can find out where your kids are and get you caught up with them." Jim started toward the door.

"But our interviews. Aren't you going to film them?" Susan asked, taking the question right out of Julie's mouth.

"Oh, they were filmed. There are several cameras in the conference rooms back here. Don't worry, we got it all."

Julie held her breath. She would never

have been quite as free with her stories or frank with her answers if she'd had any idea she was being filmed. She looked toward Susan, wondering if she should apologize in advance or just hope that they cut a lot of what she'd said.

Then she saw Susan's face. Her expression of horror left little doubt that apologies might be needed from both directions. Julie didn't think she wanted to know what had been said in the other room. In fact, she was certain of it.

CHAPTER 2

Susan spooned the balsamic reduction sauce over the pork chops, then created an arc of sauce around the edge of the plate for effect. The color of the julienne vegetables made the perfect complement to the plate, as did the hint of couscous peeking from beneath the chops. A couple sprigs of rosemary across the top added the final touch to the presentation. She took a deep breath, stomach churning, and carried the plates into the dining room.

"Wow, even for you, this looks amazing. You've really outdone yourself." James sat in his usual chair, the soft glow of the candles washing his face in an amber light.

"I hope you enjoy it." She set the plates on the table, knowing that she most certainly would not.

She pulled the knife slowly across the meat, gathering her thoughts, waiting for the perfect time. But how did one find the perfect moment for a conversation like this?

"Delicious." James put the fork in his mouth, and suddenly Susan could bear the taste of unspoken words no longer.

"Who is she?"

"Mrs. Reynolds, you nodding off on me there?"

Susan jerked awake, and it took her a moment to realize where she was. Her face burned as she looked up toward the hairdresser. "I'm so sorry."

The girl waved her hand dismissively. "Not to worry. Lots of people get sleepy when they're getting their hair done. I don't take it personally. Come to think of it, I don't take much personally."

Two years ago, Susan might have made the same statement. That, of course, was before she'd asked the question whose answer changed everything.

"This is where you get out." The man behind the wheel of the black Suburban pulled to the side of the dirt road and motioned his head toward the passenger door. It was only the second time Julie had heard his voice since beginning this journey almost two hours ago.

"You can't be serious." She looked toward

the driver, waiting for the punch line. His black wraparound sunglasses made it difficult to read any kind of expression, but the firm set of his jaw showed no hint of a smile. Julie glanced toward the backseat.

Whitney's blue eyes were huge, and she shook her head in small, quick snaps. Brian's mouth was open, but he managed to stab Julie with an "I told you this was a bad idea" expression.

Not for the first time today, Julie wished that Thomas had come with them. He would know how to handle this. But Thomas wasn't here, and her kids needed her to summon up some courage and stand up right now. "You can't just leave us here." Her voice wobbled, betraying any pretense of authority she hoped to convey.

"Sure I can. Haven't you ever watched reality TV before? This is what happens."

"We're in the middle of nowhere, and we have no idea where to go from here." She looked out the window for any sign of life — a farmhouse, another car, anything. There was nothing but rolling green hills dotted with a couple dozen cows on the right and a crop of . . . something green and leafy . . . to her left.

The driver pointed slightly behind his left shoulder. "You see that mailbox back there?

That's yours. Your new home is down that dirt drive a ways. Start walking. You'll find it."

"Then you need to drive us to the house." Julie managed to at least keep her tone even this time. "Otherwise, I'll have to report you to the producers."

"Mrs. Charlton, the producers are the ones who told me to drop you here."

"Oh."

There must have been a more intelligent response, but at the moment, it eluded her.

"How far?" Whitney had her arms crossed across her chest and was leaning back hard into her seat. No self-respecting teenaged girl was going to take off walking down a dirt road without at least a hint of a fight.

"You'll find out when you get there. Now get moving. We've all got a schedule to keep."

Julie grasped the door handle but couldn't bring herself to pull it just yet. "I . . . uh . . . what about our things?"

He reached down and pulled the release. "Back's open. Now, you've got sixty seconds to get your stuff out of there before I drive away and take it with me."

The entire car shook with the force of Whitney's door flying open. Before Julie had even processed what was happening, Whitney was at the back pulling out her duffel and backpack.

Julie opened her door a bit more reluctantly. "Come on, Brian, get your things. You don't want to lose your telescope, now do you?"

Once again the car shook. "Hurry up, Whitney, my telescope's more important than your stupid old shoes."

"Shows what you know." Whitney didn't look at her brother, but she did reach in and pull out the hard telescope case and hand it back to him, soon followed by his bag. "Hey, what about our . . ." Instead of finishing the sentence, Whitney raced around to the driver's-side window and pounded. "What about our phones? We want our phones back."

The driver rolled the window partway down. "My job was to confiscate them and deliver them to the appropriate person."

"If that's true, then why aren't you taking our luggage to the *appropriate person?*" Whitney looked toward Julie. "Mom, he's going to steal our phones."

His window began an ominous ascent, but just before it reached the top, he called out, "I wish you all the best of luck." Then the SUV with blacked-out windows pulled away, leaving them all alone, two thousand miles from their home and with no idea of what to expect.

"That guy's a jerk." Brian stared after the car with squinted eyes.

"He's just doing his job, like they told him to." Julie studied the empty country road and tried to smile brightly as she gripped her suitcase. "Well, I suppose this is where our adventure begins. Why don't you pile your duffels on my rolling bag, and let's get moving."

"I told you this was going to be a disaster." Brian put his bag on Whitney's, then wrapped his right arm around the telescope case. "This is heavy. Hope it's not far."

So do I. The driveway was mostly dirt, a much deeper red color than Julie had ever seen. Pulling her suitcase onto it from the pavement immediately made it more difficult to pull. There was no house in sight, and the temperature had to be in the high eighties. She'd heard about the humidity of the South in the summer, but it took today's arrival in late-May Tennessee to make her fully understand it. She suspected they would see much worse before this summer ended. Still, there were worse things than heat.

"Tell me again why we're doing this?" Whitney adjusted her backpack to the other shoulder and looked toward Julie.

"I told you, I think it is a good idea for all of us to slow down a little. Living simply for a few months will give us a chance to de-stress and think about what it is that's really important to us."

"Getting dumped on the side of the road, in this kind of heat and humidity, in a place I've never been, doesn't exactly seem the ideal way to de-stress to me. There's just nothing logical about it." Brian mumbled just loud enough that Julie knew he meant for her to hear.

"I already know what's important to me," Whitney put in. "It's the travel volleyball team that I can't be a part of this summer, because I'm here. Now all the other girls will be way ahead of me for varsity. Not to mention the City College biology class I'd planned on taking."

"We've been over this already, Whitney. You're sixteen years old and it's too much pressure. When I was your age, it never even occurred to me that I needed to take college classes in the summer, or that we should play a single sport year round or risk losing our spot."

"Things were different then," her daughter said, and Julie tried not to take it as, *Yeah and look at you now.*

30

"When's the last time you really enjoyed volleyball, Whitney? The way you talk about it sometimes, it's become just another chore in your day."

"Mom, volleyball is what I do — it's who I am."

"I'm missing astro camp, and you don't hear me back here whining about it — even though I think we all know that my hopes for this summer have been decimated." Brian coughed from behind them. "Mom, could you maybe roll that thing somewhere a little less dusty? I can't even breathe back here."

Julie turned to see puffs of dust coming from behind her suitcase wheels. Somehow it reminded her of smoke signals. SOS, indeed.

"Sorry. Why don't you walk ahead of me?" Julie paused and watched her son struggle past her with his load, his face already beginning to redden from heat and exertion.

"I really don't see the necessity for coming all the way out here if you just want us to slow down," Whitney started in again. Her words were beginning to pick up speed. "All you had to do was tell me you didn't want me to play volleyball this summer. At least I'd still be near my friends. I could even work that summer camp for the West-side kids. It just doesn't make sense."

Julie said nothing. She knew better. The kids' lives had become so high-pressure, so overly scheduled, that it was going to take more than just telling them they needed to slow down. They needed this. A radical life-style change. All of them — maybe Julie most of all.

But there was much more at stake here. "This is about more than us slowing down for a while. You know it's important to Aunt Susan that we do this. We're a family, and families support each other."

Whitney nodded, her face suddenly soft. "You're right, and we will."

"Yeah, we will." Brian wheezed. "I just think there must have been a way to help her that was a bit less" — he stopped walking and took a couple of deep breaths — "disruptive to our lives. Where are Aunt Susan and Angie, by the way?"

"Good question." Julie had no idea why the producers had been so insistent that the two families travel separately. Somehow, she'd just gone with it, like she always did, without asking too many questions. Without asking enough questions, perhaps.

Whitney grabbed Julie's arm and whispered, "Mom, look, there's a man up in that tree. The third one on the right."

Julie looked toward the dark shape in the tree line. It certainly was a man. She could see his jeans and tennis shoes dangling near the trunk about halfway up, his face hidden behind a leafy branch. "Let's speed up a bit."

She caught up to Brian and whispered, "We need to hurry."

"Why?" His face was bright red, so that his freckles barely showed. "It's too hot to go any faster."

Whitney grabbed his arm and pulled. "There's a man up in that tree, dumbo. You want to stand here and wait to find out whether he's looking for a fresh-off-the-plane California family to rob? Maybe he likes telescopes." She looked toward the tree again, then turned back, a hint of panic in her eyes. "Mom, I think he's got a gun."

Brian jerked around, stumbling over his own feet as he did so. He somehow managed to catch himself before he or his telescope fell. As he straightened up, he began laughing hysterically. "That's not a gun, it's a television camera, dork-o." Brian continued to laugh, but whether it was from relief or showmanship at the idea that he might be getting filmed, Julie didn't know.

Whitney blew out an irritated breath and

stomped away. A few seconds later when they caught up with her, she turned to Julie and said, "So tell me the truth, how bad do I look? I'd rather hear about it now than be caught off guard when I see it on television."

"You look just beautiful." Julie reached over to pull Whitney's hair behind her shoulder. Always a bit wild and wavy, it was taking on a life of its own. Her daughter's face was damp with perspiration, and orange dust spotted her legs and arms. "And I'm sure they're just warming up. That won't be for the show."

Brian, who was now in front, reached the top of the hill and pointed. "Hey, look, there's the house."

Julie caught up to him and almost gasped. Nestled into a lush emerald nook stood the most charming farmhouse she thought she'd ever seen. It was white and gleamed in the sun, waiting for them. Just off the house was what appeared to be a small storage barn, and there was a much larger barn just behind that, surrounded by fences and corrals.

"Doesn't it just figure that we'd have to get all the way to the *top* of this hill, to see *down* to where we're going? Don't you think they could have given us a ride to here at least?" Whitney laughed as she said it, her voice suddenly higher-pitched, the intoxication of cameras and crews and a completely different life obviously affecting her, too.

Julie nodded. "You read my mind."

The house was made entirely of planked wood painted white, no shutters, with a tin roof on top. It was neat and tidy and appeared freshly painted. Julie had read enough about the Amish way of life to know this was more or less what to expect, but the simplicity of the place carried a charm that fancy accoutrements just couldn't bring. The red paint was peeling on the little storage shed . . . barn . . . whatever it was, as well as the much larger barn farther back on the property. "It looks like a Norman Rockwell painting."

"Norman who?" Brian leaned a bit to his right side with the weight of the telescope in his hand.

"He was an artist from a long time ago — before my time even."

"Was paint even invented back then? Were there dinosaurs, too?" Brian grinned up at her through reddish-orange lashes. His face had gone so red from heat and exertion, his freckles had nearly vanished.

"Brian, you refrain from the old-people humor and I won't call you 'kiddo' on national television." Julie smiled at her son, happy to see him in such good spirits.

"It smells funny here." Whitney wrinkled her nose.

Julie took a deep breath. "That, my darling, is clean, fresh air."

"Perhaps." Brian sniffed the air. "But I'd say there's also a bit of freshly turned earth, the sweet smell, I think, is honeysuckle, and there's just a dash of . . . hmm . . ."

"Manure?" Whitney cocked one eyebrow at her brother.

"Most likely. Animal waste of some kind is nearby, likely near the barn Mom thinks looks like a painting."

Honeysuckle or horse manure: Which one was the summer going to be?

Julie looked again at the scene ahead, took a deep breath, and said, "Okay, you two, let's go do this."

CHAPTER 3

"Lift your chin up just a little and look over my left shoulder."

Susan did as the photographer — whose name she hadn't been told — said, hoping she didn't look like a complete amateur. She concentrated on presenting a polished and in-control demeanor for the camera but couldn't be sure it came across that way.

"Just a minute." The stylist rushed over to dust Susan's forehead with a bit of powder. Then she took a comb and painstakingly adjusted what felt like only a few strands of hair. "There now, that's better." She hurried behind the photographer, and the camera began to click once again.

The photographer pulled the camera away from his face, tilted his head, and stared. He nodded twice, forehead wrinkled in concentration. "Hmm. Let's try a few without a smile. Show me your best power pose." He pulled the camera back up to his face, ready for action.

Susan had no idea what a power pose might look like, but she tried to visualize magazine photos she'd seen of women CEOs over the years. She folded her arms across her chest and turned sideways a little, pretty certain she'd seen this one before.

"Umm, no, I don't think that works." Kendra Stern, the segment producer for the Lisa Lee show, stepped from the shadows. "We do want to portray her as competent, but we want to keep a homey edge to it. Maybe something a bit more relaxed."

"Right. How about turning that chair a quarter turn, rest your elbow on the back of it, and your chin in your hand."

Susan did as she was told and waited.

"It still looks a little . . . stilted," Kendra said.

The photographer squinted, "Maybe if you don't sit quite so straight. Try to look relaxed, like you've just arrived at your cozy home after a hard day's work."

Susan tried to ease back a little. Somehow she felt a bit slumped, but she did as she was told as the camera began clicking again.

"Okay, I think we've got enough to work with here. Thank you, Carl." Kendra took a step forward. "You'll email the proofs this afternoon?"

The photographer loaded his camera into its case. "Yep." He looked toward Susan then and nodded. "Good luck."

"Thank you." Susan watched him leave the room, followed by the stylist, and wondered what to expect next.

"Now, a few more things we need to talk about." Kendra walked over and popped the latches on her leather briefcase. "I've been speaking with the publisher we're planning to use for your *Simple Hospitality* book. They've created a couple of mock-ups for a potential book cover."

She held up a full-page glossy showing a rustic table set with a checked tablecloth and covered with a bounty of meat, bowls of vegetables, baskets of breads, and at least three latticed pies.

"This one has potential, but there's nothing that really pops. It looks like any other book already out there." She shuffled the papers to reveal the next choice.

A twilight sky hovered over a barn that looked much like the barn in this very place. Off to the left, in the foreground stood a white farmhouse, no shutters, a colorful flower bed still visible beneath the fading sky. Yellow light shone from a window, an oil lamp visible inside. The title was written across the top in white script letters, *Simple*

Hospitality.

"That one's nice," Susan said, leaning forward to study it more closely. A shiver of excitement ran up her arms at the thought that this really might happen.

"Yes, it is." Kendra paused for a moment. "Here's the thing. As you are undoubtedly aware, last year we did *Going Almost Blue Blood* with Abigail Phreaner and her family."

"Yes, I remember." Susan had tuned in every Friday to watch the progress of an ordinary family who had been put in New York social circles for the sake of the show.

"Those episodes drew large ratings. But when we partnered in the publishing of *Upper Crust Living for Everyone,* well, the sales were not as stellar as we'd anticipated. In follow-up surveys, it turned out that many of the viewers didn't really identify with Abigail, per se, and never felt that she changed or became more refined — she just got to live in an interesting situation. In other words, she failed to gain a perceived level of expertise."

Susan tried to keep breathing. This *had* to work out for her. "So what does that mean for me?"

Kendra shrugged. "It means the publisher has indicated they might reconsider the book if things aren't absolutely ideal."

"And what is 'ideal?' " Whatever it was, Susan would do it. Although she was getting paid a small stipend for being a part of the show, the big payoff was to come afterward. The cookbook or lifestyle book. Recurring segments on the Lisa Lee show. Maybe her own show one day? That was the goal.

Susan might have lost her husband to a twenty-years-younger home-wrecker, but that was the last thing she'd lose. Not her house. Not her dreams. Angie needed stability in her life, and Susan was the only one left who could provide that.

Kendra looked directly into her eyes. "You need to be the best possible *Almost Amish* person this world has ever seen. You need to make certain that the viewers see you in that light. That they all want to be more like you. We want to see you embodying the simple lifestyle."

Susan straightened her back. "I won't let you down."

"Good." Kendra put the mock-ups back in her briefcase. "Now let's step out and get a few shots outside the house. I've just been notified the rest of your family has arrived."

"Oh, really? I didn't hear the car pull up."

"That's because it didn't. They were

dropped off at the head of the drive, about a half mile out."

Susan looked at Kendra. "You mean they're having to walk? In this heat? With all their things?"

The left side of Kendra's mouth twitched oh so slightly. "It wouldn't make for good reality television if there wasn't a little bit of discomfort, now would it?"

"But you drove Angie and me right up to the house."

"We needed you for the photo shoot. And remember, you'll make simplicity look easy. . . ." She tilted her head to the left and smiled. "Everyone else will show just how hard it is."

CHAPTER 4

A group of people spilled out of the storage barn, talking amongst themselves. Julie scanned the group until she saw Susan in their midst, dressed to the hilt and styled to perfection. She practically glowed.

"There's Aunt Susan. Wow, she looks beautiful. Look at her hair, her clothes." Whitney's smile was huge. "I have to admit, I was afraid they were going to make us live so *au naturel* that I'd be stuck with my hair sticking out in all directions for the next three months." She paused for a moment. "I don't want to get quite that fancy, though. I hope they won't make us dress up like that."

"I think we're about to find out," Julie said as the crew suddenly turned in unison.

"I should've brushed my hair." Whitney put a hand up to her frizz and pulled at a strand. "Like that would help at this point. I'm doomed."

"Girls." Brian let out a long and disgusted sigh. "You don't hear me whining about not brushing my hair."

Susan waved up toward them, then hurried over to join them. "Oh, I'm so glad you're here." She hugged Julie. "Can I help you with anything? Whitney, Brian, so good to see you."

"Oh, there you are. We'd begun to think you'd gotten lost on the walk over." The woman wore a perfectly tailored white shirt and dark jeans tight enough to show that not an ounce of fat lingered underneath. Her hair was short and layered, with blond highlights that framed her elegant cheekbones and jawline. "I'm Kendra Stern, the onsite segment producer."

"I'm Julie Charlton; this is Whitney and Brian."

"So pleased to finally meet you." Kendra's gold loop earrings glinted in the sun.

Julie became keenly aware of the bermuda shorts and polo shirt she'd chosen for traveling, the unstyled ponytail, the ten pounds that she'd been meaning to lose forever.

Susan was wearing a sleeveless top the color of pale butter, and black linen pants that didn't seem to understand they were supposed to wrinkle. "We just finished up a little segment that will air this Friday." Susan's smile was huge, and there was something about her eyes, something besides the professionally applied makeup that looked different. It took Julie a moment, but then she realized what it was she was seeing.

Hope.

Excitement.

Things that had disappeared from Susan's life this last year. "I'm so glad we get to experience this with you." She looked around. "Where's Angie?"

Susan smiled and nodded toward the barn. "I think she's checking out the animals."

"Can we go, Mom?" Whitney had already taken a step toward the barn.

"Sure. Go put your duffels on the porch first."

"Actually, we'll take care of those for you." Kendra raised her left hand and motioned toward the film crew. "Chris, take the Charltons' things, please."

A young man stepped from the crowd. Likely somewhere in his late teens, he looked almost gothic, but not quite. His asymmetrical hair was so black Julie suspected it was dyed, and the right side dipped long enough that it partially covered one of his incredibly blue eyes. His T-shirt was black with a white guitar across it, but his jeans were blue and he wore surfer-style flip-flops.

He took their bags without comment, tossing Whitney's backpack over his left shoulder. When he reached for Brian's telescope case, Brian shot out his hand. "Be careful with that. It's a delicate piece of scientific equipment."

Chris grinned and returned a single nod. "You got it."

The kids walked off in the general direction of the barn, and Julie returned her attention to Kendra. "So what do you need for us to do?"

She extended her right arm, making a sweeping motion in the air. "Make yourself at home. For now, you just settle in and relax, get used to the place. Tomorrow we're going to take a tour of the real Amish country near here and see how that all works. It'll be a few days before we get serious about your weekly assignment."

"Sounds good."

"There are a couple of things you need to be aware of."

"Okay."

"Anything upstairs — bathrooms, bedrooms — is off-limits for our cameras and

46

recorders. However, anywhere that is considered a public area is fair game. Our goal is to catch some true snippets of what this lifestyle is really like for a modern family, complete with all the frustrations."

Julie shivered at the thought of being watched, but this was part of the deal. She'd known that from the beginning. "In other words, when we come downstairs, we'd better mind what we say, and we'd better have clothes on."

"I would definitely recommend the clothes part — we're a family-friendly show, you know. However, I'm really hoping that you won't always watch what you say. Those are the things that make for good television, aren't they?"

"Uh . . . I guess so."

"Also, there is to be absolutely no contact with any of the crew. You do not speak to them; they do not speak to you."

"You mean we can only talk to each other?" Julie had never considered anything this rigid.

"You can always talk to me when I'm on set. And we'll be sending in various helpers for different tasks. These are locals, not crew members, and they're fine. Any friends you might make in your limited activities in town or at church are also fine, but remember, you may not go anywhere with them in their vehicles. Automobiles are off-limits unless you are with one of our drivers."

For years, Julie had fantasized about a slower life. A quieter life. Somehow, in this agreement, she wondered if she might have gotten a little too much of a good thing.

"Thank you so much for being willing to do this. There aren't many women I know whose sisters-in-law would uproot their kids like this for an entire summer."

I'm the one who should be thanking you. "Of course they would. That's what families do."

"I'm glad you're in my family, then. I saw the kids head for the house. Let's go inside. I haven't even seen it yet."

She hadn't even been inside yet? "How long have you been here?"

"We got here several hours ago, but we spent the entire time in that little storage shed, which they've turned into a production office and our official interview set. They're calling it 'the shack.' Oh, and we did make a quick foray into the barn, which is where I lost Angie. Last time I saw her she was petting a little calf."

"Cows, really?" Julie looked toward the barn. "This experience is going to be so great for the kids." And for all of them.

"Yes, it will." As they started walking toward the farmhouse, Susan said, "Think what an interesting college application essay this experience could make."

"College essay?" So much for slowing down. "Are you already thinking about that?"

"Of course. Angie will be a senior next year, and early applications will be due shortly after we get back. Whitney's only a year behind Angie. It wouldn't do her any harm for you to start thinking about it, either. These days, you need every advantage possible if your kids want to go to a top-notch school."

The old familiar pressure clamped across Julie's shoulders.

Susan kept talking. "Even the UC schools today — the competition is incredible. I read UC Santa Barbara had almost forty-five thousand applications this year for less than four thousand spots. It's even worse for UCLA. Of course, Ivy League has always been our goal for Angie." Susan fanned herself with her left hand. "It is hot here, isn't it?"

"Yes it is." Julie stopped. "Won't that be . . . awfully expensive? I mean, with the divorce . . ."

"It's what we'd always planned for her, long before James went into his second childhood. Besides, part of our settlement was that James would pay for college." She raised both eyebrows. "I wonder what his new bride will think about paying for four years at Princeton? Maybe it'll make her wonder what she was doing messing around with a married man." Her voice caught on the last couple of words.

A clattering sound came from behind them. Julie turned just in time to see the kids emerging from the house, the screen door slamming behind them. Susan called out, "Hey, careful! We don't want to break anything on our first day."

"Our first day and our last." Whitney came to a stop in front of Julie, arms folded. "They lied to us."

Julie did not like the sound of that. "What happened?"

"Ask her." Whitney pointed behind them as Kendra emerged from the farmhouse.

Kendra had the indulgent look that said she clearly thought whatever the kids were talking about was of little significance. She glided over to the group. "The kids are all a bit upset about their wardrobe."

"Wardrobe?" Julie asked.

"They've confiscated our suitcases and

filled our closets with a bunch of *Little House on the Prairie* hand-me-downs. Mom, do you have any idea how ridiculous we'll look wearing this?" Angie's eyes were moist with indignant anger. Since Angie was usually shy, to the point of almost painful quietness, for her to speak up this way spoke volumes about just how upset she was.

This was Susan's deal, so Julie waited for her to address this issue. And she waited. And waited, well past the point where the silence had grown long and uncomfortable. Susan's eyes were narrowed in concentration, as if she were trying to decide something, but she still didn't speak.

Finally, Kendra said, "I just tried to explain to the kids that those are not Amish clothes hanging in their closet. Amish wear solid dark colors. Your girls have floral skirts and puffed-sleeved blouses that the Amish would never allow."

"Mom, those skirts are down to our ankles, and they're gathered all around. We'll look like we weigh an extra fifty pounds in those things." Whitney chimed in this time. "And I won't even mention the complete lack of style."

Since Whitney was stick thin, Julie doubted the first argument was terribly valid. Given the fact that her idea of style usually involved athletic shorts, T-shirts, and tennis shoes, Julie couldn't help but smile at the second assertion.

"The point is" — Kendra kept her focus on Susan — "that even though this is not the week of true Amish dress, if our show is about your family attempting something close to this lifestyle, we can't have the girls running around in California summer apparel. Simple living means a simpler wardrobe. I don't think people will want to see them in tank tops and short shorts. It will totally fly against what this whole experiment is about."

"Can I see the clothes in question, please?" Finally, Susan joined the conversation and started toward the house, soon followed by the others.

Brian walked up beside Julie and whispered, "Did you hear her say they took our suitcases? That includes my telescope."

Once again, Julie found herself wishing Thomas were here. He was so much better at dealing with situations like this. But he wasn't here, and Brian needed her help. She jogged forward to catch up with Kendra. "What about Brian's telescope? It was part of the agreement."

"You shipped his telescope ahead. Remember?" Kendra's superior attitude grated against Julie's nerves. "The box is in the shed at the back of the property — we decided that would be convenient for Brian's stargazing yet out of the way of the cameras."

"We shipped the *reflector* scope ahead, the bigger one" — Brian said this in a tone that left no doubt he thought Kendra was a complete idiot — "but I brought a *refractor* scope with me. I want to keep it in my room."

"So you're telling me there was another telescope in the bags that Chris took?" Kendra rolled her eyes.

"Yes, it was a black hard case, and I carried it all the way up the driveway with me."

Kendra pulled a small walkie-talkie from her belt. It beeped when she pushed the button. "Chris, where'd you put the Charltons' bags?"

Seconds later, another beep was followed by Chris's voice. "I locked them in the storage trailer."

"I need you to retrieve the black hard case and bring it to the farmhouse."

"What about our personal things?" Julie knew the kids were nearing meltdown, and she was going to help them if she could. "There are some things in our bags that we need." She thought about the family pictures she'd brought from home, the note Thomas had written to send her off.

"Your wardrobe has been provided."

"Well, I want my medicated face wash, and I want my own underwear." Whitney turned toward Julie. "Honestly, Mom, we did not agree to this."

Julie looked at Kendra. "She's right. The kids . . . and Susan and I . . . need some of our own things. We did not sign up to do *Survivor.* There is no million-dollar prize here, and I see no reason why we can't live simply, yet still have some of our own personal things."

Kendra glared at her long and hard. Without ever changing her expression, she lifted the walkie-talkie again. "Bring the rest of the bags, too." She looked at Susan. "I'll give everyone five minutes to get any necessities from their bags." Then she turned back toward Julie. "*Necessities* only."

"In five minutes, we can dump out our entire bags. We'll get our stuff, one way or the other." Julie barely heard Whitney's whisper and Angie's answering snicker.

She started to turn around and tell the girls that this type of defiance was not acceptable, but something held her back. In fact, she decided that maybe she agreed with Whitney. Five minutes was plenty of time. She smiled as she followed Kendra and Susan into the farmhouse.

CHAPTER 5

The air inside the house was hot and hung thick with the odor of dust, decay, and neglect. Susan sneezed several times, which only drew more of the musty, stale heat into her lungs.

"It's still a bit warm in here." Kendra fanned herself. "We just turned on the air-conditioning units this afternoon. There are three window units in the house, but they're rather small and the house is a bit drafty. I think it will take them a while to catch up."

Susan nodded, still trying to catch her breath. They entered into what she assumed was the living room. It was a fairly large area, with a stone fireplace on one end and the door to the kitchen on the other. The wood floors were old and scarred and dusty. In fact, the whole place was grimy. There were cobwebs in the corners. The white lace curtains were yellowed at the tops and bottoms. The only thing that didn't look as if it might fall apart was the furniture. Rustic, no doubt, but not crumbling. She looked toward Kendra. "I wasn't expecting the place to be so . . . dirty."

Kendra touched a yellowed wall and nodded. "No one has lived in this house in several years. A well-known record producer in Nashville bought it a few months ago, thinking he might do something with the place someday. One of his friends on our production staff knew about it, so when the idea for this particular segment was born it was a win-win. We gain, for free, the perfect place to film, and he gets the benefit of some much-needed maintenance on his place."

She touched the kitchen table, which was simple and looked as if it had come from a secondhand store. "We did take out all the old furniture and replaced it with something a bit more Amish looking, but we decided to leave the cleaning to you. Amish people are known for keeping their homes spotless, you know. This will be a good test for your family, to see how well you can actually pull all this off. Our second segment will be about the Amish home, complete with before and after pictures."

The earlier conversation still rang through Susan's mind. Failure here meant failure at everything she had left. She could almost see the smug expression on *her* face, could almost hear the "no wonder he left her" whispered amongst *her* group of not-yet-thirty friends. That couldn't happen. She would make this a success if it killed her, and if making this place clean was what it took to be the best almost-Amish person possible, then no one in this house would rest until it was spotless. She began mentally forming a to-do list.

Julie walked into the bedroom that Whitney and Angie would share. The two beds were covered with simple quilts, one eggshell blue and the other a soft apricot, and each had an antique-looking cedar chest at the foot. So pretty and quaint. She made her way over to the closet, prepared to calm the situation as quickly as possible.

Whitney held the door open, tapping her foot and waiting. "See what I mean?"

Julie looked into the closet, giving her eyes a moment to adjust to the dim light. Then, in spite of her best efforts at being the adult, setting the good example, she began to giggle. Then laugh. Then all-out guffaw.

"What's so funny?" Susan came into the room, followed closely by an obviously annoyed Kendra.

"Uh, well . . ." Julie shrugged, and her embarrassment at being caught quickly squelched the laughter. She pulled a skirt and shirt from the closet and held them up to show Susan, ready for her take-charge sister-in-law to handle this situation.

Susan reached out to touch the tan muslin skirt with brown and white flowers and the beige cotton blouse. She cut her eyes nervously toward Kendra, then back at the clothes. "These certainly are a bit . . . dated . . . but, Kendra, I understand your point." She stood in place, nodded silently a couple of times, then said, "I don't really see a problem with these. I'm sure the kids will adjust soon enough."

Julie looked at her, searching for a trace of the sister-in-law that she'd known for the last eighteen years, the one who never backed down, never placated. "So you're okay with this?"

Susan nodded crisply, once again cutting her eyes in the general direction of Kendra. "I think it will be good for the girls."

Julie looked at the gathered skirt in her hand, knowing how Whitney and Angie felt about them, having at least some clue what it would mean to them in a social sense, then looked back at Susan. Was this really the same woman who when Angie had felt self-conscious about her bunny costume for the fifth-grade play had taken it to a tailor to have it fitted into something more flattering, albeit less bunny-like?

Julie wasn't sure how this would be "good" for the girls, but could see how it might be embarrassing. Still, it wasn't a stand she wanted to make. Part of this summer was about helping Susan, and it wouldn't hurt the kids to make a few sacrifices to help out their aunt and mother. Still, she hoped this would not go much further.

"Well, I've got collared shirts and blue pants, and you don't hear me whining about it." Brian walked over and dropped down on the closest twin bed. "Coolness is a state of mind, not the clothes you wear."

"And you would know that, how?" Whitney folded her arms and leaned against the wall, glaring at her brother.

"I've got the stuff." Chris came into the room, leaving a pile of luggage behind in the hallway. "I believe these two go in here." He set the girls' duffels inside the room, then went out for another load.

Whitney dove across the room to reach her bag. "Everybody clear some space. If we've got a limited timeframe; we need some room to move in here." She yanked open the zipper and started rummaging.

"Here you go, sport." Chris brought Brian the telescope case. "I'll bet you'll see some really sick stars this far out of the city."

Brian's face lit up at the validation from an older and cooler boy. "Yeah, I think so, too. You want to check it out sometime?"

"Chris, you know the rules about talking to the families." Kendra scowled from the doorway. "Now everyone take out any *necessities,* then bring your bags back down to the porch and Chris will take them away. You have five minutes, and it started ten seconds ago." She looked at the silver watch on her wrist, as if to emphasize the point.

"Okay, girls, I'll leave you to pick your things. I've got a few necessities I need to get out of my bag, too." Julie grabbed her rolling suitcase and made her way to her own room. There was a pine-framed double bed with a green-and-brown quilt, a simple bedside table, a sad, small, worn dresser, and the closet door. Curious as to what her own wardrobe might entail, Julie opened the door to see essentially the same thing she'd seen in the girls' closet, just a few sizes larger. Blah. She didn't relish the thought of walking around looking like Mother Hubbard either, but in some ways, it was less embarrassing than today's clingy styles.

She opened her suitcase, pulled out the

framed photos she'd brought with her, a few books, and her stationery. Then she thought about what Whitney had said. She tiptoed to her door, closed it quietly behind her, and emptied her suitcase on the bed. She then quickly began stuffing the dresser drawers and the bottom of the closet with her own things. You never knew when you might need these things, after all. She closed the suitcase and latched it firmly before carrying it back downstairs and setting it on the porch.

Whitney and Angie soon appeared, obviously empty duffels in hand and sheepish smiles on their faces. Julie looked at them and couldn't help but grin. They might have gotten off to a rocky start, but now it was time to slow down. Enjoy each other. A whole summer full of quality time with the family. "All right, now that we've got that behind us, I think you two should give us all a tour around the barn. We can walk down to the creek" — the screech of the screen door announced Brian's arrival with yet another suspiciously empty-looking duffel — "and we need to go find the shed where they've put Brian's larger telescope. I'm thinking this place will make for perfect star viewing, don't you think, Brian?"

"By the end of this summer, you'll know

more about astronomy than you ever dreamed possible."

"As if we've ever dreamed about astronomy." Whitney nudged her brother from behind.

"All right, you two —"

Susan pushed through the door and set her suitcase beside the pile. "Whew." She tucked her barely long enough hair behind her ear. "Okay, everyone, I've made a list of chores that we all need to tackle. This place is a mess, so there's no time to waste."

Julie studied Susan's face, hoping there was some sense of joking in her eyes. She saw none. It looked more like panic. "Don't you think we ought to look around first? Let the kids show us the barn, check out the creek?"

Susan ran her pointer finger over the top of the front doorjamb and held it up to show a greasy black smudge on her fingertip. "There's a lot to do to this place before it's halfway livable, and this seems like the best time to tackle it. The crew's caterers are providing our meals for the next couple of days, so we need to get this done while we don't have other responsibilities pressing on us."

Julie debated telling Susan that the dust would still be there tomorrow, but she didn't say any such thing. The creek would still be there tomorrow, too, she supposed, and the place did need some deep cleaning. She was here to help Susan, and that's what she planned to do. "Aunt Susan's right. Everyone take a look at the list and get busy on your assigned task."

"But, Mom, we —"

Julie held up her hand to silence Whitney. "Let's get a good chunk of our work done now. Perhaps we'll have time to look around later this evening. We want things to look their best for the cameras, and besides, we've got almost three months here. There will be ample time to see everything." She hoped her words sounded like she meant them in spite of the fact that what she wanted more than anything was to set every single responsibility aside and just explore.

CHAPTER 6

Susan went straight to the kitchen. The old farmhouse sink had rust stains at the bottom and the ancient stopper had likely been white once, but that had been a few presidents ago. Like maybe Lincoln. But if the producers wanted the perfect Amish household, then she was going to give them perfection like they'd never imagined.

She opened the cabinets beneath the sink and found an assortment of bottles, each labeled "earth friendly." Dish soap. Window cleaner. Wood polish. She breathed a sigh of relief when she found one that said Mineral Cleaner — for hard water and rust stains. Perfect. She sprayed a little in the sink, then left it to do its work while she turned her attention toward the search for just the right scrub brush.

Footsteps pounded into the room behind her. "Let's start with the window by the kitchen table." Whitney was in full-fledged leader mode.

Susan couldn't help but smile. For all of Julie's good qualities, domestic skills were not among them. This summer would be the perfect chance for Whitney and Brian to learn the value of a well-kept home. "Good job, you three. Way to work as a team."

Whitney smiled and saluted toward her. "At your service, ma'am. Okay Brian, you know your assignment." Brian opened the window next to the kitchen table and unhooked the old triangular-shaped latch and pushed the screen outside. He repeated the process with the window near the cabinets, and finally approached Susan. "Excuse me, Aunt Susan, could I reach past you for just a minute?"

Susan backed away, pleased with how this was working so far. "Be my guest."

"Okay, women of the farm, if you need me, I'll be outside cleaning screens with the menfolk."

"So, in other words, you'll be outside by yourself?" Angie's voice sounded light. Carefree.

"I guess that's the truth of it." Brian rubbed his chin. "It's going to be a lo-ong summer." He hurried out the kitchen back door before Whitney could swat him, the screen slamming behind him. Susan bit back a reminder to be careful. She didn't want to dampen their enthusiasm.

Across the room, the girls got busy with their work, so Susan headed back to work on those rust spots. The cleaner had actually made a pretty fair start on the stains. She scrubbed at what remained — discoloration embedded for all these years would not be removed without more than a little bit of hard work. Well, hard work was what she was all about.

Some time later, she found a detail brush and began cleaning around the sink's edge. An old toothbrush would probably have worked best, but at this point, she'd make do with what she'd been provided. It wasn't ideal, but that was the point. You could do great work even with less than ideal circumstances.

"Ick. This is *disgusting*. I wonder how long it's been since someone wiped these windowsills?" Angie rinsed her sponge in the bucket the girls had between them. "Or painted them, for that matter. This paint is all cracked and peeling."

Susan walked over to get a closer look. The sills reminded her of a map, with cracks providing roadways, bubbled-up areas of mountains, and bare wood looking much like a barren desert. "The outside looks freshly painted. Why didn't they paint the inside, too?" Before the words had even left her mouth, she knew the answer. They wanted to see what she would do with this run-down place — whether or not she had what it took to take a simple lifestyle and make it something beautiful. Well, she was going to show them exactly what she could do. "I think I'll ask Kendra for some paint and painting supplies."

"Mom, we're only going to be here for three months. I think it would be a little excessive to repaint the place, don't you?"

"I think it'll be good for all of us. A little hard work, some elbow grease, and this place will be perfect." And hopefully, all of America would agree. It was the only hope Susan had.

One by one, the kitchen cabinets were beginning to gleam. Well, not gleam perhaps, as they were old and scarred, but they were cleaned and polished to the best level possible under the circumstances. The girls had gone outside to check on the "menfolk" and the screens, and Susan stood on the counter scrubbing the top shelf. She could almost picture this episode when it aired.

She began to visualize the snippets they might show — the before and after pictures of this place, the kids all pitching in and helping, the way that hard work could make even the most run-down place look so much better. The show would be a success, the book would be a success, and James would come to realize that he'd made a mistake. But it wouldn't matter. She was going to prove she didn't need him.

She heard the sound of the kids coming back into the kitchen, almost tiptoeing, whispering quietly amongst themselves. "How are the windows coming?" She turned around, surprised to find Julie there, too.

"Great. Just great." Whitney smiled, looking a bit sheepish. "Aunt Susan, don't you think we could all take a break now? Maybe walk down to the creek before it gets too dark to see it? Go check out the barn? Mom hasn't even seen it yet."

Susan looked at the set of cabinets yet to be cleaned and thought about her plans to clean the floors on her hands and knees. Doing this all well, and doing it quickly, was going to earn her big points with the producers and big ratings with the viewers. "There will be so many other times we can see all these things, and this place is in such need of a good cleaning."

"And we have been cleaning for over two hours." Angie folded her arms across her chest in that know-it-all teenager way.

"Work before pl—"

"I think it would be fine to take a little break, just to walk around the place, don't you, Susan? I mean, after all, that's what this whole experiment is about — slowing down, spending quality time with the family. Right?"

"Yes, and we can do all that in a couple of days, after we get this place all ready to go."

"Mom, this house will never be clean enough, or good enough, to meet with your satisfaction. We'll spend the entire time here doing nothing but trying to make this place into something it's not. Let's just accept it for what it is — old and run-down — and have a little fun while we're here."

"But we need to do this right. It's important for me . . . for all of us . . . that we do a good job."

"And we will, Susan, don't you worry," Julie said. "Let's just take a little time and smell some of the beautiful roses while we're here. Come on down off that counter and let's go enjoy our kids for a little while. We can come back and do some more chores before bedtime . . ." Her voice trailed off, a bit wistful sounding. "Or we just start again tomorrow — spend tonight playing a board game, or cards, or something."

"Mom, you promised me that you would ease up during this . . . this . . . whatever it is," said Angie.

"We've been here all of eight hours, I hardly think —"

Julie reached up and grasped Susan's hand. "Come on down. We'll all pitch in and do some more when we get back. Promise."

Susan looked from the cabinets to her family and back again. Taking a break now would spoil her rhythm, and theirs too, but she didn't want a mutiny this early in the game. She decided to compromise this time. "Okay, but we can't stay out for long, and you've all got to promise me you'll work all that much harder when we get back."

Susan didn't miss the kids cutting their eyes at each other, but Julie smiled, perhaps a bit too brightly. "Of course we will."

A symphony of gurgling and splashing led them down the path through the wooded area and directly to the creek's bank. It smelled of moss, and all things green and glorious, with perhaps just an undertone of fishiness to add contrast.

There was a small beachhead, mostly covered with pebbles and twigs, with occasional patches of what looked like clay

71

showing through. To the left, a long set of shallow rapids led to a calmer pool near the beach. To the far right, there was a set of slower, deeper rapids, which led around the corner and on to who knew where? Julie watched as the kids ran toward the water.

"This is so awesome. I wonder how deep it is. I bet we could swim right here." Whitney had already pulled off her sandals and started for the water's edge. "Wowser, it's cold." She drew her foot back, only for a second, and then plunked it back in. "I'm saying this place has some major fun potential." She took another step in.

Brian walked right out of his flip-flops and knee-deep in the water before nodding in satisfaction. "Yes, I think this will do quite nicely."

Angie reached down to pick her sandals up off the ground. She carefully placed them higher on the bank, then put the toes of her right foot in the water before yanking back. She laughed, then took a step in. "Yeah, definitely refreshing!"

Julie looked at the scene, buzzing with joy to see the kids enjoying themselves. And they weren't using electronics, or organized activities, or even a chock-full schedule. They were kids doing what kids were meant to do — learning about the world around them by experiencing it. Not just reading about it in their mounds and mounds of homework, not just seeing it in a movie or a video. She turned, prepared to share the happiness of this moment with Susan.

Susan's right hand held her chin, her mouth moving, although no sound was coming out, and she was slowly shaking her head back and forth. Her forehead crinkled together in worry lines that Julie had rarely seen. She reached out and touched her sister-in-law's arm. "Are you all right?"

Susan's eyes regained focus, and she looked toward Julie. "Fine. I'm fine. I was just thinking through all the work we should be doing."

Julie put her arm around Susan's shoulder and leaned her head on top of Susan's in a playful manner. "We've got to teach you how to relax a little. That's what Amish living is supposed to be all about, right? Living simply? De-stressing?"

Susan shrugged. "Their living may be simple, but I'm guessing that the workload on the average Amish farm leaves very little time for actual relaxing. If we're going to really do a good job of living like them, then we need to work as hard as they do, too."

Julie squeezed Susan's shoulder with her hand. "Nobody wants us to become Amish,

Susan. It's about balance. We're not going all out with all their rules — otherwise this wouldn't be part of a television show, now would it? Besides, I read some Amish-based novels before we came here, and what captured me — and I bet what captures a large part of our target market — is reading about the small things — their homemade pies, their quilt making, spending time with the family. Not working their fingers to the bone. Although" — Julie pulled her arm away — "I don't disagree with you that true Amish life has a harder reality than that. It's just not what we're here to do. I'd say the three window air-conditioning units in our house confirm that."

Susan nodded. "I know we're not going all-out, but we've got to be good enough. Better than that. We've got to do this amazingly well. We *have got to* make the best almost-Amish family that America has ever seen."

"And we will. We're all here to do this, and we're all going to do whatever it takes to make this a success."

The kids started skipping rocks across the surface of the water. Julie reached down and picked up a couple of flat stones, handing one to Susan. "Come on, let's go stick our feet in, too. Then I'll help you corral them back toward the house."

That night, after everyone had gone to bed, Julie lay staring at the ceiling as usual. Yet the yellowed paint and road map of cracks across the plaster helped remind her this was not the usual. At all.

She stood up, pulled on her robe, and walked outside. It all seemed so unreal.

From the general direction of the creek, a dull chorus of bullfrogs serenaded the dark. Closer by, the cricket choir added their own twist to the tune. A glass dome of stars twinkled above, creating the most beautiful scene Julie could ever remember.

This place was all so new, not yet comfortable in a familiar way, but as Julie stood beneath the sky, she felt warmth begin to seep into her tense muscles. She took a deep breath and felt her shoulders relax. It had been so long she had forgotten what this felt like.

Peace.

She remembered that day in her car when she'd thought about driving away to another place. A place without all the burdens of her regular life.

I think I just might have found it.

CHAPTER 7

"This is going to be interesting, don't you think?" Julie nudged Whitney, trying her best to get a spark of excitement out of her daughter.

Whitney shrugged noncommittally. "Maybe." She'd been in a grumpy mood all morning. Julie suspected it was a combination of last night's evening-ending chores, poor sleep the first night in a new place, and the withdrawals from twenty-four hours without texting or Facebook.

"Come on Whitney, I'm counting on you to be the leader of the kids. If you go into this with a bad attitude, you know that Brian and Angie will follow."

"Angie's older than I am, and this is her mother's deal. Why isn't it up to her to lead?"

"You're the most outgoing of the group. You know Angie's always looked to you. Come on, it will be fun. Besides, you're wearing your own clothes, aren't you?"

Whitney actually grinned now. "I have to admit, Mom" — she tossed a frizzy blond strand of hair over her left shoulder — "it was a stroke of genius when you 'suggested' " — she put air quotes around the word — "to Kendra that it would make a nice contrast for the cameras today, showing us in our California clothes and them in their Amish stuff."

Julie tried her best to make her shrug seem blasé, but in truth, she, too, was proud of her brilliance. "A mother does what she can."

They walked down the stairs to find the rest of the family already assembled in the living room. There were several additional crew members, one holding a camera to his shoulder, the other what looked like a long stick with a microphone on the end. It was obvious from the way Brian and Angie never looked directly at the camera that they were all too aware of it.

Susan looked up from the baseboard she was dusting. "At last, our stragglers have arrived. Is everyone ready for a tour?"

There was nothing but silence for the space of a couple of seconds. Julie looked toward Whitney, wide eyed, and nodded slightly — slightly enough that the cameras

wouldn't pick up on it, or so she hoped —
and said, "This is going to be fun. Isn't it?"

Whitney walked over and put her arm
around her brother's shoulders. "Sure is.
Don't you think so, Brian?"

"Let go." He shrugged her arm off of him,
glanced toward Julie long enough to understand the message in her eyes, and said, "I
always enjoy learning about new cultures,
so I'm sure this will be enjoyable. Don't
you think so, Angie?"

"I can't wait." She spoke the words almost
like a sigh . . . but a happy one. Well, after
the faked enthusiasm from her own family,
it was nice that at least one of the kids
seemed truly excited.

"Okay, people, let's load up. Reynolds
family, you're in the first Suburban, Charltons, you're in the second."

"Why can't we ride together?" Whitney
twisted a strand of hair around her finger.

Kendra looked at her with that annoyed
expression that was becoming too familiar
for Julie's liking. "Because you won't all fit.
Now, come on, everyone. We've got a schedule to keep."

"What do you mean we won't fit?" Brian
rubbed his chin. "Suburbans hold eight
people in relative comfort. There are only
five of us, plus a driver."

Kendra didn't bother to turn toward him when she answered. "Camera crews and equipment take up space, too — not to mention producers."

Brian rolled his eyes and shook his head. Whitney nodded her agreement with her brother.

Angie followed Kendra to the cars. "About those cameras. The Amish don't allow their pictures taken, isn't that right?"

Kendra checked the fingernails on her left hand. "Not usually, but they'll make an exception in this case. I'm sure of it." She turned and climbed in the front Suburban without ever looking back.

The man wore faded jeans and a gray T-shirt, which fit too tightly across his ample midsection. The stubble on his chin was gray, as was most of his hair, and something about the way he looked told Julie he'd lived in the country all of his life. "Hi, everyone. The name's Joe. I'll be leading your tour today." He looked at the cameraman. "Film what you want now, but you can't have those cameras out once we hit the Amish areas. They don't believe in having their picture made."

"Let me talk to them," Kendra said. "I'm sure that once we explain what we're doing

— trying to show the average American about their more simple way of life — they will be more than happy to let us do our thing."

He shook his head. "No, ma'am. It all comes down to respect, and that's where I draw the line. I don't allow photography or videos of Amish on the tours I'm leading, and that's the end of it."

Kendra folded her arms and glared at him. He stared back evenly and didn't even blink, as far as Julie could tell. Finally Kendra threw up her hands in exasperation. "Okay, okay. But the cameras can come with us, right? As long as they're only filming our families during the tour."

"So long as you put all those things away when I say so."

"All right." She walked away and pulled the crew over into a huddle. There were several nods from the group, but Julie couldn't hear what they were saying until the very end. As the huddle was dispersing, Kendra stood whispering to one of the cameramen and Julie caught the word "naive." He snorted a response as they walked toward the group.

Joe called for attention and pointed them to what could very well have been a trolley, except that the motor was two large horses.

"Everyone take your seats and we'll get started." Joe extended his hand toward Kendra, in an offer of assistance.

She turned her back to him. "The camera crew goes up front with Joe. Susan and Julie, I want you on the bench just behind them, and then the kids."

Soon, they were moving down a narrow country road, dotted with farms and pickup trucks and barns. The horseshoes made a pleasant rhythmic sound against the well-worn pavement as they wound slowly along the road. After several minutes, Joe turned around. "See them white houses up ahead? Those are some of our Amish homes." He turned to the side then. "I'd like for you fellas to put your cameras away now."

The men nodded their compliance and began the work of properly stowing their equipment into hard black cases. As they passed the first house, Julie noticed multiple lines of laundry — line after line of dark blue trousers and white shirts, ruffling slightly in the light breeze.

To the right of the house rested a large vegetable garden with a dozen or two neat rows of young plants. Two women stood out in the midst of it, hoes in hand.

"It seems awfully hot to be out gardening in the middle of the day like this. Especially in all that dark clothing." Julie looked at the women in their black caps, dark long-sleeved dresses, and aprons. The morning's humidity was already pressing on her, and she was wearing a knee-length khaki skirt and a sleeveless cotton top.

"This ain't nothing. It's nice today compared to what it'll be in a month or two. Up in the nineties, air so thick you'd think you could drink it. Them women'll be out there in it every day — gardening, doing laundry. They're always working. It's their way. Kids too. Those kids don't sit around playing video games in air-conditioned comfort. They work."

"Oh, the poor things." Whitney leaned toward the other side of the buggy to get a better look. "That must be so miserable." She glanced toward Susan and shrunk back a little. "The heat, I mean, not the video games."

"That part sounds pretty bad if you ask me," Brian mumbled, mostly to himself, but he did look up and grin at Julie before turning his gaze outward.

Joe shrugged. "I reckon it's all they've ever known."

They rode on, passing white house after white house. They all looked very much the same — comforting and homey in a way Julie found appealing.

"We'll make a stop at this next house. They sell molasses and homemade candy. There's also a woodshop out back I'll show you."

Julie climbed down, excited to see true Amish wares. They walked inside a little shed. On one wall hung dozens of woven baskets. Julie picked one up, considering where she might use it in her home. She turned it over and saw that it was signed and dated. "That one was made by Sarah. She's the youngest . . . 'cept for the baby." Joe looked over her shoulder at the baskets. "They make some nice pieces here."

Julie nodded her agreement, then turned. Opposite stood shelves of neatly aligned jars of molasses with homemade jelly. She turned to Joe. "Will someone come out so we can pay?"

He pointed toward a simple hinged box on a table at the back of the shed. "Honor system. You just put your money in there. If someone's around when we pull up, they'll tend the store. If not, then you do it the old-fashioned way."

"Somehow I don't think that system would work in L.A.," Kendra said.

Julie laughed, looking out the window of the little store. She noticed one of the cameramen walking around the side of the house. "What's he do —" Only then did she notice the camera in his hand.

Kendra immediately picked up a basket. "What do you know about who made this one?"

Joe turned to look at it. "Oh, that's Hannah's. She's somewhere in the middle, maybe ten. Anytime I pull up and she's around, she comes running out to say hi — I give her a grape soda from time to time." He grinned. "She likes those a lot."

Kendra continued to fire question after question about the family and then, after glancing quickly over her shoulder, said, "Can we see that woodshop now?"

"Okay." Joe set the basket back on the shelf. "Everyone follow me, and watch your step."

Julie was the last to enter the woodshop, turning in time to see one of the men shooting footage of the little store they'd just been in. She looked around for the other and saw him on the front porch, this time taking still photos.

Julie entered and found the space too tight to do anything other than stand behind the group. The heat of the day combined with the tightness of the quarters and the thick smell of freshly sawed cedar made the air even heavier. The group was looking at a crib and a king-sized bed frame, both made by the family who lived in the house. Sawdust covered the floor and a good bit of the workbench as well.

"Okay, let's make our way back to the buggy. There are lots more things to see."

Julie was the first out the door, but she waited for Kendra to exit. "Kendra, your cameramen were out here shooting, in spite of the fact that they were asked not to."

"Were they? I didn't notice." Kendra continued walking, so Julie hurried to catch up. "I know that you know they were. I saw you distracting Joe. These people have asked that no photographs be made."

"They won't even know about it. We're being very discreet, and I specifically said to focus on the setting. The shed, the house. Not the people. What's it going to hurt?"

"It hurts because, aside from these people's beliefs, you told Joe you wouldn't do it."

"They won't know about it, and he won't know about it. Right?"

In spite of the heat of the day, a chill ran the length of Julie's spine. She knew a warning when she heard one. If Kendra was willing to lie so openly about this, what else was she capable of?

CHAPTER 8

Susan looked at all the Amish homes, their front porches neat as a pin. This level of perfection would be no small task for them to attain and maintain.

"They're adding onto that one." Joe pointed ahead. "She's got another baby on the way, so they're adding a couple of bedrooms upstairs, and they just put in a new outhouse on that end. See how it's disguised so it almost looks like part of the house?"

"Outhouse?" Kendra leaned toward the building as if trying to determine whether or not Joe was telling the truth. "I thought Amish had a modified version of indoor plumbing."

Joe laughed then and clucked at the horse to go faster. "Different groups have different rules. The ones we got down here — they're called Swartzentruber Amish — are a lot less modern. They don't have all those configurations to get water into their house. It's all hand-pumped outside and hand-carried into the house. I think some of the ones up north use refrigerators and such, powered by propane. Here they don't. They use iceboxes. And coolers. You'll see that when we stop at one of the houses down the way where the girls make candy to sell."

"Where do they get the ice?" Julie asked.

"They buy ice from the local stores. But, for the most part, they pretty much eat their food fresh or can it."

"That'd be an interesting challenge," Kendra mumbled, more to herself than anyone else. "Tough, but doable." She looked toward Susan. "I hadn't considered a week without indoor plumbing. That would be extremely interesting, wouldn't it? Not only the aspect of a modern family having to use an outhouse, but also having to bring their bath water in from the well and heat it. Hmm . . ."

"What? *No way!*" Whitney leaned forward. "That was part of our deal in coming here: no outhouses."

"Are you sure about that?" Kendra cocked her head to the side and looked at Whitney. "I'll have to pull out my contract and see what it says. I'm not sure I remember that part."

"Well, I do." Whitney's head was directly between Julie and Susan now, she was leaning so far forward. "No Amish clothes except for one week — you've already broken that part of our deal as far as I'm concerned — Brian gets to have his telescopes, and no outhouses. Those were the three conditions that the three of us" — she nodded her head back toward Angie and Brian — "agreed to."

Kendra shrugged. "As I said, I'll have to pull out my contract as a reminder."

Susan tried to remain calm, but it was growing harder. Whitney's teenage attitude had the potential of ruining everything if she kept pushing Kendra like she had for the first twenty-four hours. Maybe they needed to have a little chat about tact.

They climbed back into the tour buggy and started on toward the next place. Julie turned toward Susan. "Doesn't it feel a little . . . weird to you? To be going up to these people's homes like it's a tourist attraction or something?"

Susan tilted her head in thought. "Maybe a little, but they obviously welcome guests or else they wouldn't have the little stores set up in front of their homes."

There was truth in that, Julie knew.

"You're right. Maybe it's just because we're not exactly the typical person who stops to buy molasses from them. I mean, the whole reason we're in this area — this part of the country, for that matter — is to pretend to be them. It's like we're exploiting their way of life for our own gain."

"Bah." Kendra shook her head. "It's no different than a professional athlete or a movie star. People want to know all about them because they're curious. Those who can offer a true glimpse into their lives do, perhaps, profit from it, but I wouldn't exactly call it exploitation."

"That's different, though." Julie tried to make herself see it from Kendra's perspective, but couldn't quite do it. "Professional athletes and movie stars thrust themselves into the public eye. If people watch them, or exploit them, well, they've more or less asked for it. But the Amish definitely don't put themselves in the spotlight."

"Look at what they wear — look at their mode of transportation. They want to be different. They may not *want* people to notice them, but by refusing to fit in, what do they expect? Like teenagers who dye their hair pink, or do the gothic look. They may say they just want to be accepted for who they are and left to live their life, but everything about them tells a different story. They want the attention."

"So if this subset of religious culture," Brian offered, "is all about drawing attention to themselves, then the most extreme in their society must do something especially noteworthy. Are there any gothic Amish, do you think?"

The others just stared at him, though Julie couldn't help but smile at his quirky sense of humor.

He shrugged, all freckle-faced innocence. "I'm just saying . . ."

"Well, in one novel I read before we came here, there was an Amish guy in it who was . . . well, he wasn't gothic . . . but he did always wear a black shirt. He was sort of dark and dangerous. And mysterious." Angie's voice took on a dreamy tone.

Whitney gave her cousin a little shove on the shoulder. "So *that's* why you spent so much time getting ready this morning. I thought it was because you wanted to look good for the TV cameras. I didn't know you were on the hunt for an Amish bad boy." She giggled. "It all makes perfect sense to me now."

"That's not at all what I'm doing." Angie's answer came quick, but the burst of deep red color in her face told Julie there might be more than a little truth to this. Besides, she'd read the same novel, and for a teenage girl, he'd been a character worth blushing over.

When they finally returned to their home that afternoon, Julie had a renewed sense of respect and wonder for the Amish people. She'd seen beautiful quilts and immaculate farms, smelled some amazing fruit pies and yeasty rolls, and watched the few Amish they'd seen go humbly about their work. What quiet dignity they all showed.

As they pulled up, a couple of crew members came out to meet the cars. Kendra climbed out and said, "Chris, we bought several containers of molasses today. Would you take them into the farmhouse kitchen for me? Make sure you Greek the labels. We'll be using them later in the week."

"Greek the labels?" Julie asked.

"Remove any kind of brand name or other identifying trademark so they are not shown on camera. We've done that with all your supplies, if you've noticed."

"The Amish have trademarks?" Brian shook his head. "Here, I'll help carry that." Brian moved around to join Chris at the back of the car.

"Me too."

"And me!"

Whitney and Angie hurried to join them, and Julie smiled at how thoughtful and well-mannered the kids were. As they headed toward the house, she couldn't help but notice Angie, walking a few steps behind, her attention clearly focused on Chris . . . who wore a black T-shirt and jeans. Julie thought back to the conversation from the tour, and a niggle of worry crept in. She hoped her niece would not romanticize Chris into the character from the book she had just read — a person Chris certainly was not.

Chris reached the door first. He pulled back the screen door, then pushed the other door open, backing up to hold the screen door for the others. Brian and Whitney each went through, offering a quick "Thanks." When Angie walked through, there was no denying the prolonged eye contact between the two of them. "Thank you."

"I'm not allowed to talk to you, but you're more than welcome." He grinned the kind of grin that would melt most seventeen-year-olds. From the sound of Angie's giggles, Julie surmised she was among them. She turned to see how Susan was reacting to all this, and saw that she and Kendra were in deep conversation, not even looking this direction. Just as well. Susan had enough to worry about right now. Julie would make certain to keep a close watch on the situation.

CHAPTER 9

"So tomorrow we will be in to shoot footage of the farmhouse for the first 'after' shot for our before-and-after segment," Kendra announced as she entered the living room.

They'd been back for just an hour or so, and Susan had immersed herself in cleaning. She'd expected Kendra to be done for the day and whirled when she heard her voice. "Tomorrow! I thought we had another week for that." Immediately, all the things they hadn't yet done clattered through her mind. "You still haven't gotten us a washing machine. Remember? I asked about it a couple of days ago, and we need it for the curtains, so of course we need more time."

"Oh, I'm glad you reminded me about that. Your brand-new washer arrived today, but we haven't brought it up to the house yet. It's quite an . . . *interesting* piece of equipment." She smiled outright.

Susan had studied enough about Amish

people to know that it would be a gas-powered machine of some sort, and that there would be a clothesline instead of a dryer. "I can't wait to see it."

"Hmm . . . yes. I'm looking forward to that, too." Kendra pulled her iPhone out her back pocket. "I'll call Gary and ask him to bring it over for you. Have you met Gary?"

Susan thought back through the photographers, cameramen, production assistants, and others whom she'd encountered over the last few days. Gary didn't ring a bell. "I don't think so."

"Gary Macko. He's your handyman."

"Handyman?"

"Yes. Obviously the Amish women have their husbands' skill sets to help them out. Since you're single" — Susan flinched at the words — "and Julie's husband will only be here for the occasional long weekend, we knew we'd need someone to lend a hand. There are some things it just isn't practical for you to do. We want you to stretch your comfort zone a bit during this experience; we don't want you cutting off limbs. He'll make certain everything else is done properly."

"Okay, sounds good." And it did. What a relief it would be to have someone share a little of the burden. Someone else who could help make certain things were done correctly.

"Oh, and by the way, the first challenge is scheduled for day after tomorrow."

"Challenge?" The words squeaked as they came out. "Already?"

"The show must go on, right? Will there be a problem?"

Calm down and act professional. "No. No problem at all. Can you tell me what the challenge is?"

Kendra nodded. "We're going to start you out slow. The challenge is simply to make an Amish staple — shoo-fly pie."

"Shoo-fly pie?" She'd heard of it but had never made one. Still, cooking was her thing. "Sounds good."

"It is . . . if it's made correctly. If it's not . . ." Kendra grinned. "Well, I'm sure Julie won't have any trouble."

"Julie? She'll be fine. She can just be my helper."

"Uh . . . no." Kendra's smile looked all too pleased. "Julie will be working alone on this challenge. We already know that you are a good cook, and so does our audience. So we decided to let someone who isn't as . . . domestically inclined . . . try out some of the old ways of doing things. You have the ingredients you need, including the molasses we bought on our Amish country tour. She'll have a few Amish recipe books to browse for tips. We'll give Julie the actual recipe we want her to use just before filming. Should be a snap."

As much as Julie disliked cooking, Susan doubted very seriously that she would even approach comfort. Judging from the grin on Kendra's face, she knew the same thing. And then Susan realized the truth — that was the whole idea. They wanted Julie to be awkward. They wanted her to fail. They thought that would make for interesting television.

Well, it might make for interesting television, but they would have to look elsewhere. It wasn't going to be easy, but by show time, Susan was going to have turned Julie into an adequate pie chef. One who could work even under primitive circumstances, and with the added pressure of cameras and all that went with them.

A door slammed and soon a voice called out "Hey, what happened to our kitchen?" Whitney leaned into the living room.

"Oh, that's right. I'd forgotten. While we were out today they did a little work in there."

Whitney jumped over the steps. "Yeah, I

97

see the stone they put on the floor and the wall, but they forgot one thing. They forgot to put the stove and oven back in place."

"The oven's not here, and we've got a baking challenge in two days?" Heat prickled across Susan's scalp. She'd been so focused on the living room, she hadn't even entered the kitchen.

"Not to worry. That old gas range was a fire hazard, so we took it out. Your brand-new oven will be installed in plenty of time for the baking challenge."

Julie picked up the amorphous piece of dough and tried to fit it into the pie tin. During the course of rolling it out, it had become less of a circle and more of a rectangle. This proved to be a problem now, because it wasn't wide enough on two sides. She cut the extra dough from the longer sides and tried to squish them onto the shorter sides.

"Julie, that looks piecemeal. Besides, it will break apart at the seam when you try to serve it. If you get it nice and round, then you won't have this problem." Susan shook her head as she said the words.

"I think it just wants to be a rectangle. And you told me not to mess with the dough too much or it would get tough.

Now, which way do you want me to play it?"

Susan thought for a second before replying, "I want you to make it round."

"It's not like I'm not trying, you know. Until this very moment, I don't think I've ever tried to make my own pie crust before."

"That can't possibly be true. You make homemade pecan pie at Christmas."

"I make the pie, not the crust. That's why they have the refrigerated section in the grocery store, for things like pre-made pie crusts."

"Okay, how about when you were in Home Economics?"

"I took World Geography instead."

"When you were a kid during the holidays?"

"Dad and I bought a box of dressing mix, a can of creamed corn, and a frozen pie and called it good."

"Wow." Susan pondered this for a minute. "I keep forgetting about your past. I guess it's no wonder you're not a very good —" Her face reddened and she looked away. "I mean, that you didn't learn a lot of the things I take for granted."

Julie turned her attention back to the pie plate, trying to ignore the sting caused by Susan's slip. She pulled the crust out and couldn't help but put some of her frustration into smashing the dough back into a ball, prepared to try again.

"Okay, everyone, your new clothes washer has arrived. Come check it out." Kendra breezed into the kitchen, followed closely by the camera crew. A broad smile lit her face as she gestured toward the back door. "Gary and Chris are about to unload it right now."

Julie wondered why Kendra would be so obviously delighted about something so mundane. And why would she feel the need to have the camera crew follow her into the house when she made this announcement?

Whatever the reason, it temporarily freed her from her doughy task, so she gratefully plopped the dough into the mixing bowl, washed the flour off her hands and forearms, and followed Kendra through the door to the back porch. She stopped short when she saw what was in the back of the rusted white pickup truck parked outside. "What is that?"

"I told you, it's your new washing machine." Kendra walked over to the truck and put her hand on what looked to Julie like a half barrel with legs sticking out of it, and some sort of device sticking up from one end. "Its design is based on the washing machines of the past, but there have been a few modifications that make it work a little better. The triangular shape of the agitator, for instance, supposedly makes the soap move through the clothes better."

Julie heard whispering and turned to see Angie saying something to Whitney, who nodded her head every couple of seconds. Then she looked up and said, "Wait just a second. We've done some research about the Amish, and this is not what they use. They use gas-powered washers. We" — she looked at Angie, who looked down — "I think they might have those wringer things, but they don't have the complete hand-wash unit like that."

Kendra's expression went from delighted to something far less civil. Whitney had been the one to challenge her, and Julie could see that the woman's face bordered on downright agitation. "Well, I'm glad to see you did some research, Whitney. That is always an admirable quality — one that is often lacking in *children* your age. I'm sure your mother is happy to hear about your research, too. You're focusing too much on the specific details. Our segment is being called *Going* Almost *Amish*. I know you know the *almost* word — you have used it yourself in order to avoid plain dresses, outhouses, and a house without air-conditioning. You've used it to barter for your brother's telescopes. Now I guess I'm using it to introduce you to your new washing machine."

"Whatever," Whitney mumbled, her face splotched red with anger. Or embarrassment. Julie wasn't quite certain.

Chris stood at the tailgate beside a man Julie had not yet seen. He was older, maybe mid-fifties. He had gray hair and wore faded jeans and a denim shirt, but something about the way he held himself made him seem a bit refined. "Where do you want it?" he asked.

"Just outside the back porch, the one off the kitchen."

The men set it in place. It was obvious from the strain of their arms that it was heavy, but neither of them gave any outward expression to show this. Chris's face remained as impassive as if he were watching paint dry, and the older man had something of a smile on his face. "How's this?"

Kendra nodded. "Just right. Thank you." She turned toward the family then. "Everyone, I'd like you to meet your handyman." She walked over closer to the older man. "You'll be seeing a lot of him. He'll be the one teaching you how to take care of the animals, repair fences, grow your vegetables — whatever it is that you need help with."

Gary nodded a greeting toward the group, and only then did Julie notice his eyes. They were that incredible shade of blue she'd always thought of as Paul Newman–esque. In fact, Gary was nice looking all around, in a rugged sort of way. "I have a rudimentary understanding of how this contraption works, if you'd like me to show you what I know. Just need some hot water and some laundry soap."

Julie couldn't help casting a glance toward Susan. Susan was looking at him, no doubt about it. Not gawking, by any means, but how long had it been since Susan had looked at any man with curiosity or interest? It was nice to see there was a little spark left in her eyes.

It didn't last long. "Angie and Whitney, go pull down the curtains from the living room. We'll clean them first and go from there."

Maybe it'd just been the machine.

Neither of the girls said anything, but they both turned to go inside and do as they were told. Julie started after them. "I'll get the hot water."

"I can carry the water out if you'll just fill a couple of large pots for me," Gary said.

"I've got this, Julie. You need to get back

on pie-crust practice. I'll be back in to help you as soon as we get things going out here."

"Oh, okay." Julie reluctantly went back into the kitchen. She rolled out the dough as Susan and Gary filled pots with hot water. This time it began to form something closer to an oval than a rectangle. Well, at least it didn't have sides. She picked it up and rolled it back into a ball and tried again. And again.

Three attempts in, Julie realized something. She was actually sort of enjoying it, and that stunned her.

She'd always hated to cook, at least for all of her adult life. And this certainly wasn't coming naturally, but it felt almost relaxing. Why? It took a moment before she landed on the obvious truth. The phone wasn't ringing, there wasn't a carpool to drive, or a practice to get one of her kids to, and no office parties she needed to be planning. In fact, the more she thought about it, the more she realized that the last couple of days had been altogether pretty wonderful. She'd been distracted enough by Susan's uptightness that she hadn't noticed it right away, but there was something about the quietness of this life she thought she just might like. A lot.

She walked away from her task and out to

the back porch, determined to savor this place a bit more. "How's the laundry coming?"

"This thing's pretty cool. Look at this." Whitney pulled a long handle back and forth, which caused the clothes in the tub to roll back and forth with a pleasant swishing sound.

Julie stepped forward and looked down through the clear lid and into the swirling, sudsy water. "You're right. That is pretty cool." When was the last time they'd ever used those words in conjunction with doing laundry?

"Hang around for a minute and you can watch us try out the wringer." Angie leaned over the washer and grinned.

"Sounds great." And it did.

"No, you better get back to work on your pie crust so Aunt Susan won't be all cranky tonight," Whitney mumbled just loud enough to be heard.

"Where is Aunt Susan?" Julie looked all around and saw no sign of her.

"She and Brian walked down to the shed with that guy Gary. He was going to help Brian get his telescope all set up."

Hmm, Susan and Gary had walked off together. There were lots of possibilities there.

CHAPTER 10

As they walked toward the shed, Gary gestured around at the rolling hills. "Ms. Reynolds, I hope you and your family will enjoy being surrounded by all this beauty. It's just amazing, isn't it?" Gary's smile seemed so serene, so content. "Just listen to the creek gurgling in the distance. This place is paradise. Don't you think?"

Susan could have told him she might have enjoyed this all a bit more if there weren't so much pressure on her. But she didn't. He was a part-time handyman; he didn't want to hear her problems. Somehow, she managed to say, "It is beautiful." She paused for just a moment before continuing with what she really wanted to say. "Listen, I was wondering, the windowsills inside really need to be repainted. Do you think you could get us the supplies to scrape, sand, and repaint?"

"I'm sure I could." He nodded thoughtfully. "That sounds like a good idea." He pulled open the door of the old shed, whose rusty hinges emitted an earsplitting screech. Gary looked toward the offending rusted metal and shook his head. "First, though, I'm charged with configuring young Mr. Brian's telescope in a satisfactory setup."

"Thanks." Brian walked inside and flipped the switch, which illuminated a single bulb dangling from a long cord in the ceiling. "The little building the show provided is nice and all, but here's the deal. My telescope is precision scientific equipment. Dust is not a good thing, neither are spiders and mice and such. We need to do something to make my observatory a bit more" — Brian wrung his hands together — "workable."

Gary nodded and smiled. "I see what you're saying. Mice and dust are never good ideas in observatories." He walked around and inspected the walls and ceiling. "I must say I'm pleasantly surprised. I assumed there would be more in the way of cobwebs in here."

"Oh, there were. I've been cleaning it all up. I don't want to even open up the box until I get this place under control."

"Got ya. Makes sense to me," Gary said. "It shouldn't be that hard to to make a more satisfactory set up. We can replace some of these boards" — he went over and knelt beside a section of wall with a couple of knotholes — "put some caulk around the window frames. A little elbow grease and it wil be almost airtight. How soon you need this thing set up?"

"The sooner the better. I'm following a couple of comets — Elenin, in particular, is moving away from the earth, and I don't want to miss it."

"Comets, huh? Sounds interesting." Gary nodded his head in true appreciation. "After we get this thing up and going, mind if I come and check it out sometime?"

Brian's face lit up. "I wouldn't mind at all. In fact, it would be great to have a man out here who actually appreciates these things. I'm living with a house full of girls who just don't get it."

Gary laughed and looked toward Susan. His eyes were so pale blue they almost glowed in this light. He tipped his baseball cap at her. "I'm sure there was no offense intended."

"None taken." Something about him was so . . . likable. But it didn't matter. He was a man, a handsome one at that, and she'd learned her lesson about trusting anyone — especially someone whose good looks could get him past where his integrity left off. "Will this project take long?"

"Two days, I'd bet. Is that all right?"

Not as soon as Susan hoped, but for right now, there were more pressing issues. "I suppose. Well, I really need to get back up to the house and help Julie practice dough rolling."

Brian waved his hand dismissively. "That might be a losing cause, Aunt Susan. Mom has a lot of good qualities, but cooking is not really one of them."

"You shouldn't talk like that about your mother." Gary sounded truly offended.

Brian shook his head. "Oh, she's the first to admit it. She tries hard, really she does, but I cannot envision something that has been true for the last forty-something years changing in forty-eight hours. It's just not logical."

"Well, I might not make her the best cook in the world, but assuming our new oven gets delivered soon, I can make her the best shoo-fly pie cook in the world — or at least a decent enough one to get us past the first week of filming without a major disaster on our hands."

"Yeah, well, good luck with that." Brian looked at Gary then. "Do you think we could get started working out here tonight?"

"Don't see why not."

"I'll see the two of you later." Sufficiently satisfied that things here were under control, Susan turned and started back toward the house.

"Looking forward to it."

Something about Gary's words, maybe the low rumble of his voice, sent a little trill of excitement shooting through Susan.

Ridiculous.

By the time she hiked back up to the house, she'd banned all silly notions from her mind and was ready to get back to the task at hand. She walked through the screened porch and into the kitchen. "I'm ba-ack." The screen door slapped shut behind her, but there was no other reply. "Julie?"

She looked around the kitchen. The dish drainer held the pie tin, washed and *empty,* the flour and butter had been put away, although there were still sprinkles of flour dotting the countertops and even a bit on the floor. "Julie?" She walked into the living room and found it empty, as well. Where was everyone?

Whitney's high-pitched laughter broke the silence. It sounded like she might be out in the side yard, so Susan went that way. She opened the door and saw Julie, Whitney, and Angie out by the clothesline. White lace curtains were stretched to cover two of the three rows of line, wooden clothespins holding them in place every few feet. "Hi, Aunt Susan." Whitney was the first to see her, and she came bounding over. "What do you think of our new dryer? It's the latest technological advance, guaranteed to dry clothes — and curtains — in the longest possible amount of time, while guaranteeing wrinkles on each and every item or your money back."

"Whitney, if you don't get a job in infomercials someday, you have definitely missed your calling. Don't you think so, Susan?" Julie's face was flushed with laughter. "I can't remember ever having this much fun doing laundry."

"How's it going down at the shed?" Angie asked, tucking a strand of hair behind her ears. "Did you get that guy all dialed in about what Brian needs?"

"I'll bet Brian tried to convince him to set up some vacuum-sealed, airtight, temperature-controlled command center." Julie hadn't stopped smiling since this conversation started. "What do you think of Gary?"

"I don't think of Gary."

The entire yard suddenly went quiet. Julie

finished pinning up the length of curtain, then walked toward Susan. "I didn't mean it like that. I meant, you know, is he going to be helpful?"

Susan shrugged. "How should I know? I hardly talked to him, but he seems sufficient for the job. Speaking of which, why aren't you working on the pie?"

"Mom, we asked her to help us, okay? Can't you relax for just one minute?" Angie's former smile had melted into the tight-lipped frown that had become all too common as her teenaged years progressed.

"Susan, I can more or less make a circular crust now. I've looked over several recipes for shoo-fly pie, but there's not much I can do about that without the actual recipe I'm going to use and an oven. Besides, I wanted to spend some time out here with the girls."

"Sometimes you just have to make sacrifices." Susan knew her voice came out sharp, but she didn't care. This was important.

Julie's smile faded, and she looked as though she might cry. She stood there and looked toward Susan, then back toward the girls, then back toward Susan. "And sometimes there are other things more important. Now, loosen up those strings of perfection for a minute and come on over here and help us do the next load of curtains in our fancy washing machine."

It took every bit of Susan's willpower not to unload everything right now. To tell them all about her conversation with Kendra, to let them know how close they still were to losing it all. No, that was her burden to bear and she wouldn't dump it on them, but she did say, "We don't have time for —"

"Yes" — Julie's voice was as firm as Susan had ever heard it — "we do. *This* is what this whole experiment is all about. It's not about pies, or even clean curtains. It's about slowing down enough to really spend time with the family."

Whitney gasped aloud. "Wow, Mom! Who knew you had all that in you?"

Julie's eyes grew wide, as if she was as surprised as everyone else that she'd actually spoken with such force. Her cheeks turned a bit pink; then she grinned and reached up to give a mock salute. "Troops dismissed."

"Aunt Julie, I'd forgotten how funny you are." Angie put her arm around Julie's waist and Julie returned the hug.

Great. No one was doing what they needed to be doing, and now even her own daughter had jumped ship.

Chapter 11

"Wow, Mom! Who knew you had all that in you?"

"Aunt Julie, I'd forgotten how funny you are."

Julie woke slowly and couldn't help but smile when she looked around her sparsely furnished room. This place was the dream she'd never even known could exist. No ringing phones. No emails asking for more volunteers. No committees. No pressure to keep up with the other moms. The reality here wasn't easy: she'd spent the last two days hand-washing and ironing a farmhouse full of curtains. But the time had been entirely invested in her family. She'd actually had fun with the girls.

She sat up in the bed, listening to the springs screech beneath her, and wrapped her arms around her knees. There were birds singing just outside the window, and the sun was already painting a rectangle across the floor in spite of the fact it was still early. She slid off the bed, then tiptoed down the stairs to the kitchen.

On the counter sat an old-fashioned percolator, and the only thing that could make this morning better would be a fresh cup of coffee. She prepped it with coffee and water, and set it on the little hot plate Kendra had provided for necessities. Within minutes it burbled to life and the smell of coffee filled the air. When it finished she poured herself a cup and took a first sip. *Not bad.* It definitely wasn't as good as the freshly ground brew she made at home, but it would more than do.

Susan walked into the room, already dressed in her assigned wardrobe — a long khaki skirt and a short-sleeved chambray shirt. It might have been a bit dated, but Susan managed to make it look crisp and classic. "I thought I heard you in here."

"I think I've finally got this coffeepot figured out. You want a cup?"

Susan went to the cupboard and pulled out a white stone mug. "Maybe just half a cup for me. I'm so keyed up over the challenge today I don't think it's a good idea to put much caffeine on top of that."

"What are *you* nervous about? I'm the one who has to do the cooking." Julie laughed as she asked the question.

Susan kept her back squarely turned, making Julie think she was avoiding the question. And she was. Her continued silence said as much.

"That's it, isn't it? You're worried I'll mess it up?" Just like that, Julie's dream morning fizzled, right back into the stress and failure she'd left behind.

Susan shrugged and kept her back turned. "This is so important to me."

"I am going to do my best, Susan; you know I am."

"Are you?" Susan turned, her face perfectly serious. "I would think that if you truly wanted to do your best, you would have actually made a pie yesterday."

"I didn't have an oven, remember? I could have assembled the ingredients and poured them into a crust, I suppose. And it wasn't like I was loafing around. You're the one who wanted all the curtains washed and pressed for the picture, remember?"

"Yes, I do remember. But I also remember that before I left to go shoot a segment downtown, I specifically asked you to practice your pie making, and you didn't. You made a point of avoiding it, in fact."

Had she been wrong yesterday? Julie didn't think so, at least she hadn't at the time. Now she felt that all-too-familiar

116

uncertainty. "Susan, I am sorry. I guess I didn't realize how strongly you felt about it."

Susan poured herself coffee. "Well, you do now." She took a sip, made a face, and shook her head. "I'm sorry, I didn't mean for that to come out so harsh. But we know everything that happens is going to reflect on me. And you know how much I need to succeed in this."

"I know, and I'm sorry I didn't spend more time figuring out the pie stuff." Julie said the words, but she wasn't sure she believed them.

Three hours later Julie sat in the makeup chair, getting powder dusted all across her face. It tickled her nose, and her eyes watered from the effort of not sneezing.

"The idea is to make it look like you're not really wearing makeup, but to make you look better in the process." The makeup artist had spiky white-blond hair with jagged dark roots, dark eyeliner that accentuated huge blue eyes, and a small nose ring. "There, I think this ought to work just right. What do you think, Kendra?"

Kendra came around the chair for a closer look. She bent over to inspect Susan's face first, gave a quick nod, and moved over to

Julie. She stared for what seemed forever and frowned. "We could really use a bit more concealer on the uh . . ." She made a semicircular motion under her eyes. "We want her to look natural, but I don't want her to look like an insomniac."

A glance in the mirror only confirmed what Kendra had said, what Julie already knew. She looked awful.

There were loud banging sounds coming from just outside the shack. Since the delivery truck had arrived an hour or so ago, Julie assumed they were making the final setup to the oven. Her stomach tightened, and she glanced toward Susan, who was looking nervously toward the door. Julie would do this well. She had to, for Susan's sake. And for her own.

"Here we go." The makeup girl, whose name Julie had not been told, leaned forward and applied something beneath Julie's eyes. "Yes, that is better, I think."

Kendra nodded. "Okay, ladies, it's time for your big debut. Let's get moving."

Julie's stomach began to flop as she stood up. It wasn't until this moment that she'd fully come to terms with the fact she was about to be on national television, on a show watched by millions of women, most of whom knew their way around a kitchen.

More than Lisa Lee or Kendra, they'd be the harshest judge of her success or failure. Well, she'd just have to show them she could do this.

Kendra led them through the back screened porch. "Along with the new stove, you'll see that we've added some additional lighting in the kitchen. It's better for the cameras." Kendra held open the door. "What do you ladies think about your new cooktop?"

A huge, gleaming piece of . . . black metal . . . more than filled the space where the old gas range had been. There were only two openings on the stove top, and beneath that, what looked like two separate oven doors. Kendra walked over to the door on the left and opened it. "This is where you put the wood." Then she opened the door on the right. "This is your oven. Any questions?"

"Uh . . . I have one." Julie looked at Kendra. "You are kidding, right?"

CHAPTER 12

"Ladies, time for our first post-challenge interview. Susan, you will sit in that chair." Kendra pointed toward an old bent wood rocker. "Now, remember, I'll be off-camera, so when I ask you a question, I want you to more or less repeat the question in your answer. I'll be completely cut out of the final product."

Susan nodded her understanding and pasted on a confident smile. Truth was, she really needed to vomit. How could this first week have been any more of a disaster? And now, she was going to have to sit here in front of all of America and try to somehow convince them that she was thriving, embodying the life of an almost-Amish person. "I'm ready."

Kendra took her place behind the cameraman. "So tell us how your life has unfolded this week. What was your first impression when you arrived here at the farm?"

Susan couldn't quite bring herself to look directly at the camera; it was too terrifying. Instead, she focused on the red light just above it, gleaming at her as if to say "it's your turn." "My first impression when we arrived here was simply, I couldn't believe how beautiful the countryside is. It's so lush and green, and the rolling hills are just breathtaking."

"Good. Now, tell us what most surprised you in a bad way."

Susan took a deep breath and considered her words. She didn't want to say anything that might make her come across as whiny, yet she didn't want to go so far in the other direction that her truthfulness was called into question. "It can be quite hot here at times. And the humidity is something I'm not really used to. . . ." Her mind kept searching for a way to put a positive spin on even the negative. "I understand the humidity is good for one's skin, which perhaps explains why southern women are known for being so beautiful — they have fewer wrinkles than those of us who come from the dryer climates." Maybe this wasn't going to be so bad after all. Somehow, so far at least, she'd been able to keep her cool. Judging from the satisfied expression on Kendra's face, she felt the same way.

"So tell us about the cooking challenge from earlier today."

Susan tried to smile, as if it were all in good humor, but in truth, she was furious. She would have to be very careful about what she did and didn't say. "The cooking challenge was a bit of a . . . challenge, to say the least." Again, she fought to produce a smile, uncertain of how convincing the results were. "Today was the first time we'd ever seen a wood stove, and apparently the internal temperature is much more difficult to control than it is with an electric or gas oven."

"Do you remember learning that the local Amish don't use gas appliances?"

"Uh . . ." Susan's tongue felt thick. "Well, I . . ."

"Let's move on. As you know, the pies did not turn out all that well. In retrospect, should you have done something differently? Do you wish *you* had been the one doing the cooking?"

Susan thought of the burned outer layer of the pie, the mushy inner layer. She could still smell the molasses as it burned onto the side of the oven after Julie tilted the crust a bit too much. "Obviously, I would have liked to have my own chance at making the pie. Cooking is something I've enjoyed for a long time." In her mind, she flashed back to Julie, dissolving the baking soda in boiling water, then forgetting to add the cold water before adding it to the molasses and egg mixture. The resulting texture was a catastrophe. "I know that Julie did her best, but in retrospect, we should have spent a bit more time practicing her baking the day before."

"And perhaps you should have explained to her the difference between blackstrap molasses and baking molasses."

"Ah, the molasses mix-up." Susan could feel her face heating with the as yet unresolved anger. "I assumed she would know from reading the labels that one was preferable to use over the other. I would think the words 'baking' molasses should have been the clue that gave it away." Susan shook her head, trying to regain her composure, but every bit of the pressure that had been placed on her was pushing down against her right now, causing her to wonder if she just might explode.

"Change of topic: let's talk about living simply. Tell us what kind of modifications your family has over a typical Amish one, and tell us the things that are similar."

"There are a few things different about our home and a typical Amish one. First of all, we do have electricity, which powers our refrigerator, water heater, and three window air-conditioning units, which don't keep the house — at least not a drafty old farmhouse — as cool as central air would keep a well-insulated home, but it does make it tolerable for us twenty-first-century softies." Susan grinned now, trying really hard to get back into the hospitable mode she'd tried to portray earlier. "Oh, and we do have indoor plumbing, which I gather some Amish families have to some extent, but some don't. The ones in this area apparently don't."

"What are the similarities, and how have they affected your family?"

"There are no telephones in our home, and we don't have cell phones — something that is taking the teenagers some time to get used to. I will say, it has been a nice change not to see them with their heads down and their thumbs texting all the time. We don't have electric lights except when the crew is inside the house filming; otherwise it's all oil lamps and candles, which is lovely, if a bit inconvenient. Also there is no television — something that is taking a little getting used to, I suppose. I miss the evening news while I'm cooking dinner, but otherwise we don't really watch a lot of television in my home. Julie and her family do a bit more, I think, and they play a lot of video games, which we don't even have at my house. So, in some ways, this is probably harder on her and her family than it is on mine."

"All in all, how would you rate your first week here?"

Susan thought back to the kids putting their dirty creek shoes on the just-cleaned porch, to the nights that she'd spent alone in her room worried about when the summer tutor was going to show up, her list of things that still needed to be cleaned, her niece's growing rebellion, her own growing panic that it was out of control, and the complete lack of anything here to distract her. She could mention none of it, so she smiled at the camera and said, "I can't imagine how it could be any more perfect."

Julie sat on the edge of her bed, looking out the tall, narrow windows at the sky full of stars. They twinkled their delight, and why wouldn't they? Stars never had to wonder why they had been created. They lit up the sky, everyone knew and acknowledged that they did it beautifully, and they never embarrassed themselves — certainly not on national television.

Everyone she knew had a special gift, or two, or even three. But she had none. Susan headed up the school PTA, a charity board, and a women's Bible study group called Lydia's Legacy, which specialized in teaching women how to show Christian hospitality. Julie had tried the group but found herself so embarrassed by her lack of skills that she'd made an excuse not to continue. In fact, it'd become such a burden that she had more or less quit inviting company over at all. The kids still had their friends over, but they were kids; they didn't care so much.

Susan, of course, was a terrific cook and housekeeper, along with her many gifts. Thomas was a terrific businessman, with an eye for investment that had kept his clients sound through some turbulent years. Whitney had a smile that could light up an entire building, not to mention a great talent for volleyball and a heart for helping others. Brian would be a great scientist someday, just like his uncle James, who, home-wrecker though he was, still was a vice-president of a company that made some kind of parts for NASA. All of them had *something* going for them. But Julie had nothing.

She looked at the brightest star in her field of vision. Brian would likely know its name, but Julie decided she'd simply call it Fred. "You know, Fred, it's not that I have a bad life. I don't. I mean, I have a great life. A nice husband, terrific kids, good health, all that. It's just that I feel like I don't contribute anything. I do everything kind of mediocre, no matter how hard I try. I want to be *good* at something, anything."

The star continued to twinkle but gave no other response. A plane flew past, way up in the distance, and Julie watched its lights until they disappeared. Then she looked back at the sky, but this time, she didn't talk to Fred the star; this time she talked to God. "Father, please help me to find myself. I feel like all I do is flounder and I'm not really good at anything. And I've been thinking that I was doing so well here, but well . . . I guess today proved just how wrong I was. Show me where my strengths lie, and help me to use them for Your glory. Help me to somehow make a difference in this world. And please, *please,* keep me from making a complete fool of myself on television again next week. Or the rest of our time here. Amen."

CHAPTER 13

The beginning of their second week arrived with a sticky heat that invaded the farm-house in a little-too-warm haze. Julie washed the last of the breakfast dishes quickly, wanting to get out of the hot kitchen as soon as possible. Even though they had installed the "summer grate" into the firebox of the stove, it still put out a lot of heat into the room. She wiped her fore-head, already thinking how much she was going to enjoy a nice cold shower.

"So tell me about this church we're going to again." Whitney came into the room, picked up a dish towel, and went to work drying a white plate from the drying rack. The shoulders and back of her green shirt were splotched a darker color from where her still-damp hair had touched it. "I mean, is this going to be a small country church, or one of those places with a gymnasium, or what?"

Julie put another plate in the rack, then picked up a couple of forks to scrub. "I gathered from what Kendra said it's going to be somewhere in the middle. It's not one of those huge churches we saw as we drove through town, but they did some checking and found a place that has a fair amount of families like ours."

"So they'll be teenagers, then?"

"I'm assuming."

Whitney groaned and shook her head.

"I'd think that you would be ready to see some other kids your age that were of no family relation by this point."

"I am. It's just" — she held up a strand of her hair — "with no electrical hair appliances, they're all going to think I'm a fuzzhead from another planet, not to mention these clothes we have to wear."

Julie turned to her daughter, prepared to argue that it really wasn't that bad. But, in truth, Whitney's hair was as frizzy as Julie had ever seen it. "You brought some of that gel, didn't you?"

"Yeah, but it doesn't work all that great without a straightener."

"What if we put just a little into your hair, to tame the frizzies a bit, and then I'll do a french braid. We haven't braided your hair in a long time."

Whitney's eyes brightened. "Will you do that one where you braid both sides, and then they meet up into one big braid in the back?"

"Sure."

Whitney nodded. "All right. Here, I'll help you finish the dishes first."

The church turned out to be a brown brick building that looked newish. It was more oval than rectangular, and the entrance rose up into a steeple above. All in all, quite nice.

Gary pulled the Suburban into a parking place and turned to the group. "Enjoy yourselves."

"Aren't you coming with us?" Brian leaned up from the backseat.

"Well, I'm planning on attending, but I supposed that your family might like a little time without all the show crew around for a change."

"Nah. We see each other plenty. Besides, I'd really appreciate it if you don't leave me sitting in a row full of all females. I mean, what would that say about my macho-ism?"

"It might say you're macho enough to gain the favor of four beautiful women. Ever thought of that?"

"Um, no. Come on, please?"

Gary shrugged. "Sure, if that's okay with

everyone else."

Whitney and Angie were quick with their agreement, and Julie followed with, "Even without my son's need for male companionship, I think it would be nice if you sat with us."

Susan was the last to respond, and Julie began to wonder if she was going to protest. Finally she said, "If you're okay with it."

"Well, I guess that's settled, then." He exited the car and came around to the passenger side, but Julie and Susan had already climbed out by the time he arrived.

As they walked across the parking lot, Whitney said, "Why didn't the rest of the crew come with us?"

"It was the original intention to bring cameras here, or so I'm told. Since a big part of the Amish culture centers around church, it would make sense. However, it seems that none of the pastors whom the show contacted were willing to allow cameras inside their churches."

"Really?" Brian asked. "Seems to me like it would make for good free publicity."

Gary nodded. "That's logical. But Hollywood's never been friendly to the church, and I'll bet there was a fear that reality TV might edit things in a . . . less than positive manner."

"I just wish we could wear our own clothes." Angie's voice was so quiet, it was difficult to hear. "It's bad enough walking into a room full of people we don't even know, without having to look like we're on our way to a costume party."

"Or a hundred years out of style," Whitney said as she pulled at the green muslin of her skirt.

"I hadn't even thought of it like that." Angie's voice was gaining in volume now. "Maybe they'll think we're clueless. No one's going to want to even come near us."

Gary smiled. "I wouldn't worry about that overmuch if I were you. In a town this small, everyone knows that the Lisa Lee show is out there filming in the countryside, and while they may not know the specifics, there are a few things they will know." He held up his index finger. "One, they'll know it has something to do with country living — in fact, they may even know it'll be something Amish-related." He held up the next finger. "Two, I'm sure everyone in this parking lot recognizes this Suburban as one of the blacked-out cars that the show is using. And three" — he held up his ring finger — "they'll all know that you are involved in the show, because there aren't many towns large enough that the teenage male population wouldn't know it if you two lived here. They'll put all those points together and realize who you are; then they'll figure out the wardrobe. I'd be surprised if it takes more than two or three seconds. So they're not going to think you're strange. I bet folks won't leave you alone."

"I don't know." Angie's voice was back to its lower volume, but something about the way she folded her arms told Julie she was far from convinced.

A set of three steps led up to the entrance, which consisted of three sets of double doors with stained glass windows. The middle set was propped open, and Julie could see people milling around in the vestibule. The brightness of the sun kept them as shadows, but soon enough she could tell heads were turning. Perhaps Gary was right, perhaps everyone did already know that the "show people" were in their midst.

"Welcome." A middle-aged man in a light gray suit handed Julie a bulletin as they entered. "We're glad to have you folks visiting with us today."

"Thank you." Julie kept walking so the rest of the group could follow her into the noticeably cooler inside. She could hear the sounds of each of them speaking to the greeter.

The auditorium was fan-shaped. The walls behind the pulpit were of brown brick, with dark wood trim. Only the baptistry in the back of the choir loft varied in shade. It was a crisp white paint with a large wooden cross hanging on the wall. *Quite lovely.*

Slowly, her attention receded from the building itself, replaced by an uneasy awareness of what was happening *in* the building. People whispered to each other, a quick head turn toward the back — toward Julie's family — then the head snapped forward. Yes, the word had definitely gotten around this small town about them. She just hoped the reception would be friendly.

"Mom, everybody's staring at us," Whitney whispered.

"It's okay, they're just curious. Just smile and hang tough. In the end, we'll all laugh about this moment."

"Somehow, I kind of doubt that."

The service started with a couple of announcements, and they sang a hymn Julie didn't recognize. Then the pastor stood up and said, "Okay, everyone turn to your neighbor and tell them what your plans are for the summer. And if you see someone you don't recognize, go introduce yourself."

"Oh no." Whitney sort of sighed the words.

"Hello there, I'm Debra." A smiling woman extended her hand to Julie. "You must be that family that is filming for the Lisa Lee show."

Julie nodded. "Yes, that's us."

"Sounds like a lot of fun. It's awfully good to have y'all with us. I hope you'll come back."

"Thank you."

By the time Debra introduced Julie to a couple more women, Julie turned to see the kids surrounded by a group of teenagers. They were talking and laughing — in a nervous, teenager sort of way, but friendly nonetheless. When they sat back down, Whitney leaned over. "What would you think about us coming to youth group on Wednesday night?"

And just that easily the kids had made acquaintances and were ready to move forward. At least, that's what Julie hoped.

Chapter 14

Susan scrubbed away the last of the stickiness from this morning's breakfast of eggs, bacon, and homemade biscuits. "I'm going to gain fifty pounds by the end of this summer," she said, mostly to herself, even though she knew Julie was somewhere in the room behind her.

"It is tasty, though, isn't it?"

"Tasty fat. Yummy cholesterol. Delicious gluten."

"Think about it, though. Kendra was right. You've never heard of an Amish person on a diet. At least, I never have. Come to think of it, I haven't heard about them doing much of anything other than farming and having romances in novels. But" — she paused for a moment, wiping at an already dry plate — "we've all been up for several hours. We milked our one cow . . . well, Whitney did, anyway . . . and fed a bunch of animals. I'm saying we probably got as much exercise as we would have if we'd gone to the gym. We're going to start on the vegetable garden today. Even more exercise. See, it'll all work out. Besides, you're always talking about the evils of overly processed foods. Well, we're eating eggs from the chicken coop outside, and biscuits from scratch."

Sometimes Julie just didn't get it. This was going to be one of those times. "We've got to start being more deliberate about what we're cooking."

Julie put the plate away, but as she turned, Susan was pretty certain she saw her roll her eyes. Honestly. How could she not care that she was feeding her kids this kind of unhealthy fare? Did she envision Susan publishing a cookbook filled with recipes full of lard and grease?

"Mom, someone's knocking at the door." Brian's call came from the living room.

"Well, open it and see who's there." Julie started out of the kitchen, laying her dish towel in a heap on the counter.

Susan reached over, picked it up, and folded it neatly before placing it squarely on its hanger. She turned and surveyed the kitchen, making certain that it was acceptably tidy before walking out into the living room. She turned the corner just in time to hear Julie saying, "Oh, please, let me help you with those. Come on inside. It's so nice to meet you." Julie backed into the room, carrying a large canvas bag.

A tiny woman followed behind. She must have been several inches short of five feet, had white-gray hair and large tortoiseshell glasses that covered about half of her face. She wore light-colored denim pants, white Reebok tennis shoes, and a blue chambray shirt. She was followed by a film crew, one of whom already had his camera rolling.

The kids were all standing around, more or less gawking, when the woman said, "Hello, children. Can you tell me your names and ages, please?"

As the kids went down the row stating their names and ages, it somehow gave Susan a flashback of *The Sound of Music* when *Fraulein* Maria first met the Von Trapp children. Except, this family was in no mansion, and this woman was no nanny. But then again, what was she? Susan walked forward.

"I'm Susan Reynolds."

The woman nodded. "Name's Rosemary. Rosemary Foil. You can call me Rose, or Rosemary, not Mrs. Foil and most certainly not Rosie. I'm here to teach you all a bit about quilting."

"Quilting?" Brian's tone was blatantly rude.

"Well, certainly not you, young man. Quilting is for women."

"Whew. I'm really glad to hear that."

"That nice young man Gary is down at the barn waiting for you."

"Yes!" Brian pumped his fist.

"The two of you are going to shovel the manure out of the barn this morning." Rosemary lifted her eyebrows all the way above her gigantic glasses, leaving Brian with absolutely no doubt about who had gotten the last laugh.

Whitney doubled over with laughter. "Well, I've got to say," she offered, pausing a moment to catch her breath between laughs, "quilting is sounding better and better all the time. Have fun, Brian."

He shook his head with no display of emotion; then he looked at the camera and grinned. "I'm off to do man's work. See you ladies later."

Julie focused on cutting straight edges and tight corners. After the debacle with the pie, she didn't want to mess up something else. Susan needed her to do this right.

The group spent the morning cutting eight-inch squares out of scraps of fabric.

"Normally, you'd cut these much smaller for a fancy quilt, but we're going to make a patchwork quilt to get started. We'll get our feet wet with the easy stuff, and then move on as time allows." Rosemary's voice was full of authority. "Okay, I think we've got enough squares now. Young ladies, now it's your job to lay out the squares on the floor in the pattern you want your quilt to be."

Whitney and Angie immediately went to work, with Angie tossing out comments like "That's too haphazard," soon to be followed by Whitney's "That's too boring." They finally reached agreement, and the finished product contained a beautiful mix of random and balanced. Both girls smiled with satisfaction as they turned to Rosemary for feedback.

"Nice work. I think you both have keen eyes for this." Rosemary carefully labeled the back of each square with row and column number and taught everyone the basics of hand-stitching. "You line two squares up, face-to-face, and then sew one edge together." She showed them the basic principles of a backstitch, which looked easy enough, at least when Rosemary did it. "We need to do a quarter-inch seam so everything lines up. I'll measure and set the pins for you until you get the hang of it. Okay, now get started; time's a-wasting."

Julie held two squares back-to-back, took a deep breath, and plunged the needle through the fabric. She went back through the same holes a couple of times to lock the fabric, then tried her hand at moving forward. Somehow, the spacing didn't look quite even or straight when she did it. She squinted and focused on making the next stitch better.

Whitney said, "My girl scout troop made a patchwork quilt, back when I was in sixth grade. We did most of the work in a single morning. Remember that, Mom?"

"I do remember. As I recall, though, there were rotary cutters and sewing machines involved. That's why it went so fast." The memory of their finished product — a somewhat lopsided collection of mismatched multicolor squares, caused something between a cringe and a smile.

"That was the coolest thing. We all still talk about how great that was."

Julie looked up at her daughter, stunned. "Really? I always thought you guys were embarrassed that it turned out crooked."

"Nah. Did you see the other quilts there? At least we tried to do it the right way. I think it was really cool."

Julie tried to return to concentrating on

her stitches, but she couldn't help smiling at Whitney's words. One of the things Julie had always considered as a failure on her part was a happy memory for Whitney. She put the needle through the fabric again. *It's not about perfection; it's about the experience. I'll just do my best and won't worry about it.*

"You have a nice, even stitch." Rosemary leaned closer to check out Julie's seam. One of the cameramen leaned over her shoulder and pointed the lens at the stitch in question. "Remember to stay lined up just above the pins." She looked toward Susan. "How are you making it over there?"

Susan's lips were tight with frustration. "Not so great."

"Let's take a look." Rosemary leaned toward Susan. "You need to relax a little. You're pulling the stitches too tight, and it's making your fabric bunch up."

Susan shook her head. "I don't know why I can't get this."

"You're not quite the natural that your sister-in-law is, but with some practice, you'll catch on."

"Me a natural? At something domestic? I've never heard those words uttered before." Julie laughed and turned her attention back to her stitches, wanting more than ever to prove that she'd earned the compliment.

"Certainly not about your cooking, eh, Mom?" Whitney grinned over the tangle of fabric and thread in her hands.

"Bah." Rosemary made a dismissive gesture, then leaned back in the rocking chair. "You remember that story in the Bible, where Jesus took the loaves and fishes from that one kid and fed the five thousand?"

"Yeah, there were all those basketfuls left over. Jesus did an amazing miracle." Whitney pulled a thread through and made a face.

"You're missing the point." Rosemary reached over and pushed the fabric back down to Whitney's lap. "It wasn't the fact that God fed them; it was that He used what the kid *already had.* He didn't say, I'd prefer it if we could find someone with filet mignon. No, the kid had something very common and not very fancy, which he turned over to God, and God used it in a powerful way. If every woman in America were a gourmet cook, then there wouldn't be any need for shows like the Lisa Lee show, now would there? She's a good cook and she uses her talent to help others. Your mom has other talents. We're each charged with using the talents we were given, not try to live up to someone else's."

Whitney nodded her head. "That's a really amazing point."

"Yes, it is." Angie set her work in her lap and looked into nowhere with a firm mouth and determined eyes.

"Hopefully it won't take you as many years as it took me to learn that and really believe it. It'll save you a lot of time and heartache if you figure it out sooner rather than later."

"Really? What happened with you?" Whitney kept her fabric in her lap and her attention focused on Rosemary.

"That, my dear" — she pushed herself to standing and stretched her back — "is a story for another day. I've got to go now."

She walked from the house without further comment.

"All right, then." Whitney giggled and soon they all joined in. Still, Julie couldn't help wondering about Rosemary's story. She looked down at her first row of stitches and smiled.

At lunch, Julie sat at the table, enjoying a ham sandwich and ice water. "I really enjoyed this morning. I hope Rosemary will be back soon." She had left them with instructions to keep working on their squares, and they would see her when it was time.

"Oh, she'll be back soon, believe me." Kendra sat next to her, wearing a white tank top and short denim shorts, a sharp contrast to the rest of them in their Peter Pan collars and long skirts. "In fact, I think it's safe to say that you'll have seen more than enough of Rosemary before your time here is through." She took a sip of her Diet Coke. "And you will have heard enough of her stories. I swear, the four of you got off easy this morning. I only heard one story the entire time. Every time she talks to me, I get at least two. And preachy . . . don't even get me started."

"I enjoyed her story. I thought it was . . . meaningful." Julie looked down and took a bite of her sandwich, immediately embarrassed.

"I did, too." Angie's voice was so quiet she barely heard it, but just hearing her made Julie glad she had challenged Kendra. If by doing so, she'd given her niece the courage to speak up, then it was well worth it. Julie looked up at her, and after making certain that Susan wasn't watching, she winked. Angie smiled just a little, then turned her attention back to the salad on her plate.

"Sounds like I missed a bundle of fun." Brian, who was showered and had on freshly washed blue pants and a button-up shirt, took a big bite out of his sandwich. "Gary's going to teach me how to —"

"Brian, don't talk with your mouth full." Julie looked at her son, cutting her eyes back toward Kendra and giving him her best "we have company" glare.

Brian shrugged, took a sip of water, and then continued. "Gary said he'd teach me how to hook up the horses to the wagon this afternoon."

"Oh, have the wagons arrived? I hadn't heard that." Susan glanced out the window as if wondering how she'd missed such a thing, although around here there were always trucks coming and going with equipment. It didn't surprise Julie at all.

Kendra's phone buzzed. She pulled it up and read a text message, then looked up. "Yes, it got here yesterday afternoon. Unfortunately, you'll have to save that for another time, as your tutor is on her way here right now."

"Oh no." Whitney said the words aloud, but it took only a quick glance at the other faces to know there was agreement among all the kids. "Tell me again why we're doing school in the summer?"

"The schoolhouse is part of the Amish fascination," Kendra said. "Even though the school year has officially ended, we wanted to bring in that aspect of their lives."

"And both of you can use the extra time to prepare for your SATs," Susan added.

"What?" Whitney's mouth hung open. "What kind of Amish kids study for the SAT? They only go to school through the eighth grade, right?"

Kendra gave Whitney her typical annoyed expression. "It was your Aunt Susan's request that there be some form of scholastic enrichment. And as I was saying before I was interrupted" — she paused just long enough to let the arrow find its mark on Whitney — "you two will prep for the SAT, and Brian will go through some science and math curriculum to help prepare him for the engineering academy when he enters high school."

"Like there's any way Brian wouldn't be the first person accepted."

Kendra shrugged. "He apparently wanted to go to a science camp this summer, and the filming of our show has prevented him from that. We're making amends in the best way we know how."

A knock sounded from the back door. Kendra stood up and started toward it.

"Come in, come in. Everyone, this is Charlotte Buchanan."

"Hello, everyone." Charlotte walked into the room. She was on the shorter size of average, shoulder-length straight brown hair, understated yet stylish. Her smile lit up her whole face, and Julie immediately liked her.

"Hi, I'm Brian." Brian had bounded up out of his seat and stood before his new teacher, his cheeks a bit flushed. Apparently Julie wasn't the only one who liked her at first sight.

"Pleased to meet you, Brian." She smiled at him and shook his hand.

"Likewise. And I'm sorry you're stuck teaching the other two this summer, but don't worry, I'll help you deal with them whenever necessary."

Charlotte laughed. "Thanks for the offer of help. I'm sure we'll all get along just fine."

Introductions were shared all around; then Kendra said, "Charlotte, why don't you take the kids on out to the schoolroom? We'll come check in after a little bit."

"All right." The kids and their new teacher walked out the door, trailing the sounds of laughter and chatting behind them.

"Is she old enough to be a teacher? She looks more like a high school student to me." Susan watched them long after they'd left the room.

"Well, you know" — Kendra folded her arms — "Amish schools only go through eighth grade, and their teachers are unmarried young women, often teenagers."

"Yes, but we agreed —"

"I'm kidding, Susan." Kendra put her hand on Susan's arm. "She graduated undergrad from Stanford, magna cum laude, to be exact. And she just earned her master's degree in education from Vanderbilt."

"Okay." Susan still looked doubtfully out the door. "Where is the schoolroom?"

"It's a small building way on the backside of the property. After you two get the lunch dishes all cleaned up, I'll walk you out there. Come find me when you're ready." She pushed open the back door and then turned. "I'll likely be down near the barn with Gary and the new wagon. If I'm not there, Gary will know where to find me." The screen door slammed shut behind her.

"I guess producers don't have to worry about whether or not the Amish thing would be to help clean up, now, do they?" Julie piled the plates together and carried them toward the large farmhouse sink. "I have to admit, I'm missing my dishwasher."

"And front-loading clothes washer." Susan sighed.

"And the cleaning ladies that come in every other week. Yes, especially them."

They both laughed then as Susan started the water running into the sink. "Didn't you think that teacher seemed a bit more like a party girl than a teacher? I think we're going to need to keep a close eye on their educational experience this summer."

Susan always kept a close eye on Angie's educational experience. Still, Julie wished she would ease up, just for the summer. "She seemed sweet to me."

"All the more reason to keep a close eye on her."

Oh boy.

CHAPTER 15

Two large brown horses stood in the paddock, their eyelids drooping in the morning sun. Several goats on the other side of the barn brayed at each other and ate at whatever was in their little trough. There were no people to be seen or heard anywhere in the vicinity. Susan stuck her head in the barn door. "Kendra? Gary?"

"Nobody here but us chickens." The reply came from behind her. She spun around and saw Gary mending a fence on the other side of the hen coop. He smiled and started toward them. "Some way I can assist you ladies?" His blue eyes glinted bright in the sun, perfectly contrasted with his gray hair.

"We were supposed to meet up with Kendra and go out to the schoolroom after we cleaned up the lunch dishes. Have you seen her?"

"They had some sort of mechanical issue and she got called away. I'm not sure when they'll be back."

"Oh." Susan thought about the young girl currently in charge of her daughter's education and decided she didn't want to wait for Kendra's return. "Do you happen to know where the schoolroom is?"

He nodded. "Sure do." He looked toward Susan with sort of a dare on his face. "But I don't think it'd be right to tell you —"

"She's my daughter, and I want to know where she is." Who did this handyman think he was? "Tell us where they are, right now."

"You didn't let me finish." Gary grinned a slow, easy smile, apparently unfazed by Susan's obvious irritation. "I said it wouldn't be right to tell you where they are, when I could show you. I've got a horse that needs some exercise, and the new wagon needs some breaking in. Now, if you ladies are up for a little adventure, come on down this way."

"Oh." Susan felt her face flush warm. "Sorry, I . . ."

"No need to apologize. Truth is, I've been itching for an excuse to hook one of these things up ever since they arrived."

They headed behind the barn where a gleaming black Amish-style buggy waited.

"This is smaller than I thought it would be. How will the whole family fit in this thing?" Susan walked around the vehicle, checking every detail.

"We got two. There's one back in the storage barn that is family-sized, with a couple of rows of seats. This one is for smaller crowds." He made short work of hitching up the horse. "Okay, ladies, in you go." He held up a hand to help Susan into the carriage. She took it and climbed in. Julie followed.

Gary came around and got in the other side. "Okay, we're about to see what this baby has under the hood." He clucked at the large brown horse, who launched into a leisurely walk. "Hmm. Not a lot, apparently."

Both Julie and Susan laughed. They started moving in the direction of Brian's observatory, then turned right at the top of the hill. From there, it became apparent that several dirt roads crisscrossed the property. Trees dotted the landscape, until they grew dense near the creek just over to the left. "This is such an amazing place," Susan said, in spite of herself.

"Yes, it is." Gary spoke the words in an almost reverent tone.

"It's interesting, though, that the farmhouse is built in the valley between two hills. In California, we would put the house right on top of the tallest hill for a better view."

He nodded. "True enough. This place was originally built over a hundred years ago. Likely the owners were thinking more about protection from the elements than a nice view."

"I suppose so."

"And it works well for our purposes. No one can see the buildings from the road, so it's nice and private."

They continued along for a moment, hearing only the muted clomps of the horses' hooves against the dirt road and the singing of the birds off in the distance. Gary held out the reins to Susan. "It's time for you to start your first driving lesson."

Susan kept her hands firmly planted at her side. "I don't think —"

"You'll be just fine. Now take the reins, and I'll tell you everything you need to know."

Susan finally lifted her hands in the general direction of the reins, still perfectly certain that she was not up to this. She grasped the reins, and Gary kept his own hands over hers for just a few seconds. "Pull here to turn right." He made a light pull on the rein and the horse started to veer off the road. "And here, to go left." He steered the horse back on course.

He released his grip but remained close beside her. Susan could feel his shoulder brushing against hers. In spite of the fact that she tried to concentrate on keeping the horse moving the right direction, she was all too aware of his closeness. It was ridiculous. They were in a tight space, that's all. It was ridiculous that she would even notice such a thing.

As the buggy reached a hilltop and started down, the small schoolhouse came into sight. It looked exactly like Julie had always pictured a one-room schoolhouse. White, rather plain, almost like an old church without the steeple. It was surrounded entirely by towering trees, as though they'd grown there solely to protect the school one day.

"How cute. Gary, do you know if this place was already on this property? I can't imagine that it was, but it looks so authentic."

"You are correct on both counts. It wasn't here, but the producers wanted a schoolhouse that looked legitimate. They found this one abandoned in town not far from here, moved it, restored it just enough that it doesn't fall in, but not so much that it looks brand-new. The schoolhouse doesn't have electricity; that's why they set it in the middle of those trees. Hopefully the shade will help keep it cool."

"I wonder how many trees they had to take out to make it fit," Julie said.

"None." Gary's answer was quick, but then he shrugged. "At least that's the way I understand it. There was a perfect spot right here, but obviously the opening isn't wide enough to bring that thing in. So . . . it was dismantled, brought in here piece by piece, then reassembled. Tell you the truth, I think they did a nice job."

"Me too." Julie leaned forward to get a better look at the place. "It's so picturesque."

"I'm just hoping there's some good teaching going on inside there." Susan's face was turned toward the building, but Julie knew she wasn't even seeing the outside. Her focus lay on the tasks that needed to be occurring inside.

"I'm more than confident that there is." Gary answered in a friendly-enough way, but Julie thought she heard something like irritation in his voice.

"We finally got the buggy, huh?" Brian seemed to appear from nowhere, his arms loaded with pine cones, nuts, twigs, and other kinds of fauna. "Can we go for a ride?" He matched his step to walk beside them.

"Where's your tutor? Why aren't you in class right now?" Susan turned to scan the immediate area, as if to find out the answer for herself.

"And what do you have in your hands?" Gary's voice was more jovial.

Brian looked down, as if just now remembering his load. "Oh, this. Well, Aunt Susan, this is why I'm not inside. Char sent me outside to gather items to be used in my summer project."

"Char?" Susan asked, her voice in full disdain mode by now.

"Our tutor, remember? Her name is Charlotte, but she told us everyone calls her Char."

"What about Ms. Buchanan? That seems more appropriate to me."

"Lighten up, Aunt Susan. This is summer, after all."

Gary leaned a bit closer to where Brian walked. "What is the project?"

"A model of our solar system in the middle, and representative astronomical structures from elsewhere in the Milky Way. We'll spend the summer studying all the things represented. Of course, I'll include Sagittarius A-star" — he looked at Gary —

"that's the super-massive black hole right in the middle of our galaxy."

"Right, of course." Gary nodded, playing along.

Brian nodded. "And the Comet Elenin will be another no-brainer when it comes to inclusion."

"I would think so." Gary grinned at Susan, then turned to Julie and said, "You've got one smart young man on your hands there."

"Yes, I do."

"Let's go see what the other smart ones are up to, shall we?" He pulled the horse to a stop.

The three of them climbed out of the buggy. Gary went around to tend to the horse while Julie and Susan started for the building, Susan leading the way.

The door stood open, to allow in air, Julie supposed. As they stepped inside she noticed that it was warm, but not unbearable.

Charlotte Buchanan was standing at Whitney's desk, looking at something in Whitney's notebook. Angie was busy writing something, her pencil flying across the paper.

"Hello." Susan made her way toward the three desks. "We came to see what was on the agenda for today's lesson."

Charlotte looked up and smiled. "Today

we're just getting our plan set and talking about what interests them most and what I feel are the most important topics for review. I've gotten everyone started on a warm-up project, but tomorrow we'll dive in full force."

"Can I drive the horse and wagon tomorrow?" Brian carefully placed the items from his arms onto his desk.

"Sorry, Brian, but that falls under the category of the true-to-life-schooling you're going to get here. Amish kids generally walk to school, just like your grandparents probably did. It's all a part of the experience," Char answered.

As the conversation and attention were drawn to Brian, a movement caught Julie's eye. She glanced toward Angie and saw her sliding a notebook she'd just been using beneath her other books. In its place, she pulled out a precalculus textbook and set it on her desk. Her entire being was focused on Susan, who, at this moment, wasn't looking toward her. What was it she'd been working on with such energy and didn't want her mother to know about? Whatever it was, Char was in on it, too, because she had moved to stand between Susan and Angie during this exchange.

Gary ambled into the classroom. "I just

got a call from the boss. She wants you ladies back at the farmhouse ASAP. Sorry to cut this school session short, but I'm sure the students and their teacher have lots to be doing anyway." He and Charlotte made eye contact, and Julie knew without a doubt there was something meant by the exchange.

"I guess we'll hear about the rest tonight at dinner," Julie said as they walked from the building.

Gary helped Susan up into the wagon, then Julie. Susan's blush still hadn't quite faded as Julie climbed up beside her. That's when Julie began to wonder how long it would be before Gary and Susan realized they were attracted to each other.

Julie watched out the kitchen window as the kids made their way from the barn and the morning's chores. They were talking and laughing, something that rarely happened at home in the morning time before school. Yet here it was not even 7:00 A.M., they'd been up and going for an hour, and their outlook was as pleasant as could be. Maybe there was something to be said about spending time in the great outdoors first thing in the morning, or having the kids do extra chores, or be electronics-free. Whatever it was, it seemed to be working.

The screen door to the kitchen porch screeched open. The kids all spilled inside, sock-footed and still laughing. Brian held up both arms to show off nonexistent muscle. "Behold King Brian. Lord of the cow milkers."

"Yeah, right. You got lucky, that's all," said Whitney.

"Nothing lucky about it. I'm the best milker in the family; admit it, both of you."

"Nothing doing. I would have had way more yesterday except that the stupid cow kicked the bucket over."

"That's operator error, not the cow's fault." Brian ducked his sister's swat and plopped at the kitchen table. "What's for breakfast? I'm starved."

"We're taking a break from the heavy stuff today. We have nuts and raisins. Some raspberries and apples. Plus we've got some oatmeal this morning, the old-fashioned kind. And some toast from last night's leftover friendship bread, and there's molasses and butter on the table."

"Gary told me yesterday to put some butter on your plate, pour molasses over it, and then stir them together. He said it's really good on biscuits that way. Maybe it'll work on toast, too." Brian spooned out a scoop of butter and started drizzling molasses over it before anyone could protest.

Whitney's nose crinkled up tight. "Ick. That looks disgusting."

"You never know for sure until you try something. That's the scientific approach. Then there's your approach . . . the blond approach —"

"Okay, you two, that's enough. Whitney, I believe it is your turn to lead the blessing."

In unison, the heads bowed. Whitney said, "Thank You, God, for this food and our family. Amen."

"That had to be the shortest blessing in history." Brian scooped up some of his molasses-butter mixture with his knife and placed it on a piece of toast and took a bite.

"There's no need to pontificate, especially this early in the morning. Besides, didn't you ever read the parable about the hypocrite who said long prayers just so he would look good?"

"Pontificate? Whitney, you just used a four-syllable word!"

Julie reached across the table and put a hand on each of her children's arms. "If I have to tell you two to knock it off one more time, there will be consequences."

Brian scooped more molasses onto his toast. "This is *really* good. Amazingly good."

Whitney picked up her fork, stuck the

tines into Brain's mixture, then pulled it back and licked it. "Hmm, not bad." She reached for the butter and pulled out her own little clump, then passed it to Angie. "Maybe we should give it a try."

"Angie, no," Susan interrupted. "Today was supposed to be healthier. And eating a tablespoonful of butter with sugary syrup poured all over it is nothing of the sort." Susan looked at Brian's and Whitney's plates and turned to Julie, her annoyance more than obvious. "I thought you were going to back me up this morning," she said in a whisper still loud enough for the kids to hear. And the cameras. "How can you let them eat like that?"

Julie froze. Once again, she'd been whiplashed by Susan. Just seconds ago she'd watched her children come inside as happy as she remembered seeing them, and now she was being scolded. For butter and molasses. Susan stared, waiting for an apology. Demanding one. The same look Julie had seen in so many eyes back home. Demanding this, expecting that from her. The life she hated. And Julie refused to let that world break in here. This place was beyond all that, and she wasn't going to take it anymore. She looked Susan directly in the eye. "It's all part of the experience. In fact" — she extended her hand toward her daughter — "pass it this way when you're done, please."

CHAPTER 16

Julie held the hoe with her left hand while she bent down to pull a weed with her right. "Some of these are so close to the tomatoes, I'm afraid I'll tear out the wrong roots."

"Who knew that weeds could grow so much faster than vegetables?" Susan removed her wide-brimmed straw hat and fanned herself. "It seems like they regenerate overnight, doesn't it?"

Hours had passed since their breakfast disagreement. Julie thought Susan might hold a grudge, but to this point she hadn't mentioned anything. And Julie certainly wasn't going to bring it up.

"I know what you mean." Julie wiped her cheek with her shoulder. Her back was aching from the morning's work, but something about being out in nature, the peace, the silence, was enjoyable despite the humidity and muscles that were not used to doing this kind of work.

"Why are the kids here already?" Susan put her hat back on. "They shouldn't be back for several hours yet."

The girls were jumping and shouting, and even Brian had an extra spring in his step. Of course Whitney's voice was the loudest and carried the farthest.

"We come bearing good news, simple women of the garden!" She reached into a large canvas bag slung over her left shoulder and extended her right hand triumphantly. In it she held lots of white paper. Julie looked at it for a moment and then realized what she was seeing. Envelopes.

"Mail call!" Whitney ran out into the garden, bouncing her way across a zucchini plant in the process. "Kendra came to the school and said we might want to take a break and walk down to the mailbox. Just look what all we came back with."

"Seems to me we could have done that after the school day was over." Susan leaned heavily against her hoe and didn't really even look at the mailbag.

Julie went to stand beside her. "Well, at least it gives a good excuse to sit in the air-conditioning for a few minutes. Right?"

Susan offered a weak smile and nodded. "Now that I think about it, a glass of ice water and a chair sure do sound good about now."

"I couldn't agree more."

The kids bounded up the back porch steps, pausing long enough to take their shoes off and put them beneath the bench on the screened porch before disappearing though the kitchen door. By the time Julie and Susan made it inside, the remains of several envelopes were strewn around the kitchen table. Brian was bent over what looked like a Hallmark card, chuckling with enough force that his shoulders were shaking. Angie was reading a letter, which looked to be about three pages long, smiling and nodding. Whitney already had one card lying on the table in front of her and had moved on to a second. She didn't bother to look up but did motion with her left thumb. "Old-person mail is on the kitchen counter."

Susan had stopped just inside the porch door, so Julie walked over to find seven envelopes. The top one was addressed to her from Thomas, so was the next. She smiled as she turned toward the third. It was addressed to Susan, so she set it to the side. So were the fourth, fifth, and sixth. There was one final envelope, addressed to Julie from one of her friends at church. She picked up her three envelopes in her left hand and took Susan's in her right. "Here you go, sweetie. Looks like even us old people get a little bit of mail."

Susan nodded, cast a quick glance to the envelope as she took it, then simply turned her attention back to the kids and their reading. They were all smiling and giggling, their eyes shining.

Again, Julie felt almost overcome with happiness. "It's amazing how much a letter means when you've been without texting or email or Facebook for a while, isn't it?"

No one answered her. They were all far too involved in the reading of their treasures to have even heard her speak.

She took Susan by the hand. "What say we go sit in the living room and read ours in comfort . . . at least the relative comfort of our hard, wooden, Shaker-style chairs?"

Susan nodded, her eyes slowly coming back into focus. "Sounds good."

Julie opened her first letter from Thomas. It was written in his usual block-style print, not quite a full page long. He wrote about being busy at work and missing the family, and then he started in on a story about his attempt to use the coffeepot.

I put the coffee beans into

the grinder, just like you showed me, put the water in the tank, and flipped the switch. It made a rather unusual sound, or so I thought, so I opened the lid to take a quick peek. Mistake! The coffee grinder sent coffee shrapnel flying through the air at Mach 3, where they eventually made safe landing in the dining room, living room, and kitchen floors. In fact, tell Brian when he's looking through his telescope tonight to see if he notices any shards of French roast in the asteroid belt.

Julie had to set the letter aside for a moment while she laughed. Thomas was funny that way. Brilliant though he was, machinery with more than an on-off switch was bound to cause him trouble. The television setup, voice mail, anything computer-related that didn't require an all-out tech, those were all left in Julie's realm. "Maybe he does need me, at least a little bit."

Whitney came into the room and dropped onto the floor beside Julie, a fistful of mail still in her hand. "Hey, kiddo, you want to hear what your father did with the coffeepot the other day?" She looked down at her daughter then and saw the tears running down her cheeks. She immediately dropped onto the floor beside her and said, "What's wrong?"

Whitney shook her head. "I should have stayed home and played travel ball this summer. Look at these pictures" She held out a half dozen pictures of the girls playing volleyball, drinking milk shakes, and sitting on the beach.

"Are you missing your friends?"

Whitney shrugged. "Did you notice there's a new girl in the pictures? She just moved to town. Coach let her join the travel team, and she's supposedly a really good setter. Mom, they say she's *really* good. That's *my position.* What if I don't even get to play next year? What if I don't make the team?"

"Honey, you've already been selected for next year's team. And who says you can't improve your skills this summer? You're not playing on an organized team, but you can practice. We'll get you a ball, and you can work on your setups against the wall of the barn or something. Remember how you used to do that against the side of our house?"

"I remember how mad Dad got when I got dirty round marks all over the off-white stucco."

"Yes, well, at least that's not a problem here. Besides, what if we put up a volleyball net somewhere out back? It might make for some fun family activity in the evening."

"Playing against you and Aunt Susan?" Whitney looked almost offended.

"Hey, we may be older than you, but we're not in that bad of shape. I'm saying we could at least give it a try." Julie glanced toward Susan, hoping she might have overheard, but she was reading a letter intently and seemed lost to the world. "Or . . . maybe some of the kids that you met at church Sunday would want to play sometime?"

"Doesn't really matter if they want to or not if I'm not even allowed to go to youth group, now does it?"

"I'll find Kendra and talk about that this afternoon. I'll insist she let you guys go."

"Insist? Really?" Whitney's face lit up. "Wow, I like this new, stronger mom I see emerging." She bounded back into the kitchen.

A new, stronger mom. Julie just sat, thrilled at the words and knowing her daughter had no idea how much they meant to her. No idea how much Julie wanted to really be that person.

After lunch, Julie left the kids to their conversations and went in search of Kendra, whom she found in the shack lingering over some sort of paperwork. The producer barely glanced up. "Do you need something, Julie?"

"Yes, I'd like to talk to you about youth group. The kids want to go tomorrow night, and I think it's important that they do."

"No. I did some checking, and they use electric guitars, amplifiers, and drums there. That's hardly appropriate in our situation." She went back to writing, subject dismissed.

Julie straightened her spine. "They need to be around other people their own age."

Kendra didn't look up. Didn't acknowledge her in any way.

"The cameras aren't allowed inside church, so it's not like the world will see it. Besides, Amish teenagers have a time where they are allowed to experience the outside world. It's called . . ." For the life of her, Julie couldn't remember the word, the one word that would help her make her case.

"*Rumspringa.*" Kendra rubbed the back of her neck. "But the Swartzentruber Amish apparently don't participate in that particular custom. Since we're in their part of the country, then your kids shouldn't either."

"Ninety-five percent of our viewers will not know the difference. Our kids need an outlet."

Kendra still didn't answer. She picked up her iPhone and pushed a couple of buttons, then said, "Could you come in here, please?"

Gary opened the door almost immediately. "What's up?"

"Would you be able to take the kids to church in the wagon tomorrow night? If they're going to do something like that, they need to go by horse and buggy to add at least a hint of authenticity."

Gary shook his head. "I've got to leave town tomorrow. Chris can do it, though. He's spent a fair amount of time around horses, and I showed him how to hook everything up."

"I don't know. . . ." Kendra shook her head.

Julie was a bit taken aback at the thought of sending the kids off with the wild-looking Chris, but she was determined to win this battle for Whitney's sake. "Kendra, the kids need to do this."

"All right, we'll try it just this week and see how it goes."

"Thank you."

"Make sure you remind the kids that Chris is a production assistant. They're not allowed to talk to him during the ride there and back.

"I'll remind them." Julie walked back to the house, excited to share the news.

The kitchen was empty, but voices were coming from the living room. She walked through to find the girls sitting on the floor, surrounded by fabric and Rosemary in the rocking chair, leaning over talking to them.

"Hello, Rosemary."

She looked up and smiled at Julie. "Hello yourself." She nodded toward the fabric on the floor. "After I got everyone broken in last time, I thought perhaps you all might enjoy your own project, so I brought over some more fabric for you all to go through. When I'm here, we can all work on the main quilt together, but I thought everyone might enjoy her own private piece to sew on in the downtime."

"That sounds wonderful, thank you." Julie hoped they would eventually get this place dialed in enough that they would be able to relax and do some sewing just for fun. At this point, the chores seemed to overwhelm all else.

"Did you sew with your mother, Rosemary?" Angie looked up at the woman, a glint of true interest in her eyes.

"Not as much as I would have liked. Mama was an excellent seamstress, and she made a big part of our living from making clothes for other people. My father had tuberculosis and spent months at a time in the State TB Hospital, so most of Mama's sewing was about earning food money. Usually, though, we'd start working on a quilt or two around Christmas. She would use the scraps from the clothes she'd made during the year, so it was always a bit wild looking." She chuckled.

"One Christmas Eve, we had just finished our Christmas quilt and were sitting bundled under it around the wood stove. It was especially cold that year. I can still feel it in my bones when I think back to that night. Since it was Christmas Eve, we burned a bit more wood than our normal allotment — Mama said it just wasn't right to be cold on Christmas — but truth was, in that drafty old house, we were cold anyway. The room hung thick with the smell of smoke, but I didn't mind. No, I was dreaming of the next morning and what I might get from Santa, and my sisters and brother and I were singing Christmas carols. Mama kept trying to get us to go to bed, but we were much too excited.

"All of a sudden, we heard this really loud sound, like a thump. We all looked around, wide eyed, when an orange came rolling across the living room floor. We stopped our singing and stared around at each other. About that time, we heard the thumping sound again, and out came another orange. Oranges in December were a treat back in those days, so we were more excited than today's kids would be about candy.

"My mother looked up and nodded. 'Santa must be in the attic. Spilled those out of his sack, most likely. Hope he doesn't come down here and find you all still awake.' "

"Did it work?" Whitney asked.

"I've never run faster in my life as I did toward my bed that night. Didn't dare move, either, until it was the next morning."

"Where'd the orange come from?" Whitney asked.

"Years later, I asked Mama about that. She said she'd had 'em hidden in the folds of her skirt the whole time. She tossed them out when we weren't looking."

"You're a good storyteller, Rosemary." Angie continued to cut the fabric, but her hands were moving slowly and she was obviously thinking. "I really enjoy good stories."

"That's one of the talents the good Lord gave me, I reckon."

"Storytelling and quilting," Julie mumbled, more to herself than anything; then she looked up at Rosemary. "I don't mean this to sound offensive, because I'm asking this question about me as much as you, but do you ever wish He'd given you talents that were a bit . . . more useful?"

"Trying to outthink God is never a good idea." She sat up a bit straighter in her chair. "Never underestimate what you have. My quilts have kept plenty of people warm over the years. And stories, well, they can be a powerful thing."

Angie nodded. "I think so, too. Your version of the loaves and fishes got me thinking a bit differently."

"Exactly my point. You've got to do your best with the things you've been given."

Angie's head was slowly nodding. Julie looked up to see if Susan noticed, but she didn't. She was busy perfecting a stitch and hadn't seen a thing.

CHAPTER 17

When the kids arrived home from school that afternoon, they were red-faced and moving slowly. The heat had really ramped up over the last twenty-four hours, and the mile-long walk was rarely in shade. They all sank down at the kitchen table with a glass of ice water.

"I don't know how people lived here before cars and air-conditioning." Whitney fanned her face with her notebook. "I feel like I could pass out right now."

"Me too." Angie took a sip of water. Her face was bright red. "It's exhausting to be this hot. I think I feel like getting a cold shower and going straight to bed."

"No early bedtime tonight, my friend. We've got youth group. Remember?"

Angie rested her chin in her hand and shook her head slowly from side to side. "By the time we finish our afternoon chores,

I just don't think I'll have the strength to-night."

"Did I hear you say that we're taking the buggy, Mom?" Brian looked up, his face so red his freckles hardly showed.

"Yes. That's the plan."

"Is Gary taking us?"

"No, he had to leave town. Kendra said she'd have one of the production assistants take you instead."

"Did she say which one?" Both of Angie's hands were locked tight around her water glass as she waited for an answer.

"Chris, the boy with the black hair. Gary's been teaching him about the horses and buggies and such."

Angie stared into her glass, seemingly mesmerized by the chunks of ice. Finally she lifted her cup, took a large sip, and said, "I'm going out to do my chores now so that I'll have time to shower and rest up before youth group. Come on, Whitney, let's get going."

Whitney turned up her glass and emptied it. "All right, I'm coming." She looked down at Brian. "You too, twerp."

After they walked out, Susan said, "I'm going to find Kendra and let her know that I want a different driver. Or I want them going by Suburban. Being out on those buggies is dangerous enough when a responsible adult is driving, much less some reckless kid who thinks he's cool."

"He's been nothing but polite and helpful every time I've been around him." Julie didn't mention that Angie's face always lit up when he was around, either. She didn't think that would help in calming Susan.

"Eddie Haskell was always polite in front of parents, too."

"Susan, why don't you go finish that wildflower arrangement you were working on before the kids arrived? I'll go talk to Kendra and let her know about our concerns and see what she says about it."

Susan looked doubtful, but she had been in major decorating mode, so Julie knew the idea was tempting. "They *will* be filming here on Friday. I really need to keep working on getting this place spruced up."

"Exactly. Now get busy, and I'll go see what I can do." Julie walked out of the farmhouse and into the shack. Kendra wasn't there, but Chris was. He was sitting on a chair, strumming a guitar. He looked surprised to see Julie.

"Sorry to disturb you. I was looking for Kendra."

"She's gone for the afternoon. Something I can help you with?" He swung the guitar to his left hand and stood up.

"Not really. We were just worr—" Julie thought better of what she was about to say, and rephrased. "We were just wondering what the arrangements are for the kids tonight, as far as getting into town."

He leaned the guitar against the desk. "I'm the designated driver for this evening's events."

Julie nodded. "Good. That's good. And you'll be driving the . . ."

"The smaller buggy. We can all fit in it, and it's easier to maneuver than the big one, plus easier for cars to get around."

Julie nodded and looked down at her hands.

"Don't worry, I'll keep it under the speed limit." He smiled. "Besides that, we've got some lanterns to put on the back. They're pretty sick, actually. I'm thinking of snagging some to take home and put on my car back in L.A."

"I'm sure they would make a big hit."

"Absolutely. So . . . you okay with that plan, or do you want me to cook up something else?"

Was Julie completely relaxed about this plan? No. But if she only allowed her kids to do things that never worried her, she supposed they would be locked up in a padded room somewhere. It sounded like a fun adventure.

"It sounds okay. So will you drop them off and come back here, then, or will you stay there and wait? In case they need to leave early or something."

"I'll stay there."

"The studio wants someone there for security, right?"

He nodded. "Yeah, I'm sure they do, but that's not why I'm staying."

"Then why?"

"I'm in the worship band."

"Oh. Okay. Great." Julie walked back into the farmhouse and found Susan arranging and rearranging the same flowers. "Well?"

"Let's just say, arrangements have been made. I think the kids are going to be in fine hands."

Several hours later, after the dinner dishes were washed and put away, Julie and Susan sat on the back porch and watched the kids loading into the buggy. Brian was about to climb in when Chris shook his head. "Ladies first."

Angie's face blushed a deep red, and in spite of obvious effort, she was unable to conceal her grin as Chris offered his hand to help her up. Whitney was next, but just clambered right past Chris's offered hand.

Brian climbed in last, but then crawled over the girls. "We men have to sit together."

"You can't even talk to him, remember?" Whitney said.

"We're men; we don't need to talk!"

Chris gave a quick glance at Angie before looking back toward Brian and giving him a thumbs-up. As the buggy pulled away from the barn, Julie was convinced that once the buggy disappeared over the first hill, any talking rules would be utterly forgotten.

"From what I've seen, that Chris is actually a nice kid."

"I don't envy the poor mother whose daughter brings someone like him home. Can you imagine? I guess someone who's raised a girl with no more common sense than to date a boy with that hairdo deserves what she's getting, though." She stood up and stretched. "You want to tackle the downstairs bathroom or the hall closet?"

Julie bit her bottom lip until she trusted herself to answer without laughing. "I'll take the bathroom, I guess." How was it that Susan could note a dirty closet from a half-mile away, and yet have no idea about what was happening in her daughter's heart? For Angie's sake, Julie hoped the attraction was short-lived, because if it ever came to Susan's attention, she didn't think the results would be pretty.

The smell of cleaning solution burned Julie's nose as she worked on all fours, scrubbing the bathroom floor. The tiny octagonal-shaped tiles looked as if they could very well be as old as the building itself. And she couldn't be certain if they were once white or if this dingy gray color was actually the color they were intended to be.

No matter. Susan was convinced that they should be white, and so this scrubbing session would continue either until the tile turned white, Susan conceded, or Julie passed out from the fumes. Starting in the far corner, she scrubbed and scrubbed and scrubbed. Her back and shoulders ached from the exertion, but she kept pushing. At least now, with the kids away, she didn't mind Susan's obsessive need to clean so much. In the evenings, when the kids were home, she wanted to spend a little downtime talking about the day, playing games, whatever it was that a slower lifestyle was supposed to entail. So far, the only thing slower seemed to be the lack of noise and the variety of activities. Now they just worked longer and harder at the same few activities, over and over again.

"My, my, my, aren't you the industrious one?"

Julie turned toward the voice, but before she could answer, she began coughing. "Hi, Kendra." She finally got the words out. "I thought you were gone for the day."

"I'm back. Where is Susan?"

"I think she's cleaning out the hall closet. Either that, or arranging more flowers, I'm not sure which."

"I'll go find her. Why don't you find a stopping point and come join us? I've got a few things to talk to you both about."

"All right." Julie wasn't sure whether she liked the sound of that. But, since there was no other option, she put her brush and gloves in the sink and went to join the others.

She found them standing in the living room, Kendra looking crisp and put together as usual. Susan, however, looked a bit rumpled — like someone who'd had her head in an old musty closet or something. Julie hadn't seen her own reflection leaving the bathroom and didn't want to think about what a person who'd been scrubbing fifty-year-old bathroom tile on her hands and knees might look like.

"There are just a couple of things I need to tell you," Kendra said. "First of all, what are you planning for dinner tomorrow night?"

"Beef stew," Susan said. Julie knew she had menus for the entire next week in her head.

"Perfect. We'll be doing a crew sampling."

"A crew sampling?" Julie held her breath and looked toward Susan, whose jaws were clenched tight.

"Yes. Periodically we'll get a bit of whatever you've cooked for dinner, or breakfast, and take it over to the shack. We'll give samples to the crew and allow honest feedback. It'll help give us an idea of whether the average American consumer would prefer more traditionally prepared foods."

"Okay." Susan's head kept nodding as she stared off in the distance. "We can do that. Sure."

"Secondly, I wanted to let you know that Thomas will be here for the weekend."

Thomas? Julie realized then how much less her thoughts had turned to him since the beginning of this adventure. "That is wonderful. When will he arrive?"

"Tomorrow night. He'll be here until Sunday afternoon."

Susan smiled and nodded. "I'm glad we're getting the place in such good shape, then."

She gestured around the room. "He would have been appalled if he'd arrived last week."

"About that . . ." Kendra walked over to the living room table and the glass cup full of artfully arranged flowers. "These all need to go. I've done some research, and especially for the more conservative Amish that live in this area, this amount of decoration would never be allowed in their home; it would be considered prideful."

"But these are from the flower garden that was already planted here, plus the wildflowers that grow down by the creek. God's creation, not man-made."

"Turns out, the Swartzentruber Amish don't grow flowers around their homes. In fact, that will be one of your tasks for this week. Tearing out the flower garden."

Susan opened her mouth, as if to argue, then shut it. She swallowed hard enough that Julie could see it; then she nodded. "Okay, then. That's what we'll do."

She picked up the plain glass full of beautiful flowers and started toward the back door. "I'll just go put these in the trash."

Julie had never seen Susan back down so quickly from anything. She wondered what kind of power she thought Kendra wielded over her.

By the time the *clip-clopping* of hooves sounded from the driveway, every trace of floral decoration had been removed from the house. The glasses had all been scrubbed clean, the hall closet was spotless and organized, and the bathroom floor was still a shade of dirty gray — although Julie would have dared anyone to find a single speck of dirt within the confines of the small bathroom. She walked into the dark back bedroom so she could look out the window without being noticed from outside.

The kids, back from youth group, were singing and laughing. This time, Brian was sitting on the outside edge; beside him was Whitney, next to her, Angie. Angie was saying something, to which Chris replied. They all laughed again.

Chris pulled the wagon into the barn, and Julie could see no more. She went into the living room and sat down with her scissors and some scrap fabric. She cut out squares from the new fabric Rosemary had brought at her last visit, thinking about all that was happening around here, and about Thomas's upcoming visit. Would he be happy to see them and simply enjoy the visit, or would he look around with eyes that noticed how much had yet to be done? He and Susan, at times, shared more than the same eye color and chin. Julie felt a clench of worry, a feeling she'd begun thinking of as her former life.

The back door squeaked open, and the kids shook the floor as they bounded into the room. Julie kept cutting, trying to appear nonchalant. "How was it?"

"Interesting." Whitney deposited herself in the middle of the living room floor.

"At first, it was a little bit . . . awkward," Brian said, toying with the hem of his blue shirt. "But still kind of fun."

"The kids were a little standoffish, especially in the beginning," Angie said.

"I think it took them a while to move past these getups." Whitney motioned toward her skirt and top. "And then the fact that we're from California seemed to make us suspicious."

"But, in the end, they mostly moved past all that and it worked out pretty well. Hey, Mom, some of the kids from the youth group help run a weekly club for some kids in one of the poorer neighborhoods. Can I start helping?"

"I don't know, Whitney. It took a lot of convincing just to get them to let you go tonight. I'll see what I can do, though."

"Well, as long as we can keep going to youth group. I really liked it." Angie smiled.

"I thought the music was excellent, didn't you?" Whitney looked at her cousin, and they exchanged a grin.

Julie looked toward Susan, who seemed completely oblivious to the exchange that was happening. "Okay, off to bed with you all. We've got lots of work to do tomorrow."

"Good night." Angie practically sighed the words as she floated up the stairs, one graceful step at a time.

CHAPTER 18

Susan stood at the counter chopping carrots into half-inch discs. Kendra's alert about the taste test — or was it a warning; everything Kendra said seemed like a threat or a warning — rang in her mind. The crew *had* to think this was the best stew they'd ever tasted; there was absolutely no margin for error. At all. Carrots done, she reached next for an onion and concentrated on dicing it into perfect, even pieces.

Next to her, obviously feeling no pressure at all, Julie hummed some tuneless melody while she poked at the fire in the stove. After a bit, she stood and stretched, then walked casually to the window and pulled back the curtain. Watching for Thomas.

The onion was taking its toll, and Susan's eyes were beginning to tear. She wiped her eyes across her upper arm. "I think we need some fresh parsley, and I'll want to mince some garlic. Perhaps we should go pull a couple of peppers from the garden. Do you think a hint of rosemary would be nice, or would that be too much?"

Julie frowned. "Susan, you've been talking about adding this, or more of that, for the last half hour. It's just stew."

"I don't want to make *just* stew, or anything else for that matter. That's not good enough. To me, cooking is like an art, and I don't want to be a finger painter. In fact, I want to do everything to the absolute best of my abilities." Julie continued to look out the window, obviously not taking the hint. "You haven't seen your husband in two weeks; don't you think he deserves more than a halfhearted attempt?"

"I . . ." Julie let her hand fall back from the curtain. She walked to the stove, opened the door and poked at the fire again. After a minute, she said, "I'll just go get that parsley and those peppers for you." She scurried out the door as if she were being chased.

Susan knew she'd hurt Julie's feelings, and she *was* sorry about that, but she had spoken the truth. Shouldn't Julie appreciate the fact that she had such a wonderful husband? Shouldn't she want to make nice meals for him? She wiped her eyes with her sleeve again. *Darn onions.*

A few minutes later, the door squeaked

behind her as she scraped the carrots and onions from the cutting board into the pot. She supposed she should try a little small talk. "Is it still hot out there?"

"Yes."

Silence. It hung in the air, like the heat that radiated from the stove.

Julie picked up a potato. She pulled out the trash can from beneath the sink and held the potato over it while she cut off the peel in long strips. She didn't say anything for a while, then made a comment or two about the weather while she reached for another potato, and then the next. "The kids seem to be enjoying their one-room schoolhouse, don't they?"

"And why wouldn't they?" Susan looked up from her work with the celery. "There's no one there but the three of them and a teacher who's barely out of high school herself."

Julie was shaking her head slowly. "When I was a teenager, I didn't have all this pressure on me like our kids do now. Angie and the SATs, Whitney and the volleyball team. I spent summers at the pool — working in the snack shack, mind you, but still, the rest of my time was free time. I didn't feel like I needed summer enrichment programs, or club sports teams, or Space Camp, just so I wouldn't be behind when school started in the fall."

"Whether or not we like it, this is today's reality."

"Personally, I'm enjoying today's reality, here — no phone, computer, or television. There's a lot of work to do, but at least it's all focused. It's all done for a reason — namely to take care of my family and the animals and crops that we're raising. I think a lot of the other stuff we do in the modern world, a lot of the stuff we have our kids doing, is really not that important."

Susan snorted. "Yeah, you'll see how important it is come college-application time. Or job-application time, even more. With today's economy and unemployment rate, how can you not want to give them every opportunity to find true success?"

"I'm just saying, I don't think we're teaching them true success."

"And I think you are looking back to what once was and burying your head in the sand about today's reality. You've got to —"

"He's here!" Julie raced out the door and was standing beside the Suburban by the time it came to a complete stop. In spite of the fact that the windows were tinted so dark that nothing or no one could be seen inside, she was waving at the windows. The front door opened, and one of the usual drivers stepped out. He nodded at Julie and walked toward the production office. A cameraman climbed out of the passenger side and walked slowly around the car. He walked all the way around Julie to stand on her right side, and then nodded toward the car. The back door flew open, and in a flash Susan's brother was out and picking Julie up, swinging her around in circles. He kissed her, just a quick peck, then hugged her tight and said something, which Susan couldn't hear from inside, but any idiot would know that it was "I missed you" or "I love you."

Julie had no idea how lucky she was to have a man like Thomas, so full of honesty and integrity. She couldn't understand why Julie didn't work harder on taking care of him. Thomas deserved excellent meals and a sparkling home. They'd watched their own mother provide it. Susan turned to put the celery and pepper in the stew, stirred the pot and put the lid back on, then took a deep breath, squared her shoulders, and pushed through the kitchen door.

"Hey there, brother of mine. 'Bout time you got here." She put on her happiest smile for Thomas, and she truly was glad to see him. He had been a rock for her this last

195

year, and it made her feel more secure just having him here.

"Hey there, sis." He hurried over and locked her in a bear hug. "So how's the simple life treating you?" He grinned and made a sweep through her hair with his left hand. "I see you've changed your hairdo. I like it."

"This is not a changed hairdo. This is what hair looks like when I'm not allowed to use a hairdryer and the humidity hovers around ninety percent."

He leaned back and nodded. "You know what, it looks good on you." He picked up his leather overnighter. "Julie was just telling me all about the creek, and the schoolhouse, and Brian's observatory. How about I take my bag inside and then we go take a look. I'm dying to see the kids."

"Well, we're just in the process of making stew." Susan cast a meaningful gaze toward Julie, hoping she would get the hint. "We're supposed to feed the entire crew tonight, so it's quite a large pot of stew. Not to mention some sourdough bread we're just about ready to bake."

Julie looped her hand through Thomas's arm and walked toward the house. "Don't worry, though, we can finish it up in a snap, and leave the stew to simmer for a while."

Susan thought about the stew. She thought about how perfect it needed to be. She thought about trying to finish it in a snap. She thought about the plethora of horrible possibilities if it turned to mush; the flavors were wrong. "Julie, I'm really not sure that we're a *snap* away from finishing."

"Really?" There was no hiding the irritation in Julie's voice. "I think it's mostly ready, except for the potatoes I still need to slice up. Thomas is only going to be here for three days. I think we can shave a little time off stew making so we can spend more time with him, don't you?"

No. She didn't. And her future life depended on this. "Why don't the two of you walk over there? I'll stay here and finish up the stew."

"Ah, come on, Suse. I don't care about the stew. Walk over with us; tell me about what's been happening."

"What's happening right now is I've got work to do, so why don't the two of you get on with your journey so I can get back to my work?"

"Susan, if you want me to stay —"

"No, no. Sorry that came out harsh. I'll just . . . I'll just be happiest if I know this was done right. You two go ahead. Have a good time."

■ ■ ■ ■

Susan watched out the kitchen window as the two of them walked away, hand-in-hand, toward the schoolhouse. She looked toward the pot of stew — a pot of stew that somehow had the potential to decide her future. It almost made her laugh. Then Angie's face came to mind. It was her daughter for whom she was doing all this. She had no Thomas. Angie's future, that burden fell squarely on Susan's shoulders and only hers. Somehow, though, she would find the strength to make it all work, and she could do it without anyone's help. She had no choice.

Squeak.

Susan whirled around toward the sound of the back porch door opening. She saw Gary approaching the kitchen door and motioned him inside.

A grin lit his face as he entered the room. "Oh my, that smells good." He closed his eyes and took a long sniff. "Really good." He opened his eyes and held up a large brown grocery bag, still smiling. "I come bearing gifts and offers of help. I thought I could — hey, are you all right?" He took a step closer, his expression suddenly serious.

Only then did Susan realize that her eyes were filled with tears. She wiped them against the back of her arm again. "Fine. I've just been cutting onions, and my eyes are really sensitive."

He nodded but studied her face for a moment as if not quite convinced. "Well, if you're cutting onions, then I think I'm just in time with this." He extended the bag toward her. "Sorry for the plain wrap-job, but I had to get it past Kendra somehow, and I was pretty certain she'd be suspicious if she saw wrapping paper and big red bows."

"What is it?" Susan took the bag, surprised by how heavy it was.

"Just a little something I made that I thought you might enjoy using while you're here."

She opened the bag, reached inside, and drew out a large wooden square, maybe an inch thick. Only when she got it completely out in the open did she get the full impact of what it was. "This is beautiful."

He shrugged, but he couldn't hide the smile at her words. "I heard you tell Kendra you needed a bigger cutting board, and I was pretty certain she hadn't gotten you one yet. I've been doing a little woodworking over the last few years, and this particular board design is called 'Amish Quilt.' I guess you don't have to guess why."

"No, I don't." The entire board looked almost like a tile mosaic, so precise was the placement of the various wood colors. The overall effect was like a quilt, made entirely of wood.

"I couldn't help but try this one. I thought it would be useful now, and maybe make a nice souvenir to remind you of your time here after you go back home."

Susan shook her head. "Thank you so much. I just don't see how I could ever use it. It's too beautiful to get all cut up."

"Nope, don't say that. No point having nice things just to put them away because you don't want to ruin them. Now, as I said, I'm here to help. I saw that your brother and sister-in-law went on a little walk, and I thought you might like a hand with getting things ready. What can I do for you?"

He leaned on the counter, and his baby-blue eyes smiled at her in a way that was totally inviting. She looked into them a second longer than she knew she should. Finally she said, "We need to set the tables."

"All right, then. Why don't you come with me, and we'll work together? Teamwork is so much more fun than working alone.

Don't you think?" Again that smile, those eyes.

"Yes, I do." *Indeed.*

Just as they'd arrived back at the house after their tour, Kendra had beckoned Julie and Thomas to be interviewed, a process Julie still felt nervous about every time. She'd discovered that staring just off-center, at the air-conditioner, made her feel less self-conscious than looking at the camera, or at the artillery of high-tech computers and equipment crammed into every available space in the shack. She hoped this would be quick, so they could get on with their Saturday evening.

"Mr. Charlton, if you can take the seat right beside your wife, we'll get started in just a few minutes."

"All right." Thomas sat down and took Julie's hand. He leaned over and whispered, "Okay, TV star. What do we do now?"

"I have no idea. Susan is the one that does most of the sit-down interviews. I'm usually just part of the live segments. In fact, I'm usually the one making all the mistakes during the live segments."

"Not true."

"Yes, it is. Haven't you been watching?"

"Well, they've only aired the pie one, but I

think a good portion of the women in America would have trouble making a pie they'd never made in a wood stove they'd never used."

"I'm sure Susan would have made it perfectly."

He squeezed her hand again. "Maybe, but cooking is what Susan does. That's her passion. You have other things you're good at."

"Like what?"

"Lots of things."

Right. He couldn't come up with one specific answer. That, in itself, was telling.

"Okay, let's get started." Kendra came to take her place behind the camera. "Now, Thomas, I'll be cut out of this, so make certain to sort of repeat the question in your answers, okay?"

"Got it."

"All right. How about telling us what you think so far about what's happening with your wife, sister, kids, and niece."

"This has been an amazing opportunity for all of them. And I've found it interesting that the kids haven't really slowed down any, at least in the way I expected. It sounded like a big summer vacation, but at this point, they're up earlier than ever in the morning because they have their farm chores to do. They are staying focused and growing a lot in the process."

Kendra nodded. "That's perfect. How about you, Julie? What are you thinking about your time here so far?"

"My time here has been amazing in so many ways. Just the quiet. I've been able to spend more time talking with my kids, not hurried time in the car, but it's dinnertime and we don't have anywhere that we're supposed to be in five minutes, and I don't have to leave in the middle of dinner to go pick up someone from practice, or take someone else to a club meeting. I understand how the Amish can be so deeply spiritual. It's not a matter of not having anything to do. Far from it. Our days are filled with work from sunrise to sunset. It's just a matter of shutting out a lot of the noise. No TV. No email, or Facebook, or texts. I hadn't realized how impersonal our lives are now."

"How about cooking the old way. How are you enjoying that?"

Julie shifted in her chair and shrugged. "I'm not a cook. I think everyone knows that. At home, I'm usually trying to whip something together that people can eat between events. But to be honest, I've grown to enjoy the process here — it's actually nice to spend time chopping and simmering when there's not a barrage of phone calls and other activities. But I think that's where it ends for me. I couldn't make it an all-day thing. Maybe it's because I don't have a very sophisticated palate to begin with. Sometimes we'll go out to a nice restaurant with Susan, and she'll comment on the rosemary flavor of the lamb, or whatever, and I would never notice something like that."

"Why do you think that is? Did your mother cook a lot when you were a kid?"

"Well, she . . ." Julie's throat closed around any further words she might have spoken. She took a deep breath, willing herself to answer the question. Another breath followed another, the silence growing long and uncomfortable.

Thomas squeezed her hand and leaned forward. "Julie's mother died when she was very young. Julie was raised by a single father — a wonderful man whom we still dearly miss — but who admitted his favorite chef was Boyardee. It just wasn't part of her growing up."

Kendra nodded. "I had no idea. Interesting." She looked at her paper, as if deciding where she might want to take the conversation from here. Finally, she looked up and said, "So, Thomas, there has been a bit of a disagreement here about the education your children are receiving. Your wife seems quite satisfied with the way things are running, yet your sister seems to believe that the teacher is not being forceful enough. Have you talked with them about this at all, and what are your thoughts?"

Thomas shifted uneasily in his seat and adjusted his shirt collar with his left hand. He glanced briefly at Julie before clearing his throat. "It seems to me, from what I've seen and heard, that the kids do need a more aggressive approach to their studies. I know that it is summer, but Brian needs to be challenged, and Whitney could always use a little extra push to get where she needs to be academically. I know Susan feels the same way about Angie."

"Why is it, do you think, that your wife is not as concerned?"

More shifting. "Well, again she just was raised differently. In my opinion, and Susan's, most kids benefit from being pushed to reach their full potential. I feel fortunate that Susan and I had parents who were always on top of our schoolwork and activities."

"Are you saying that Julie didn't reach her full potential?"

"No, of course not." He looked toward the side walls, as if composing his thoughts.

"Julie's terrific just the way she is, but there is that unknown factor of 'what if.' "

This opinion was nothing Julie hadn't heard a hundred times, and yet the hearing of it never grew less painful. The two of them argued about pushing the kids too hard versus letting them coast through life on a semi-regular basis. Still, the implications never failed to hurt, because the take-away Julie always got from this conversation was "Julie is not good enough." Now all of America would hear it, too.

CHAPTER 19

Susan scrubbed the countertops. Hard. She felt a growing confidence that the house was coming under order — Kendra admitted as much during their interview earlier — but this was not the time to let off. Eight more weeks and her future, and more importantly Angie's, would be secure.

"That was a fine dinner, ladies. Nothing compares to fresh-out-of-the-garden vegetables." Thomas bent down to hold the dustpan in place for Julie and her broom, moaning as he did so. "I think I'm too old for the simple life."

They all laughed, but a bit uneasily, Susan thought. This life was hard.

"Okay, everyone, into the living room, please." Whitney stuck her head in the door, a big goofy grin on her face.

Susan still needed to prep the dough for tomorrow morning's cinnamon raisin bread. "I'll be just a bit."

"You need to hurry or you'll be late for opening ceremonies." Whitney sounded whiny, as was too often the case. Hopefully Thomas would shut that down while he was here.

"I'm sure —"

"Come on, sister of mine. I'll help you with the dough after we see whatever it is we're supposed to see. We don't want to miss the opening ceremonies to — whatever it is — that much is certain." Thomas put his arm around her shoulder and began to pull her toward the living room. So much for his help.

"But I really need to get this done."

"And you will, and I'll help, but we're just going to wait a few minutes."

Susan walked into the living room, prepared to force a smile through whatever silliness it was that Whitney had planned. After that, she could hurry back to her bread dough.

The kids all stood in the center of the living room, flanked by a couple of checkerboards. Whitney picked up a wreath of magnolia leaves and put it on her head. "Welcome to the first annual Checkers Olympics. Each person will be representing a different country. Mom, you'll be Austria, Dad you're Switzerland, Aunt Susan is

France, Angie is England, Brian is Chile, and I'm . . . well, I'm America, of course."

"How come you get to be America?" Thomas asked.

"Well, because I'm the most patriotic."

Brian snorted something that sounded like "yeah right" from behind her. Whitney cut a quick glance at him and grinned. "And . . . I'm the one who picked the teams. But all the countries were picked for a specific reason."

"Why am I Switzerland? Because I'm neutral?"

"Yeah, right, Dad. You're wound tight as a Swiss watch, but . . . I decided that every stockbroker should have a Swiss bank account, so I let you keep it."

Thomas laughed. "Well, I like the bank account part."

"This is how it works. There are two checkerboards, and Brian has already worked out the brackets. All we have to do now is draw numbers for your country's position on the bracket. The amazing Angie, also known as Great Britain, or GB for short, has placed all the numbers in the bonnet. Switzerland, since you're a guest here, we'll let you draw first."

Thomas stuck his hand into the bonnet. "Five."

"Okay, you'll be sitting out the first round. France, you're next."

Susan stuck her hand into the bonnet and prayed for a six. She could go work in the kitchen while everyone else got started. She reached in her hand and pulled out a two. Great. "How about I trade with Thomas? I really need to get started on that dough."

"Mom, come on. Even the Amish sit down and enjoy family in the evenings."

"But the recipe calls for letting the dough rise for two hours, rolling it out, then letting it rise for another hour."

"I'm thinking scrambled eggs and biscuits sound good for breakfast tomorrow. Let's spend some time with our kids."

Susan was just about to tell Julie what she thought of that idea when Angie walked over and grinned up at her. "Looks like it's you and me." She dropped to the floor beside the closest checkerboard. "Okay, France, let's see what you've got." She moved a black piece one step closer to Susan's side.

Susan sighed and sat down. Might as well make the best of it. "I've got enough to take on the Brits, that's for sure." She counter-moved and waited for her daughter's response. It had been a long time since she'd played checkers.

Whitney sat between the two boards so she could see both of them; Thomas sat opposite her so he could do the same. "A mother-son matchup. This should be interesting. Hmm." He nodded his head slowly, as if thoroughly intrigued by the idea. Julie sort of groaned.

"Hey, you're the one that raised him," Whitney laughed. "If he's an overachieving genius, then it's your fault."

Brian made his next move. "Is it her fault that you're an underachieving dum—" Brian glanced up toward Julie and stopped himself just a fraction of a second too late. "Sorry."

"Brian, tell your sister that you're sorry, not me." Julie glared at him until he broke eye contact.

"Sorry." He wasn't overly convincing. "But really, I want to know. If Mom's raising made me a genius, then why aren't you one, too?"

"Your sister is plenty smart. Knock it off." Julie slid another checker forward.

"Yes, I am, and I am smart in more than just books, unlike some people in the family."

"You shouldn't talk that way about Dad," Brian quipped, and the entire room erupted into laughter. Then he triple-jumped Julie's checkers and everyone laughed again.

As annoying as those kids could be at times, Susan did admire the easy conversation that always seemed to flow in their family. She looked at her daughter sitting across the checkerboard from her and was thankful for the time they had together. "So, Angie, what are you most enjoying about our little experiment?"

Angie blushed and glanced at Whitney before she answered. "It's all been kind of fun, so far." She looked down. "Except for these clothes. It's kind of embarrassing when we go places. I can't begin to imagine how the true Amish people must feel, with people staring at them all the time."

Susan nodded. "I suppose they get used to it, but I agree, there must be times when it is really hard."

"You remember when they told us we couldn't make any pictures when we went on that tour? In the book I just read, a tourist actually jumped into a buggy with a couple of Amish people and started taking pictures. It wasn't a true story, but still, I bet there are some people who are just that thoughtless. How could anyone think of treating people with such disrespect?"

Susan flashed back to the day of their tour. She'd seen the cameramen sneaking around the Amish houses that day, but out of fear of complaining she made the decision to stay quiet. It could only have caused trouble because it wasn't her place to . . .

She was merely an employee of the show, she had no right to . . .

Not her place . . .

Time to change the subject. "You read a book about Amish people?"

Angie nodded. "Yeah, a trilogy actually — Aunt Julie read them, too. They were on the *New York Times* list, and I figured that would be a good way to get some background on what we were going to be doing."

"Why didn't you tell me you'd read those books? We could have talked about what you were learning, and about what we were expecting from our time here."

Angie shrugged and turned her full attention to the game board. "I thought you might be mad at me for wasting my time reading something that wasn't going to further my education. Besides" — she slid a checker into Susan's home row — "you never asked. Now crown me."

Susan put a second checker on top of Angie's, but her mind was no longer on the game. *I thought you might be mad* and *you never asked* pinged around inside her head over and over and over again. Hours later, as she lay in bed beneath the blue-and-white quilt, the words had gained in volume, making it impossible to sleep. Were there other things she didn't know about her daughter?

"Okay, ladies. I think today we'll try to finish this one up, and maybe next session we'll start on something a little more complicated." Rosemary held a magnifying glass up to a section of stitches, then looked up at Julie. "This is nice work. Haven't seen many folks pick it up this quickly."

Julie couldn't stop her smile. "Thanks. I've been practicing in my spare time."

"It shows."

"In my case, you've probably never seen anyone pick this up quite so slowly." Whitney shook her head and stared down at a knot in her thread. "I just don't get it. How can I be so utterly bad at something?"

"Don't give up; you'll learn it in time." Rosemary moved to help her. "You're the one that came up with our color pattern for the quilt, and you cut the straightest edges of anyone."

"Big whoop. I'm the great straight-edge cutter." Whitney sort of sighed as she pushed the needle through the fabric again.

"You say that like it's not important, but

someone has to do the cutting. It doesn't matter how well your mama sews if the pieces aren't cut out, or if they're cut so poorly they won't line up. Never let someone make you feel like whatever gift you have is less important than someone else's. Do you know who Stephen is from the Bible?"

Whitney looked up. "Sure. He was the first martyr."

"Hmm." Rosemary rocked forward in her chair and leaned toward Whitney. "He was that. But do you know what he was before?"

"One of the disciples, I guess."

"Do you know what his job was?"

"Teaching people about Jesus, right? I mean, that's why they killed him."

"He was a waiter."

"Huh?"

Rosemary began a slow rock. "The Greek believers started complaining to the apostles that their widows were being overlooked in the distribution of food. You know how that goes — get a large group of people together and there's always someone who thinks something is unfair, and maybe it was." She stared toward the wall as if seeing the scene right through it, slowly shaking her head as she did. "Maybe it was."

"So what happened?" Whitney asked, her

sewing temporarily forgotten in her lap.

"The twelve basically said, 'We've been called to teach and to pray, not to *wait tables*,' but — and here's the important part, don't miss it — they didn't say that waiting tables or feeding widows was not important. They said, 'Appoint seven men to head up the food distribution, men that are full of wisdom and the Holy Spirit.' "

"And Stephen was one of those men?"

Rosemary nodded. "Yep. Sure was." She rocked back, then forward, then back again. "Waiting tables doesn't sound terribly important in the scheme of things, does it? Yet it freed the apostles up to do what it was they were supposed to do. And Stephen didn't just wait tables; he served God with all his heart. And God rewarded that by enabling him to perform great signs and wonders, just like the apostles. But, my point is, as much as we all think of the apostles being the most important, I'm saying that they would not have been effective if those in jobs of lesser honor had not performed the work they were called to do. So if cutting straight edges is your call and stitching is your mother's, then I say they're both important. Don't you?"

Whitney nodded. "I guess so. But I still wish I could stitch better."

"You keep practicing, and you'll get better at it."

Julie rocked back and forth, considering what Rosemary had just said. She knew there was wisdom in the words, but she wished that somehow God would just show her what it was she did well, what it was that she was supposed to do. Somehow she didn't think a nice hand-stitch was going to serve her well when she reentered the real world.

CHAPTER 20

Rosemary's story and things she'd been saying about giftedness didn't leave Julie. In fact, it nagged her, roiling around and making it impossible to enjoy Susan's baked chicken and mashed potatoes. Even the perfectly prepared green beans, picked from their garden not five minutes before cooking, didn't tempt her the way they usually did. They just all reminded her how much that seemed to be Susan's gift. Along with keeping a spotless house. And keeping her daughter well on track to being accepted to any college in the country.

Sure Julie could hand-stitch better than most twenty-first-century beginners to hand-stitching, but what did that matter, really? Back home she felt as though she spent most of her time in a chaotic fog, always reacting to things, but never acting with a purpose. Busy, but accomplishing nothing. It was a never-ending cycle that left her exhausted yet unfulfilled.

"Okay, I think we need to get ready for youth group. Can I go ahead and start doing my part of washing the dishes?" Angie turned the full force of her huge chocolate eyes on Susan.

"Angie, we haven't even finished eating yet."

"Well, I have. And we need to leave in a little while, and I really want to change clothes before we go, and I know I'm supposed to be the one who cleans out the pots and pans tonight. So can I go ahead and get started, please? I'll still be able to talk to everyone and everything." Angie cut her eyes in Whitney's direction for less than a second, but Julie noticed the unvoiced plea.

"Yeah, Mom, me too. It takes awhile to get all this done, and we want to make certain we get to youth group on time, so . . ." She stuffed the last bite of chicken in her mouth and stood up. "Come on, Angie, I'm finished eating, too. Let's get this done together."

"Wait a minute." Susan cocked her head back and smiled. "I get it now. There's a boy, isn't there? There's a boy you like at youth group, and that's why you're wanting the extra time to get ready."

Angie turned pink, but she shook her

head. "Mom, I can tell you beyond the shadow of a doubt that you are mistaken. There is not a single boy in that youth group that interests me."

There could be no doubting the sincerity in her voice, and Julie knew that she was telling the truth. The trick was in the wording. There wasn't a boy *in the youth group* that interested Angie. She didn't say anything about the worship band, or their driver for the evening.

By the time she heard the horses clomping up the driveway, Julie was having trouble staying awake. Susan sat in the rocking chair, recipe books in her lap, working out their menus for the next few days. Julie had been writing in her journal and reading in the Psalms, searching for something that would give her some guidance about gifts. She had found none. "I think I'll go out and welcome the kids home."

"Mmm-hmmm." Susan didn't even look up from her task.

Julie walked out the kitchen door just as the kids were starting to climb down from the carriage. As she suspected, Angie was sitting next to the driver, and after Chris jumped out, he reached up his hand and helped her down. Whitney and Brian exited the other side.

As soon as Whitney noticed Julie she ran up to her. "Hey, Mom, have you talked to Kendra about me working with the Kids' Club? They're short several people, and they really need my help tomorrow night."

"I really haven't."

"Can you please just tell her I have to do it? You know that's something I always wanted to do in Santa Barbara, but practice got in the way. Now that I'm not getting the benefit of team practice, at least make them let me do something worthwhile with my time."

"You really love working with kids, don't you?"

Whitney nodded. "Yes."

"I'll talk to Kendra first thing in the morning and tell her it's something you're going to do. It's a good thing, and it's something you're really good at." It was one of Whitney's gifts. One of many gifts that Whitney possessed and used whenever possible. How was it that even Julie's kids seemed to understand their place in the world, and Julie herself did not? She knew that if she couldn't change that, she had no hope of ever being truly happy.

The sun still lit up the entire hillside as

Susan put the last of the dinner dishes into the cupboard. The window air-conditioning units were no match for the Tennessee summer heat and a wood stove. She wiped her forehead. "Whew. A few more nights like this and we'll be having raw vegetables the rest of the summer."

"Some Amish have what they call summer kitchens, which are not directly attached to the house," Angie explained as she wiped the last spot off the countertop. "And a lot of them also move their living area into the basement during the summer months, where it's cooler."

"And is this what fictional Amish do, or the real ones?"

"Mom, you know that most novelists try to stick to facts on those kinds of things as much as possible. Besides, I said some, not all." She folded up the towel and hung it over the rack. "Can I ride with Whitney tonight when she goes into town?"

"You mean, work at the Kids' Club with her?"

"No, I wasn't planning on staying — that's more Whitney's thing than mine — but I enjoy getting out for a nice buggy ride in the evenings. It's . . . nice."

Susan thought about the young man who drove them to youth group, his too-long artificially black hair, and his anti-establishment look. She did not want her daughter riding alone with him on the way back from dropping off Whitney at the housing complex. Then again, she really didn't want Whitney going alone with him, either. "Let me think about that. Perhaps the entire family should ride along — you know, spend some time together."

"No!" Angie's answer came out very fast and very loud. She paused just a moment before continuing. "I mean . . . no . . . there's no need for everyone to go, just because I want to get out."

Susan turned to lean against the counter and look at her daughter. It seemed like she was up to something, but there was very little she could get into at this point. Still, there was enough of a nagging doubt that she wasn't willing to hand over free rein. "You're right, we don't want to inconvenience everyone."

Angie's breath came out in one slow, relieved expulsion. "That's exactly what I think."

"But I've been wanting to get out and go for more rides anyway, so I'll come along with you. Just me. Then no one else is inconvenienced on our behalf."

"But, Mo-om . . ."

The sound of footsteps coming up the back steps stopped the conversation. The screen porch door creaked open and seconds later Gary could be seen standing at the kitchen door, preparing to knock. Susan opened the door before he raised his hand.

He looked up, surprised, and then grinned. "Well, hello there. And how is everyone this beautiful evening?"

Susan nodded. "Fine. We were just having a talk about riding into town with Whitney. Is Chris about ready to take her, do you know?"

"Nope he's not. This is his night off, and so I'm the official chauffeur for the evening. Did you say that you were planning on riding with us?"

"Well, I . . . Angie and I were just talking about riding, but I . . ."

"You know what? I think I really need to stay here and work on some schoolwork. I'll just run up and see if Whitney is ready." Angie disappeared before Susan could argue.

"Well, I don't have to come along. . . ." How much more awkward could this be?

"Please do. I was planning on running a few errands in town while she's at the Kids' Club. Would you like to hit Walmart with me? We can hitch our horse and buggy to the post beside the real Amish."

Just the thought of going somewhere familiar, and modern, sounded wonderful. "I'd love it. Julie, don't you want to come with us, too?" Julie had been talking about a trip into town for several days now.

Julie shook her head. "Not this evening. I want to work on my quilt and do some journaling."

"I'm ready." Whitney bounded into the room.

Gary smiled. "You seem excited."

Whitney nodded. "The only problem is I'm afraid the little kids will see me in these clothes and think I'm weird, and they won't want anything to do with me."

"I'd say a girl with your personality could overcome anything, especially a minor fashion issue. Those kids are going to love you." He opened the back kitchen door and held it. "Shall we, ladies?"

Quickly enough they were out in the buggy and on their way. Whitney fell quiet for the first time since they'd arrived — probably feeling awkward sharing a ride with them — and so they all rode in silence, accompanied only by the soothing clack of horse hooves. After a long half hour, they pulled up in front of the apartment complex. A group of small children came running out. "Horsies are here, horsies are here."

Gary hopped down and walked around the buggy, smiling toward the group. "Who wants to give him a carrot or two? I just happen to have some in my pocket." He pulled a plastic bag out of his jeans pocket, which held several carrot pieces.

Whitney took a deep breath, smoothed down her skirt, and said, "Wish me luck."

Susan reached over and squeezed her arm. "You'll be amazing." A group of teenagers walked past on the far side of the road, headed toward town. They were laughing a bit too loud, making it seem to Susan they were more concerned about appearing to have a good time rather than actually having one. Things were so hard at this age. She was thankful that Angie was doing so well in spite of the divorce and all the changes. Still, she couldn't help but worry about her.

Gary climbed back up into the buggy. "All right, next stop."

A few minutes later, they walked through Walmart's long aisles, and for a few minutes Susan felt utterly overwhelmed. Having been isolated for a few weeks, it seemed huge and loud and crowded.

Gary picked up the items he was after,

and then went to stand in the self-checkout line. "You seem distracted."

Susan shrugged. "I'm just a little worried about Angie, is all. You know, teenagers. That's their job, to keep their mothers distracted and worried."

He laughed. "Yes, I think you're right. Tell you the truth, it doesn't get a lot better when they get older. My oldest daughter is twenty-seven. She just went through a nasty divorce. The whole thing just ate me up." He shook his head. "Only thing you can do is just trust them to God."

"That one's easier said than done sometimes."

"You won't get an argument from me there." He picked up the plastic bags filled with tools and sandpaper and started toward the door. "Angie has a good head on her shoulders, though. I wouldn't worry overmuch about her. She'll be just fine."

"I hope so."

They made the return ride also in silence as Susan turned the words over and over in her head. She had no idea how long they'd been riding when Gary reached over and put his hand on top of hers. It jolted her out of her thoughts, at least for long enough to be shocked. "You know, you can talk to me about anything. I'd like to help you in any way I can."

Susan looked down at his tanned hand, still resting atop hers, and for just a brief moment allowed herself to think about how nice it would be to share some of her burden, not carry the entire load by herself. But that wasn't reality — not her reality anyway. In her reality, Gary was just a hired hand who knew nothing about the struggles she faced. Still, his offer stirred something inside her that made it impossible to rebuff him completely. She drew in a deep breath and exhaled slowly. "Thanks, I'll keep that in mind."

He pulled his hand away and clucked at the horse. As they reached the apartment complex, the sounds of laughter and squeals grew louder and louder.

"The horsies are back. The horsies are back." Several kids ran toward them until one of the counselors called them back.

"Bye, everyone, see you next week." Whitney waved as she started toward them.

A little girl broke free of the group, ran up, and threw her arms around Whitney. "I wuv you, Whitney."

"I love you too, Jasmine." She returned the hug before sending the girl back to the group. She was still waving after she climbed into the buggy. They started moving and immediately Whitney said, "I think that might have been the best night of my life! You know, they didn't even notice my weird clothes. All they cared about was having someone to give them a little attention. None of the other stuff really seemed to matter."

Somehow it all came out in one breath.

"Too bad the rest of the world's not a little more like that. Hmm?" asked Gary.

"Yeah." Whitney yawned. "That was fun, but I'm beat. Tomorrow morning's going to come a little too early for me."

They pulled up beside the house, and the lights were all off downstairs. "Looks like everyone else must be worn out, too," Gary said.

Susan climbed down from the buggy. "Thanks for taking me with you. It was nice to get out."

"I enjoyed the company. Maybe we can do it again next week?"

CHAPTER 21

The smell of bacon lingered in the house long after the eggs, cantaloupe, and biscuit-and-gravy breakfast had been consumed. The kids had already left for school, and Susan had headed to the shack for her sit-down interview.

Julie savored the silence.

This week's filming had been all about Amish breakfast, everything from cinnamon rolls and raisin bread to the more hearty fare of this morning. Thankfully, it had been a team effort, instead of all the pressure being on Julie or Susan to perform. The meals had all turned out rather well, Julie smiled to herself. Susan would have to be happy with that.

Julie saw the shack's door open and Susan emerged, headed back to the house with her typical, purposeful stride. No doubt she would have a list of assignments for the day, so Julie took a seat at the kitchen table and waited.

"Kendra wants you to come over for an interview. Meanwhile, I'm going to get busy sanding down the windowsills. We got some paint on our trip into town last night." Did Julie just imagine it, or did Susan blush?

"What's the interview about?"

Susan shrugged. "She didn't specify."

"Okay." Julie ran her fingers through her hair as she walked across the way. She must look a mess. But she supposed this is the way she looked through all the live-action filming as well. Why should a sit-down interview be any different? She pushed open the door. "You wanted me for an interview?"

Kendra crossed two things off a clipboard and said, "Yep, just for a few questions. Have a seat; we'll get you all set up."

A stylist ran a quick brush through her hair, but other than that, Julie was left untouched. Not for the first time, Julie thought she might be glad she couldn't actually watch these episodes.

"How have you enjoyed the traditional breakfasts this week?"

"I love all the traditional breakfast food. It's not something I eat much of at home, so this was actually a treat."

"Why don't you make traditional breakfasts at home?"

"No time. And they're messy. It's interesting to me, though, since they lack all the modern conveniences, that Amish women don't cook food that is less labor intensive. It's funny, isn't it, that so many people envy the Amish way of life? We say it is simpler. But simpler is harder. A lot harder. We've got all these great tools — computers, electric mixers, blenders. All these things are supposed to simplify are lives, so why is it we believe that it's those who *don't* use any of these things that have the simplest life of all?"

Kendra and the cameraman looked toward each other. They exchanged a smile between the two of them that Julie did not at first understand. Then she realized she'd been rambling. "Sorry about that. I got a little carried away."

"No, no. That was perfect." Kendra made a couple of notes on the paper in front of her. "You're free to go back now. Thank you for coming."

"Sure." Julie stood up and started for the door, feeling like a complete idiot.

"Did Susan tell you what next week's adventure is?"

"No." Julie was hoping it had something to do with spending quality family game time, or something like that. "What is it?"

"No electricity."

"You're kidding."

"No, but I'm guessing that by the end of the week you'll all wish I was."

"I'm pretty certain I already do." Julie could hear the sound of their laughter as she walked from the room. This week was going to be the hardest one yet.

The kids sat around the living room, each staring at the walls of the farmhouse as they absorbed this latest piece of news. They sat in miserable silence for what seemed like forever.

"Maybe it won't be all that bad. I mean, we don't use electric lights or cooktops anyway." Whitney twirled a piece of her hair around her index finger.

"Have you noticed that it's a *bit* hot and humid in this part of the country? What do you think it's going to be like in here without air-conditioning?" Brian tried to spike up his hair with his fingers. Since Kendra had confiscated his gel last week, it was wasted effort.

"Hot." Whitney sighed and put her chin in her hands. "So when does this fun phase begin?"

"Midnight." Susan rocked the chair in

short, rapid clips. "And we're going to make the best of it. We're going to show America that we are not just a bunch of soft Californians."

Silence.

Julie looked around at the group, saw the panicked look on all the kids' faces. "Well, let's make the best of this. Angie, what was it you were saying about a lot of Amish people moving into their basements for the summer?"

She nodded. "That's what I read. But we don't have a basement here."

"No, but we could move our bedding downstairs where it will be a little cooler. We could have a giant camp-out in the living room for the week."

"Oh boy." Whitney snorted. "That sounds dandy." She looked at the other kids and shook her head, causing a ripple of giggles. "How are we going to keep our food cold?"

Susan began to rock a bit more slowly as the details began to come together. "I think the original plan was to bring in an old-fashioned icebox, but somehow that fell through. Kendra said they will bring us a large cooler, and keep us supplied with enough ice blocks to keep our food from spoiling." She rocked back and forth. "Of course, we'll have to use caution and not open it any more than we have to."

Brian stood up and stretched. "Well, that's that, then. Hey, Whitney and Angie, you want to come check out Saturn? It should be positioned for optimal viewing right about now."

"May as well." The slump in Whitney's shoulder was purposeful; Julie knew that. She wasn't going to say any more about this, but she wanted everyone to know she was displeased with the situation.

Julie sat down with the quilt and began to sew the next row together. "Susan, you want to help me work on this?"

Susan shook her head. "No. I think I'll go scrub the bathroom one last time. That floor just drives me crazy."

Julie was left alone with her sewing, giving her time to think about what lay ahead for them this next week. It wasn't going to be easy; that was for sure. But how many people in the world lived in hotter temperatures than this and had never even heard of electricity? How many people lived in this part of the country without air-conditioning? She assumed a fair amount of them did. Of course, a good portion of California, including their own home, went without air-conditioning, but the humidity was much less, and the nights far cooler.

No, this would be a good reminder for them to appreciate what it was that they took for granted on a daily basis. She focused her attention on making short, precise stitches.

She wasn't sure even how much time had passed when the kitchen screen door opened.

"Knock, knock."

"In here, Kendra." Julie wondered why it was that Kendra bothered to say the words, when she was already inside anyway. It wasn't like they could keep her out.

"Where is everyone?"

"The kids walked down to check out some stars, and Susan is cleaning the bathroom." She resisted adding the word "again."

"I see." Kendra took a seat on the wooden bench. "Your sister-in-law is intent on keeping this place spotless, isn't she?"

"Yes, she is." Julie felt exhausted just thinking about Susan's self-imposed house cleaning.

"Do you think she cleans to excess?"

Julie shook her head. "No. I mean, look at this place. It is spotless."

"But you personally don't spend as much time cleaning as she does."

There it was. The same old "you're not doing enough" type statements that inundated Julie in her regular life — not enough hours at the school, not enough work at church, not enough house cleaning at home, not enough time with her family, not enough, not enough, not enough . . . the words were all around her. Julie shrugged. "I guess not." She returned her focus to making an even backstitch.

"I've been hearing you're really good at that." Kendra came closer and looked at Julie's project.

Julie pulled a stitch tight. "Apparently I have the most nonmarketable skill of any woman in our generation."

Kendra laughed. "So . . . how did the family take the news about no electricity?"

"They're not thrilled about it, of course. But I'm sitting here thinking it will be good for all of us. Not fun, mind you, but it's just one week. We'll see how spoiled we really are in our daily lives."

"I bet a lot of our viewers will agree." She moved toward the bathroom. "I'll just go check in with Susan."

Julie stood up to stretch, then went to the window and looked out. The night was especially dark, and it was difficult to see anything past the security light over the barn door. She thought about the kids and wondered why they'd been gone so long. It shouldn't take that long to look at Saturn, especially Whitney, who had long since tired of those kinds of things.

Then piece by piece, a puzzle began to assemble in her mind. The night was dark. Very dark. Because the sky was full of clouds. Which meant that they weren't actually looking at Saturn, and hadn't been, in spite of the fact that they'd all been gone for over an hour.

She went to the door and looked out, but saw or heard nothing. They were up to something; there was no doubt about it.

It was another hour before they all came home. "Well, we're tired. We're going to head to bed. See you all in the morning." Whitney didn't even look her way as she said the words, neither did the rest of the kids. "Yep, we're tired." They all made a show of yawning and stretching the whole way up the stairs.

"Well, they certainly calmed down. After all that initial bellyaching, I thought they would come in with some new tactic to get us to change our minds." Susan shook her head and looked toward them. "I don't know what happened, but whatever it is, I'm glad."

"Yes, glad." *Then again . . . maybe not.*

CHAPTER 22

By the time Susan woke Saturday morning, the house had been without air-conditioning for five or six hours, and the air already felt thick and oppressive. How bad would it get by the end of seven days? She walked into the bathroom and splashed cold water on her face, bracing herself to go downstairs and light the stove for breakfast.

She tiptoed down the steps toward the kitchen. Normally, she didn't try overly hard not to wake the kids because they had to get up and do chores, too. Today, with the heat already pressing in, she thought she might give them a bit longer of blissful unawareness.

She checked to make certain the grate was as high as it would go in the woodbox, then searched for the smallest pieces of wood possible. After she got the fire going and put the coffeepot on the burner, she stepped out onto the screened-in porch. It was definitely cooler out here. Not by a lot, not yet, but after the stove had been used throughout the day, that might change. Yes, they were going to need to move their beds somewhere else.

When she went back inside, the water for coffee had not yet even begun to boil. Perhaps she'd been too sparse in her use of wood. Reluctantly, she added another piece. She probably should just go with milk, fruit, and cheese for breakfast, as none of those things needed heat. But what would the viewers want her to do in the situation? Taking the easy way out was likely not the answer. So she pulled out the griddle and went about making pancake batter. She added another piece of wood to the fire to make certain she had enough heat to cook bacon as well, hoping that the viewers would appreciate this effort.

"Ew-wee, it's hot in here." Whitney came tromping through the kitchen, followed closely by Angie and Brian.

"Good morning, Aunt Susan."

"Good morning, Aunt Susan."

"Good morning, Mom."

The kids passed through the kitchen in quick progression, then disappeared out the back door on their way to the barn and morning chores.

"Hurry back. I've got pancakes about to go on the griddle."

"Sounds delish," Whitney called back over her shoulder.

Julie came traipsing in from the front door just then. "Whew. If this morning is any indication, this is going to be the hottest day yet." She carried a basketful of berries from the garden. "Doesn't it just figure that it would be the week we don't have electricity?" She went to the sink and washed the berries, then set them in the strainer to dry. "I bet Kendra has been watching the weather reports ever since we arrived, waiting." She pulled the butter out of the large cooler, which had been brought in last night. "Which is not going to make the week a lot of fun, but in the long run, this will be good for us all."

By now, Susan was standing over the steaming griddle, wiping her forehead with her pajama sleeve. "You're probably right." Footsteps on the back porch announced the kids' return. "Everyone hurry and wash your hands. Breakfast will be ready in about one minute."

"Oh, sorry, it's just me. I didn't mean to interrupt breakfast." Gary's voice came from the other side of the screened door. Susan glanced up to see him standing there, looking all fresh and cool in a pale blue T-shirt and faded jeans. "I was just stopping by to see if y'all would like some help moving the beds around today. I heard a rumor that this was the no-electricity week, and I thought we could at least move the beds downstairs. It'll make your living room a bit crowded, but it'll make sleeping more comfortable."

Susan was suddenly all too aware of the fact that she was standing there with her hair a mess, still wearing her shapeless blue cotton pajamas. It wasn't like she cared what she looked like for Gary, in particular, it's just that she really didn't want anyone to see her looking this way.

"You read our minds." Julie walked over and swung the door open. "Come on in. Join us for breakfast."

Oh, great. That was easy for Julie to say. She'd obviously gotten up in time to wash her still-damp hair and put on some clean clothes.

"Ah, thanks for the offer, but I don't want to impose. Besides, I ate a bowl of cereal a while ago, so I'm plenty good."

"Nonsense, nonsense. We're all about hospitality, right, Susan? Here, let me pull you up another chair."

Susan turned to see Gary looking at her,

waiting for her response. She looked down at herself and shrugged. "You're welcome to stay" — she glanced down again — "but you may want to sit facing the other direction. I obviously wasn't expecting company this morning."

He walked up beside her, close enough that she could feel his shoulder as it brushed up to hers. "I think you take the first-thing-in-the-morning-rumpled look to a whole new level of chic."

"Liar."

"Not even a little bit." He pulled a loose strand of hair away from her face and tucked it behind her ear.

Susan looked into those baby-blue eyes of his and wanted so badly to believe him. She knew better, but would it hurt just to let herself go emotionally, just for a while? Just while they were here?

The kids came clattering up the back stairs at the same time Julie returned to the kitchen with a chair from the living room. "Wash up, everyone. Breakfast is ready. Gary is joining us this morning."

Julie pulled out the chair from the head of the table. "This one's for you, Gary. Everyone else, shift down a place, starting with you, Brian. We'll keep the adults on one end of the table." She carried over a plate of pancakes to put on each end of the table.

Susan sat at her place, still so embarrassed to be sitting here looking like this that it took her a few seconds to realize the room had fallen silent. She normally led them in grace.

Julie finally spoke up. "Gary, would you like to say grace, or would you prefer that I do it?"

"I'd be happy to." They all bowed their heads and closed their eyes. "Dear Father, thank You so much for this amazing family You've brought to us here. Help us not to take for granted what a blessing we're experiencing right now. Thank You for this food and the cooks who worked so hard to prepare it. Amen."

The table fell more or less into silence as everyone began to eat their pancakes. The clank of fork against plate and the occasional "pass the pancakes, please" testified to the fact that the pancakes were a hit.

"So why are you eating with us this morning? I think I missed that part of the conversation." Brian stuffed another bite of pancake into his mouth, his expression showing nothing but innocent curiosity at his question.

"I invited him," Julie said. "He's going to help us move some of the beds downstairs, so perhaps we'll be a bit cooler tonight than we would be upstairs."

Brian nodded. "Oh, great. Thanks for doing that."

"You are most welcome, Brian. And I still want to come check out that fancy telescope of yours sometime."

Brian choked on his milk but nodded. "That would be great. I'm pretty busy working on a class project this week, but next week would be great."

"All right. Next week it is."

CHAPTER 23

Susan swept the living room while Julie and the girls pulled out all their quilting supplies. They were chatting and laughing, and with every single word, Susan's blood pressure crept a little higher. The stack of mattresses against the wall looked haphazard at best — far from the Amish standarad of neatness. Just because it was Saturday and the kids didn't have school didn't mean they could just goof off. There were always things to be done — certainly more pressing things than quilting.

"Aunt Susan, I don't know why you're sweeping the floor now. It's just going to have strings and thread all over it by the time we're done."

Susan wondered if her face and neck were bright red, the way her mother's used to get when she was about to have an explosion. Susan stopped sweeping so she could look Whitney directly in the eye. "Why make the bed if you're just going to sleep in it again tonight? Why wash the dishes if they're just going to get dirty again? For that matter, why even cook the dinner, if you're just going to have to do it again the next night?" Her voice gained volume with each repeated question.

"Susan." Julie set down a pile of fabric and walked across the room. "Are you all right?"

"I'm fine. But I'm sick and tired of being the only one who does anything around here. If it weren't for me, nothing would ever get accomplished. Why can't all of you take a little more initiative instead of just counting on me?"

"I . . . uh . . ." There were tears in Julie's eyes as she looked from the girls back to Susan. "Girls, why don't you put that fabric up on the chairs. Angie and Whitney, go get the supplies and scrape another sill. I'll just go get another broom and help Susan."

A silence so heavy had descended on the group that the sound of each footstep across the wood floors sounded painfully loud. The swooshing of the broom against the floor, the scrape of metal against wood, grew louder with each passing second. Nobody was speaking or even glancing up, and certainly none of them were looking anywhere near Susan. She looked at the group silently involved in their chores, faces set, and knew that she had been too abrupt. But everything she'd said had been the truth, too. She was tired of having to push and prod to get anything done around here.

Julie stepped out of the room for a second, returned with a rag, and began dusting around the fireplace. Susan finished sweeping and went to get her own rag. At least she could help Julie, perhaps build a little bridge between them. She walked over to the mantel. "Have you done this side yet?"

"No." Julie's voice was soft and low.

From the corner of her eye, Susan saw Julie's hand go up to her face, and she glimpsed tears on her cheeks.

Susan ran her rag across the mantel, and just as she'd expected, it came away dusty. It had been two days since they'd done this, and since they were leaving the windows open all the time this week, a fine covering of dust and pollen had spread throughout the room. She hoped that Julie and the kids were noticing this and realizing that this had indeed been necessary.

"My, my. Aren't you all a bunch of worker bees today?" Rosemary stood outside the screen door of the living room, since the wooden one was propped open. "You're about as quiet as I've ever heard ya, too. We'll have to see if we can't do something about that, now won't we?" She came inside, then stopped and fanned herself. "It's a tad stuffy in here. What would you ladies think of taking our work outside on the porch?"

"I'll . . . just go clean off the table and chairs real quick." Whitney disappeared into the kitchen, reappeared with a rag and bottle of cleaning solution in her hands, and headed to the porch.

"I'll help." Angie went out the door, never looking back.

"What's the matter with everyone around here? You'd think your last cow had just died or something."

Julie walked toward the older woman. "Oh, sorry, we're not being very hospitable, are we? Rosemary, would you like a nice cold water?"

"Sounds wonderful." She picked up her large bag and started for the door. "I'll just go see if the kids need my help." As the door swung closed behind her, Susan heard her say something that included the words "prickly" and "uptight."

Well, someone around here had to be. Nothing had changed from their life in Santa Barbara, only the setting. Once again, she carried the full burden of making certain that things were done correctly.

Julie breezed past her, three glasses full of water in her hands. She used her hip to push open the storm door. "Here you go, ladies. A round of water on the house."

There was faint laughter from the girls before Julie said, "I'll just go get some for Susan and me, and then I'll be back and ready to stitch."

"I'll get it." Susan set the dust rag aside and went about preparing a couple of glasses of ice water. She carried them outside, put one glass beside Julie's chair, and brought the other with her to the last chair on the porch. She picked up a couple rows of fabric and began lining them up, just like Rosemary had taught her. She hated this. It was tedious, and boring, and a complete waste of her time. There were so many other things that needed doing.

"I've been thinking," Julie said, looking up from her work. "I know that everyone in this town is well aware that we are out here filming, and they are all more than a little intrigued by that. So, I'm thinking, maybe if we actually finish a quilt that is good enough, we could auction it off to the local residents. The money could go to help with that Kids' Club Whitney worked with the other night, or maybe the hospital here, or some other local charity that needs help."

Rosemary nodded. "That's what I call a terrific idea. I have a friend who's an auctioneer. I bet he'd help us with it." She rocked back and forth. "You've got a true gift, Julie, a true gift."

"I may be good for a beginner, but even I know enough to know I'm not great."

"I wasn't speaking of sewing. You think that one over for a while." Rosemary turned her attention to Susan. "So . . . you're looking a little stressed over there. Needin' some help with your stitching?"

"No, thanks. I'm fine."

"I see." Rosemary leaned forward, her elbows on the arms of the rocking chair, her watery blue eyes fixed on Susan. "Don't look so fine to me. You carry a lot of burdens that you really don't need to carry."

Susan did not have the time or the patience for another Rosemary-the-shrink session. "I carry the burdens I have to carry in order to make certain my daughter and I survive in this world."

"You think?" Rosemary stared at her, completely still, just waiting. Julie and the girls all sensed it too and looked up, as if waiting for this grand revelation. "I think you have a lot in common with Martha in

251

the Bible. You can choose to either drive yourself crazy, striving for that unattainable perfection, or you can remember what you're doing it all for."

"That all sounds very wonderful, but I don't think my goals are unattainable. They just require discipline and hard work. That's my job . . . and I know what I'm doing it for — my daughter — who needs my example so she can learn to apply herself fully to have the kind of future she wants to have."

"What kind of future do you want to have, young lady?" Rosemary turned her attention to Angie.

Angie's face turned bright red, and she suddenly became very interested in her stitching. She shrugged. "I don't know. A good college and good job, I guess."

Rosemary nodded. "I see. Well, it seems to me like the two of you have it all figured out, then." She went back to rocking.

Susan waited for her to say more, but she just rocked and stared. Somehow, she knew there was an indictment in that silence. But it didn't matter what some small-town woman whose life was sewing quilts thought. She knew nothing of the real world.

The day did not get any cooler, and even as

the sun began to dip, the heat remained unbroken. Worse, the stove still radiated warmth from dinner, and now steam rose from the sink as Julie and Susan finished washing the last of the dishes. Neither had talked about the morning's spat, and Julie hoped it was behind them.

Handing over the evening's final plate, Julie wiped sweat off her brow and said, "Well, on the bright side, think of how much money people pay for a steam room. We're getting the spa treatment for free here."

"Somehow I'm not feeling the rejuvenating effects one would expect from such treatments." Susan chuckled and put the plate in the cupboard.

From outside came a shuffle of footsteps. "Evening, ladies," said Gary, appearing at the screen door. Susan waved him in, but he said, "As I can feel the heat coming off the stove from here, I think I prefer to stay outside. That should start cooling down soon, but I thought I might offer an evening ride. Feel the wind on your faces. It's the least I could do after this morning's wonderful breakfast."

"That does sound nice." Susan closed the cupboard door and leaned against the countertop. "But I'd feel guilty going out for a ride, with the kids all down at the observatory working on their school project."

Julie had been pondering Brian, and the observatory, and all of the kids' reactions since breakfast this morning. Something was up. Brian should have jumped when Gary asked to see it, and Whitney had certainly never before been in a hurry to spend time with her brother. Yet all of them — including Angie — were all suddenly overwhelmed by a mysterious school project. Whitney had volunteered, "Since Brian has to work on the telescope for his project, Angie and I will go there and do our work, too. That way we're all together if anyone needs help."

The whole thing was extremely suspicious.

"Oh, I'm sure they won't mind if you get out for just a little. They all know how hot it is in here after you've cooked a meal. In fact, if it would make you feel better, we can swing down that way and see if any of them want to go for a quick ride with us."

"I don't know. It sounds wonderful, really, but there are things . . ." Susan's voice trailed off and she stared into the distance, as if thinking intently.

Something about the way Susan and Gary were looking at each other made Julie wonder whether it was the ride in the evening air or the company that sounded so wonderful to Susan. "I think a ride is a splendid idea. Let's get out of here and give this place a chance to cool down." She grabbed Susan by the arm. "Come along, now."

Susan was laughing more than protesting, so Gary went into the barn to get the wagon and horse. He emerged a few minutes later. "Ladies, shall we?" He offered a hand up, and Julie discreetly took a step backward so Susan would be the first in. It was probably a juvenile thing to do, but whatever it took to get Susan back into life, she would give it a try.

Gary clucked to the horse, and they took off down the road in the general direction of the creek and the observatory. No one spoke, but an overall feeling of well-being and peace surrounded Julie so closely, she wondered if they all felt it. When was the last time she'd felt this way in her old life?

Just before they reached the top of the hill, Susan said, "I bet the kids wanted to do homework in the observatory because it's probably a lot cooler down there — it being so close to the creek."

"That's likely true." Gary pulled the horses back to a walk that was so slow, they were barely moving forward. Step by step they finally crested the top of the hill. The lone window of the observatory had a dim light shining out of it, casting eerie shadows through the leaves of the swaying trees.

Gary clucked at the horses once again, and they sped up, becoming noisier in the process. "What are we doing?" Susan asked.

The light in the window of the observatory seemed to flicker and dim. "Just, uh . . . checking out the horses. That's all." Gary's smile was huge as the wagon drew closer to the observatory. "Why don't you ladies just wait here, and I'll go see if the kids want to join us?"

"No, let me do it. I'm on the end, and you need to control the horse." Julie climbed down before he could argue.

She crossed to Brian's hideaway, pulled the door open, and found all three kids sitting on the floor, a couple of oil lamps in the middle of their circle. The air inside felt cool — amazingly cool. "Hello, everyone. I can see that you are all certainly working hard."

"Oh, hi, Mom. I didn't even hear you guys."

"I'm sure you didn't." Each and every kid was showing undivided attention to the notebooks and textbooks in front of them. *Right.* "Aunt Susan, Gary, and I are going for a little buggy ride, trying to cool off a bit. We stopped by to see if you wanted to come with us."

The kids all looked at each other, then quickly back down toward their books. "Well, we've really got a lot of homework this week." Whitney kept her eyes focused on her notebook.

"Yeah. Mom must have had one of her talks with Charlotte," offered Angie. "Or something."

"Well, good for you three. Way to keep at it."

"Sure."

"Sure."

"Yeah."

The words followed her out the door. She bit her lip, trying to keep a straight face as she walked back out to the buggy. "The kids all seem rather overwhelmed with school-work, so they've declined."

"Wow. Charlotte must finally be getting serious about their studies. I'm glad to see it." Susan fanned herself with her hand.

"Yes, they certainly do seem industrious," Gary said and, catching Julie's eye, gave a wink. "Looks like it's just us old folks for tonight's ride, then."

Gary clucked his tongue, and the horse began its leisurely stroll. Just the little momentum stirred a breeze, and when the buggy pulled into the shadow of some poplars, it almost felt cool to Julie. On they went, down past the schoolhouse, then to the far end of the property before heading down a back driveway and out onto the main road. A few cars rushed by, but the evening was quiet and the sound of tree frogs and cicadas began to fill the night air. Eventually the horse veered down the front drive, returning them all to a stop in front of the farmhouse.

"I'll let you ladies out here and then go put the horse away."

"Are you sure?" Susan asked. "We can help you."

"I know you could and you would, but it's been a big day for all of you, and I suspect it will be a long and sticky night. Besides, this is man's work."

Susan actually giggled as she climbed down from the buggy. "Far be it from me to interfere with man's work."

Light suddenly spilled into the area as the door to the shack opened and Kendra came walking out. "Oh, there you are. I've been looking for you, Susan. Why don't you come over, and we'll talk about what the plans are for next week."

"Okay." Susan made one last turn back

toward Gary. "Good-bye. And thanks again."

"My pleasure." The smile on his face left Julie no doubt that he meant it.

Julie waited until Susan and Kendra had disappeared and closed the door before she walked closer to Gary. She leaned toward him and whispered, "How did you know?"

He snorted. "I was down at the creek trying my hand at gigging frogs last night. I heard the kids whispering and figured they were up to something. So I snuck up the hill and watched for a while. I've got to say, that boy of yours is something of a genius when it comes to electrical wiring. There's not a soul on the production crew that will ever realize that one of their lines has been bootlegged."

"I hope that someday he will use that genius for good and not for evil." She laughed.

"Got to admire their ingenuity in the face of the current situation. Fact is, if I were you and Susan, I'd be trying to figure out an excuse to get myself down there, too. Although," — he rubbed his chin — "I'm guessing you didn't tell her for a reason."

"I don't want to put her in the position of having to lie to anyone, should it get discovered."

"That's what I thought, too, which is why I didn't say anything."

"Good night." Julie watched him disappear into the barn, then pivoted on her foot and turned back toward the house. By the time she reached the back steps, she was giggling. Those kids — she had to admire their resourcefulness.

"You're not going to believe this one." Susan jogged up behind her.

"What?"

"Next week, Lisa Lee is going to be here! She's going to tape the entire Friday segment *here*. On site."

"Oh. Is that good news, then?" Julie thought so, but given the stressed tone of Susan's voice, she didn't really think so.

"No. I mean, maybe, but the day we get electricity back, she'll be here. The queen of perfect domesticity, seeing us after sweating for seven days."

"Susan, I'm sure she understands that we —"

"First thing tomorrow morning, we've got to work on getting those windowsills painted, heat or no heat. We've got to make sure this place is perfect."

Julie looked at her sister-in-law and knew that nothing would ever be perfect enough for Susan. The bar would keep changing and there'd always be one more thing to do, and she would keep working at it until it consumed her.

Maybe tonight's buggy ride was a sign, though, that she could step back for at least a minute. Julie hoped so. If not, she couldn't imagine what the next days might bring.

CHAPTER 24

Sunday morning dawned hot and sticky. Even having their mattresses downstairs hadn't helped that much. Now, after a cool shower, Julie couldn't help but wish for some sandals to wear to church and wondered how reticent the girls would be this morning. But she heard no complaints, and they all loaded up into the buggy, all wearing long dark skirts and black flats. At least Kendra had loosened the stipulation about wearing heavy work shoes and nylons; she supposed they could be grateful for that.

"Did you notice the cute sundresses that all the girls at church were wearing last week?" Whitney sighed and sat down. "I can't wait until we can wear cute clothes again."

"So are you telling me that you actually want to wear a dress? I never thought I'd hear those words come out of your mouth." Julie looked at her daughter and waited.

Whitney shrugged her left shoulder. "Maybe." She paused for a minute to think about it, and then said, "Probably not. I just don't like to stand out. I feel like everyone is looking at us in this."

Gary climbed up after everyone had loaded in. "Okay, here we go."

The horses clopped down the road, making a pleasant sound. In spite of the fact they were traveling down a country road, cars still came up behind them at a fairly regular rate. Gary would wave them around if he could see the road ahead was clear.

One particular car came up beside them and began honking, and honking, and honking. It was an old muscle car, painted black, loaded with boys who appeared to be in their late teens. One of them rolled down his window and shouted, "Hey, girls, want to come for a real ride? We got the ride of your life, right here." More honking followed.

Gary kept the horse moving forward at an even pace. His head never moved to the side, but he did say, "Just ignore them. Don't give them the satisfaction of a response."

It took every bit of Julie's self-control not to jump out of the buggy and onto the car and go after some boys who'd dared to disrespect her daughter and niece. She noticed that Susan had put a hand on Gary's arm and was squeezing, a sure sign she was facing the same struggle.

"Come on, what ya waiting for?" *Honk. Honk. Honk.*

The horse jerked forward, but Gary kept him under control by use of the reins. Another car rounded the curve from the other direction, headed straight for the muscle car. Gary pulled the reins back sharply and said, "Whoa." The buggy stopped and the car moved forward and pulled in front to avoid being hit by the oncoming car. "Keep on going, fellas, just keep on going," Gary whispered under his breath.

The car came to an almost stop, then in a flash of squealing tires and flying gravel took off down the road at a high rate of speed. One of the boys stuck his hand out the window as if to wave good-bye. Gary clucked the horse back into motion.

"Whew, I'm glad that's over." Julie's body was shaking from toes to fingertips.

"Me too," Whitney said. She leaned forward toward Gary. "Why didn't you do anything to stop them?"

Gary looked over his shoulder. "That, young lady, was a true Amish experience.

There are jerks like that who harass the Amish on a regular basis. It makes you wonder what is so lacking in their own lives that it makes them feel better to pick on someone they know will not fight back."

"I'll say." She sat back and shook her head. "I'd never thought about that. Or maybe the way we all feel kind of funny dressed in our less-than-stylish clothes. Amish people must feel that way a lot."

Gary nodded as he pulled the horses around to the back of the church. "I'd say we've all had one of those 'learn by experience' moments this morning, wouldn't you?"

"I hope we don't have many more of those." Whitney climbed down, still shaking her head.

At the church, Gary helped Julie and Susan to climb down and then hitched his thumb back at the road. "I'm going to stay out here for a bit, just to make certain those bozos in the black car don't come back looking to make some trouble."

"Do you think they know where we are?" asked Julie. Her nerves had just began to calm, but now she felt her hands shaking again.

"Nah. And they couldn't see us from the

road even if they drove by right now. Still, I'm going to play it safe. I don't want anyone messing with our wagon, and especially not Popcorn." He rubbed Popcorn's muzzle as he said this, his eyes soft. "We don't want anyone bothering you, do we, girl?"

"That's probably a good idea." Susan's face didn't quite show the conviction of her words. "We'll see you after, then."

They walked around the corner to the side of the church, staying close to the edge of the building and inside the line of shade from the roof overhang. "It's going to feel good to sit in an air-conditioned church, isn't it?" Julie fanned herself, trying to focus on the strands of hair sticking to her neck rather than her still-jangled nerves.

Susan nodded. "Yes, it is. I'm never going to take our California weather for granted again."

"I know just what you mean."

"Or the safety of being in an actual car, with a cell phone. After what just happened, I can't understand how Amish can stand to live that way."

"I suppose it's faith." Julie took another step. "I've never considered myself lacking in faith, but I was scared out of my mind this morning."

"Me neither, and me too."

They were approaching the corner of the front of the building, and the sounds of laughter and squeals seemed louder than normal. Julie supposed that her senses were just heightened after this morning's ordeal. Just then, Whitney appeared at the corner and beckoned with her arms. "Come on, you two slowpokes. You've got to come see this."

Julie and Susan picked up their pace. When they made it to the corner, Julie began to smile, and then outright laugh. "What happened?"

Brittany, one the girls Julie had met from the youth group, smiled and looked down at her long denim skirt and white short-sleeved button-up shirt, then looked back up and grinned. "A bunch of us were sitting around eating pizza the other night, texting our friends, you know . . . stuff. And we were talking about how we wished we could invite Whitney and Angie and Brian to join us, and how hard it must be not to be able to text or anything. Then we all decided that as a show of support, we would go down to the thrift store and see if we could find some clothes like they wear." She waved her hand around at the assembled group of teenagers, the girls all wearing long skirts, the boys all wearing button-down shirts and dark vests.

"That was a really nice thing for all of you to do."

Brittany shrugged. "Nothing to it."

"I wish I had a camera so I could take a picture of this," Angie said. "I think it will be one of my favorite memories from this summer."

"No worries. My phone takes pics. After you're back in civilization, I'll friend you on Facebook and put these on your wall." Brittany held her iPhone high above the crowd and took a picture, then began taking random shots of different kids in the group.

"Make sure you don't post those now, or it'll get them all in trouble."

Julie recognized the voice before she even turned to see Chris. He was wearing a dark T-shirt and jeans — apparently standing out in the group didn't bother him at all, because in this conservative congregation, he was definitely underdressed.

"Oh, you've got to be kidding." Whitney's mouth scrunched up into a tight ball of annoyance.

"I just said she can't post 'em *now*. Didn't mean she can't take 'em."

The music started playing from inside, warning all of them that church was starting. The kids hurried into their usual rows on the far right near the back, and Julie and Susan went to their usual spot on the left near the middle.

Julie couldn't help but turn to look. Angie and Whitney were sitting together; Brian was a couple of people down. Chris sat in the row behind them, directly behind Angie. Hmm . . .

The music director made his way to the podium. "Let's all stand and sing 'Amazing Grace.' "

They started singing the familiar hymn, and Julie had to make a conscious effort to focus. Between the harrowing ride to church, and the thrill of what the church youth had done for the kids . . . well, her emotions were charged in every direction, it seemed.

"When we've been there, ten thousand years, bright shining as the sun." Finally she calmed enough to really focus on the words and revel in their deep meaning.

At least, until she heard the male voice joining in the song. She looked to see that Gary had entered the church, and had come to sit beside Susan.

CHAPTER 25

Julie splashed cold water from the kitchen sink on her face, one of the only surefire ways to escape the heat she'd discovered over the past few days. She'd never known five longer days in her life. Long days and shortened tempers. And the heat was responsible for both.

Susan held back the curtain so she could watch the kids walking up the hill. "I think we should definitely check in on their school again. I just don't think Charlotte is pushing them hard enough."

"Really? What makes you think so?"

"Well, for one thing, have you checked out the homework they've been working on?"

"No, but they've been out at the observatory every night this week working on it." Julie bit back her smile, not wanting to give anything away. "Around here I've seen Brian drawing sketches for his project, and both of the girls writing in their journals, which I know was an assignment from Char."

"My point exactly. Writing in journals? Of what benefit is that? In elementary school, maybe, it helps them practice their cursive. At their age, they need to be buckled down and learning. Angie has a hard enough time keeping up in her classes when she goes to school full-time and works with a couple of tutors at home each week. This is only going to hurt her next year. If I don't see signs of something significant, I'm going to ask Kendra to find a better instructor."

Acid burned the walls of Julie's stomach. "Susan, one of the main appeals about the Amish way of life is that it is so much slower than modern life — at least it's perceived that way. If we are simply going to turn this into a modern-day pressure-fest in a rural setting, what's the point?"

"Yes, well, Amish children only go to school until the eighth grade, too. Our kids will be going back to real life, where an eighth-grade education would mean no job, or at least not a job that could sustain a family. We have to remain practical in the middle of this."

The screech of the screen door, followed by the thump of footsteps across the back porch, preceded a knock at the kitchen door. "I'll get it." Julie was thankful for a

271

reason to get out of this conversation. She opened the door to find Gary standing there.

"Good morning, ladies. Hey, I found a little something I thought your families might enjoy. In fact, I am so convinced your kids are going to enjoy them, I thought I'd better give you two a head start or you'll never get a turn. You want to come see?"

Susan had made her way toward the door. "What is it?"

"Right this way." He held the door open and gestured toward the barn.

As they walked toward the barn, Susan's step was its usual brisk I-have-places-to-be pace. Gary matched her step for step. "So how is your day going?"

"Fine." She kept her pace and barely offered a turned head with the response.

Just as Julie was pondering how rude that came across, Susan must have realized it, too. She slowed her pace and turned toward him. "That came out a little short, didn't it? I am sorry, it's just that Lisa Lee is coming to visit in a few days, and it's hot, and I'm concerned about the kids and their schooling while they're here, and all that seems to manifest itself in an ugly way. Apologies."

"I can't help you with Lisa Lee or the heat, but I would tell you not to worry about the kids. Char is an excellent teacher. I absolutely believe that."

"I wish I could be so convinced. I'm planning to go out there this morning and see what they are working on. I'm just not sure that she is sufficiently motivated to move the kids in the right direction."

Gary's smile faded just a little, but only until he reached the door to the storage shed beside the barn. "If you are determined to go out and check on things this morning, then you will find my surprise especially useful, I think." He swung open the door to reveal a trio of scooters. At least, Julie thought they were scooters. The wheels were much larger than she'd seen on the scooters at home — almost the size of bicycle tires. "Most of the Amish don't use bikes, but apparently some allow scooters, as long as they are not fancy. They're not exactly Razor scooters like you see at all the schools these days, but what they are lacking in form, I believe they will make up in function."

Julie stood beside one of the contraptions, wondering if she could possibly ride it without killing herself. She put her right hand on the handlebar and squeezed the brake. "I wonder why Kendra never mentioned these."

"She didn't know about them. I found out

about them and brought some back myself." He adjusted the Atlanta Braves cap around his gray curls. "Didn't think I was ever going to convince her to let y'all use them."

"I'm surprised you did," Julie said.

"Thankfully, she doesn't know that some forms of Amish forbid inflatable tires." He grinned and looked toward Susan.

Julie laughed. "That's a good thing." She gave herself a small push and glided forward. "I know the kids will love these."

"I hope I survive them." Susan kept her feet firmly planted. "Will you come with us out to school? You can give us a lesson along the way."

He tipped his cap. "Sounds like a plan to me."

Seeing the expression on his face as he looked at Susan told Julie all she needed to know about why Gary had done this. She couldn't help but smile thinking about what more surprises this summer might bring.

When they reached the tree line, the sound of Whitney's laughter drew them away from the school. They looked down onto a little grassy clearing near the water's edge. A large canopy of gray canvas was strung from a tree on the clearing's edge, to what looked like a couple of large branches braced together, forming two other corners, making a perfect triangle of shade.

Charlotte looked up as she saw them approaching. "Ah, Mrs. Reynolds, Mrs. Charlton, Mr. Macko, so nice to see you. Have you to come to see what we're working on, today?"

"What is *that* you three are riding on?" Whitney hopped up and walked over.

"Mr. Macko bought them for us to use around here. We thought we would check them out and make a trip out to see you at the same time," Julie said.

By now, Brian had made his way over and was checking out the new ride. "Interesting piece of equipment. My personal thanks."

Gary smiled. "I hoped you all would enjoy them. They may not be terribly cool, but they will make your commute to and from school much faster, I think."

The creek burbled happily as it hurried on its way, birds chirped their own working songs back and forth in the trees, and the smell of damp earth and wildflowers added richness to the outdoor symphony. Julie looked at Charlotte. "What a nice idea to have class out here. It's a beautiful place, and so much cooler than the schoolhouse today."

"The hanging of the canopy made for a

nice physics and logic problem." Brian grinned at his teacher.

"Charlotte," Susan said, "I wonder if we might have a meeting today so we can discuss your academic plans for the rest of the summer. Just to make certain we are all on the same page."

"Of course. We were just about to take a snack break. Would you like to do it now?"

"Yes." Susan's jaw was firm, and Julie couldn't keep her own stomach from clenching in response. Why couldn't Susan ever relax? "Why don't the two of us go talk privately? Unless you want to join us, Julie?"

Julie considered for a moment. "No, I think I'll stay here with Gary and the kids."

"Suit yourself." The disapproval was obvious in Susan's voice. The two women walked off in the direction of the school-house.

"Woo-ee, someone's a little uptight."

"Whitney . . ."

"Just saying." She grasped the handlebars of Susan's scooter. "Can I take it for a spin?"

Gary nodded. "You bet. Here, why don't the three of you try them out?"

"All right." The three of them were soon zooming up and down the dirt road, laughing and having a blast, seemingly oblivious to the heat and dust.

"It appears your gift is much appreciated, especially by the younger generation." Julie thought about how that might have sounded. "Not that us old folks don't appreciate it, too. Just seems like a disaster waiting to happen."

He laughed. "I know what you mean. I was praying I wouldn't break my neck the first time I tried one of those things." The phone jangled in his pocket. "Excuse me." He took a couple of steps away to answer. Seconds later, he waved the kids over.

"It seems you are all needed back at the farmhouse right away. They want family groups, so Charlton family, why don't the three of you take the scooters? I'll walk back with Susan and Angie when the meeting is over."

"Why do they need us?"

Gary grinned. "You should know how things work well enough by now to know that I'm not going to tell you anything."

"Okay, Mom, let's see how well you can ride this thing." Whitney stood beside the scooter Angie had just vacated.

"Not very well, I'm afraid." But Julie climbed on board. "Are you sure Angie shouldn't take this one?"

"Positive."

Julie tried to somewhat keep up with her kids, but quickly gave up and allowed herself to lag behind. They were way too young and fast; no reason to kill herself to prove the obvious, especially going uphill.

Whitney reached the crest of the hill first, then hit her brakes and stopped in a cloud of dust. Brian soon followed suit. "Hey, Mom, there's a black car pulling up down there. Lisa Lee is not supposed to be here yet, is she?"

"I don't think so." *Oh no. Surely not.* Julie caught up to the kids and looked down at the farmhouse and the Suburban just coming to a stop in the driveway. This was going to shove Susan right over the edge.

The back door opened then, and Julie could see someone climbing out. The figure backed away from the door and then it closed behind him. "Oh, my goodness, oh, my goodness. It's your father." She clamped her hand over her mouth, the sheer joy of the unexpected visit causing tears to run down her cheeks. "Race you to the bottom." Julie climbed back on her scooter and started pumping her left foot as fast as she could. After about three repetitions, she realized that this might have been a mistake, as it was downhill and she was going much faster than was safe for someone with her skill level. Still, she didn't care.

"Slowpoke." Whitney sailed past, looking like she was barely even exerting effort. "Dad, Dad! Dad, look up here." She was using one hand on her handlebars and waving with the other, while Julie was holding on for dear life with both hands. Brian passed her, too, but he at least seemed to be exerting effort in the process.

Julie eased up on the hand brakes and found herself gaining on the kids. By this time she had no idea whether or not Thomas had seen them yet, because she was too terrified to look anywhere besides the road directly in front of her. She had almost caught Brian when they reached the car.

"My, my, what has happened to the wife I used to know? I don't recognize this speed demon I just watched tearing down the hill at Mach 1 speed."

Whitney threw her arms around Thomas's waist. "You might not recognize a lot of things. Mom has started to come out of her shell in a major way. She's almost . . . almost cool." She leaned back and squeezed Julie's arm at the elbow.

Julie looked at her daughter, waiting for the punch line, but saw nothing other than a serious expression on her heat-reddened face.

"Well, all right." Thomas grinned as he reached out and included Julie and Brian in the hug. "It's so good to see the three of you. The house is just plain boring without all of you around."

"Yeah, but I bet the house is finally tidy to your satisfaction, right?" Whitney looked up at him. "If not, you've got no one to harp on but yourself, 'cause we didn't do it."

Julie couldn't help but stiffen a little as she waited for his response. Thomas and Susan were definitely from the same gene pool, and it was a constant source of stress in their home. Right now, she wasn't sure what she wanted to hear — something between the harsh truth and a complete lie.

He finally cleared his throat as he pulled away from the hug. "Well, that part is nice, but I still miss all of you."

Ouch. Ouch. Ouch.

Didn't this work in reverse in most families? Wasn't the wife supposed to nag the husband about these things?

Thomas interrupted her thoughts with another enormous hug. And she embraced him back. It felt good to be in his arms, and for the moment, she'd just focus on that.

Still, she couldn't help but think a few hours later that while an organized house was nice for Thomas, there was another side to that equation, because in a lot of ways, the last few weeks had been a nice break for her, too. An escape from the constant awareness that she did not live up to her husband's expectations. In this place, she was very aware of not living up to Susan's standards, but because things were so extreme here, it didn't feel as depressing.

After a festive dinner, Whitney and Brian said they'd take care of dishes, so Julie and Thomas headed out for a walk together. She had so much she wanted to share — about Whitney at Kids' Club, Brian and his observatory, gardening, sewing. And Rosemary. She told Thomas the woman's stories and how they'd gotten her thinking about using her gifts. She looked at Thomas. "Thomas, what would you say are my gifts?"

"Your gifts? Besides being beautiful, you mean?"

"That's a lie, and you know it. I'm not being facetious; I want the truth."

"It's not a lie. You are beautiful, and I suppose I need some clarification of the question. How, exactly, would you define the word 'gift' as you are using it in this sentence?"

"You know good and well what I mean. What am I good at?"

"You're a terrific mother, a great wife, and

one of the nicest people I've ever met."

"Those are all too general to be completely true or completely helpful."

"All right, then. I'll be more specific. You're a great wife because you constantly deal with my ever-changing schedule with good grace and good humor, and I know from the talk around the office, this is not the norm for many of my coworkers. You are a terrific mother because you encourage the kids to follow their own dreams. That part about you being one of the nicest people I know is true, too, and one of the ways I know this is that you truly see people. You notice when someone is sad, or uncomfortable, when most people would not give them a second glance."

Julie knew there was a flip side to all those statements. She might adapt to a schedule well, but his coworkers' wives maintained meticulous homes. She let the kids follow their dreams but perhaps was too lax with them. She noticed people, but did she do anything to really change things?

Maybe Rosemary was wrong. Maybe there was a group of people who really just didn't have anything much in the way of gifts. They were the group of people, like her, who just floated through the sea of this life, waiting for the tide to pull them in, or push them out, or the next wave to crash into them.

Still . . . maybe there was a bit of truth to his words. *God, if I really do have a special gift, any gift, please show it to me. Please help me use it to the best of my ability.*

"Now, let's get back to that part about me being a terrific wife." She wrapped her arms around his neck. "What was it you were saying again?"

CHAPTER 26

The Friday morning of Lisa Lee's visit had been a train wreck. Nothing had gone right, including spilled coffee, which had splattered underneath the stove, a backed-up kitchen sink, and burned pancakes that still smelled up the entire farmhouse. All the makings of a disastrous day were firmly in place. Susan pulled out her to-do list. "We've got to work fast. We're already almost half an hour behind schedule, and there are a few additional things we have to add to the list now." Susan would make certain things were as comfortable as possible for Lisa Lee's visit today — just like a good Amish woman would do for her guests.

"The kids sure must enjoy their school. They seem to be in an awfully big hurry to get there." Thomas turned from the window and looked at Susan, as if waiting for a response.

Since she didn't have time for chatter this

morning, she gave none. "Okay, Thomas, you're in charge of sink duty. Let's see, Julie . . ." She started to tell her to work on the coffee clean-up detail, but it was too important to have that job done correctly today. Better just to get Julie out of the way. "Why don't you go on out to the garden and start weeding at the green bean row?"

"Don't we need to do a load of laundry this morning?"

"We certainly don't want Lisa Lee showing up with our laundry hanging out on the line. It's got to look perfect around here, and we are a far cry from perfect right now."

"Okay." Julie turned and started for the door.

Susan heard Thomas mumble something to her as she walked by. It sounded something like "I want to go to school with the kids," but she couldn't be sure, and it didn't really matter. They didn't have time to talk.

Susan got down on her hands and knees and looked at what she had to face. Julie had wiped up the bulk of the coffee after she'd spilled it, but it had streamed underneath the stove and all around the front stove legs. This was going to require a toothbrush and some scrubbing. She looked under the sink and pulled out her cleaning supplies while Thomas continued to work with the plunger in the sink itself.

"So how are things going here?"

At least he was working while he talked. "Fine. Just busy."

"Fine? Really? Because you seem about as uptight as I've ever seen you."

"Of course I'm uptight. Today's visit is crucial for us, and it's started as a nightmare."

"No worries, sister of mine. We'll have it all straightened out and ready to go by the time Lisa Lee arrives." He looked at his watch. "We've got a couple of hours yet, yes?"

"Yes, but plenty of things to do." She pulled out the brushes and cleaner and went back to the stove. She knelt down on the floor and started scrubbing with every bit of her energy. Hopefully things would get better from here. "This is make it or break it for me today. It has to be perfect, and given the start we're off to, I'd say that's likely not going to happen."

"We'll give it our best shot." A loud gurgling sound coming from the sink was the first hopeful sign. "One down, what's next on my list?"

It was good to have Thomas here.

A few hours later, Susan watched through

the farmhouse window as Lisa Lee emerged from the black Suburban. Kendra and the camera crew had been standing in the driveway as the car approached. Kendra held out a restraining hand toward the crew and approached Lisa, shook hands and began telling her something. Lisa nodded politely, tucked her hair behind her ear, and smiled without comment. Finally, she shook her head and pointed toward the house.

Kendra was obviously still arguing the point as Lisa Lee came to the front porch and knocked. Susan ran to the door, accompanied by the cameraman, who was waiting inside. "Welcome. Please come in." It felt strange inviting her in, as if she were a guest, rather than the reason for all of this.

"Hello. How nice to see you again." Lisa walked in and hugged Susan. "I hope you are enjoying your adventure here."

"Yes, I am." She hoped it sounded convincing.

"Julie, so nice to see you again. Thomas, thank you for being willing to adjust your schedule to be here today." She walked over and hugged each of them.

It was amazing that even in this heat, Lisa Lee was every bit as perky as she was in her Los Angeles studio. She looked around the living room and smiled. "I am so happy to be here so I can see for myself how this is all working. We've had feedback from the segments that is absolutely amazing. Haven't we, Kendra?"

Kendra, who had entered silently behind Lisa, nodded. "Yes, we have."

"So for today's taping, we're basically going to do a general tour of the place. We'll go out and check out the kids in the schoolhouse, look in the barn and see the animals, look at the vegetable garden, and do a lot of talking to each of you. Then we'll film my first attempt at cooking in the wood stove, during which time I'll prepare a three-course meal for your family."

"That sounds wonderful." Julie beamed up at Thomas. "Can you believe it? A three-course meal prepared by Lisa Lee."

Susan couldn't help but wonder what that might mean. Did they have Lisa cooking because she had not performed adequately? Would she be expected to do that much better during the upcoming weeks?

Lisa fanned herself. "Whew. It's hot in here."

Yes, it was.

Julie sat at the table, pondering the odd sense of peace that had begun to build inside her today. She wasn't certain if it was

288

because of her talk with Thomas last night, or the unexpected easiness of being around Lisa Lee, or the fact that Lisa had also burned the shoo-fly pie she'd made for dinner tonight.

"Ladies" — Lisa Lee looked around the table, then nodded toward Thomas and Brian — "and gentlemen. I would like to thank you for one of the most enjoyable and challenging days I've had in a long time."

"I'm so glad you enjoyed it." Susan said the words in perfect grace, and with a beautiful smile on her face. Only because Julie had known her so long did she know that Susan was stressed to the breaking point right now.

Lisa looked down at her watch. "Let's see, Kendra. I believe you said that electricity could be restored at 6:00 P.M., and according to my watch, it's 6:02. What do you say we get a little air-conditioning going in this place?"

"A good idea." Kendra nodded and pulled out her ever-present walkie-talkie. "Joe, turn the power back on to the farmhouse."

The whirring sound of the window-installed air-conditioners quickly filled the room, and a cool breeze began to stir from the backside of the house. A collective "aah" went around the table.

"It'll take it a long time to cool off, I imagine. I must say, you are all awfully good sports about living this way for a week. I think all of us who live on the California coast tend to forget what real weather feels like. Susan, I'm amazed at all that you accomplished in this heat."

Susan just continued to give her perfect smile.

"And, Julie," Lisa said, picking at the piece of pie on her plate. "Julie, I have to say, I'm impressed with how well you did cooking that shoo-fly pie on the first week of being here. That stove is more difficult to control than I had thought it would be."

"No offense to you, but it definitely soothed my ego a little bit when you burned the edges today."

Lisa laughed. "Glad I could help you out. Kendra, what is the task for this coming week?"

"Authentic Amish clothes." Kendra looked around the table until she fixed her gaze on Whitney. "All week long."

"Oh no." Whitney covered her face.

Kendra smiled outright. "Starting in about an hour. As soon as the dinner dishes are sufficiently washed and put away, we're going to make a trip into town. We want Lisa to experience this firsthand."

Whitney moaned and shook her head. "This is going to be awful."

The grin on Kendra's face left little doubt that she was counting on it.

CHAPTER 27

There were already three buggies lined up at the watering rail when they arrived. They sat dark and empty in the fading evening light, their horses taking no notice of the new arrival. Julie shifted uncomfortably in her seat, hoping this outing wouldn't last long.

"Isn't this wild? We're parking our horse and buggy in an actual horse-and-buggy parking spot at Walmart." Whitney shook her head. "The kids back home would never believe this one."

"They're not going to believe you in a black bonnet, either, but I'm guessing they'll get to see a little of both if they watch the episodes." Brian adjusted the straw hat on his own head. "I guess that's one of the advantages of being the only boy on this adventure. I know *for a fact* that none of my friends are going to be watching."

"Neither will mine." Thomas nodded

toward his son. "But I'm still glad I get to dress normally."

Whitney reached up and touched the side of her neck, tucking an imaginary loose hair back inside her bonnet, and glanced toward Julie. "Mom told me I had to keep a positive attitude in the midst of this horror, so I'm not going to say what I'd really like to say right about now." She looked down at her black skirt and apron. "Suffice it to say, we'll just have to pray for low ratings for this particular episode."

Chris laughed as he climbed down from his place in the buggy. "Have a good time, you guys," he whispered as he helped Whitney down from the buggy. He looked up at Julie then, a hint of panic on his face.

She smiled and whispered, "Don't worry. I'm not the 'no talking' police."

"Glad to hear it." He helped her down from the carriage, then turned his attention toward the smaller buggy, which had arrived beside them, carrying Gary, Susan, and Angie. He hurried around to the far side to assist Angie while Gary helped Susan.

The two Suburbans had taken parking spots near them, and Lisa Lee, Kendra, and a full barrage of cameramen emerged and stood at the ready.

Julie made certain her bonnet was sitting

securely on her head as she started toward the front door of the huge shopping center. She looked at Thomas. "A little part of me thinks that it is sort of nice to be allowed back into the modern world for a while."

"What does the bigger part think?"

She shrugged. "It's embarrassing. The outfits, the cameras, all the attention this is sure to garnish." By the time they reached the inside of the store, people were already gawking. They pointed, and whispered, and giggled.

Kendra turned to the group. "All right. Adults, we're limiting you to the grocery section of the store. Kids, you are free to go wherever you like as long as you stay together."

"Woo-hoo." Whitney did a fist pump. "Come on, everybody, let's go check out the music." Angie and Brian followed in a whirl of excited chatter, followed by a couple of cameramen.

A tired-looking, bone-thin woman approached the group. Her gray hair frizzed in various directions, in spite of the ponytail she wore. "Hey, you're Lisa Lee, aren't you?"

Lisa smiled graciously. "Yes, I am. What is your name?"

Within seconds an autograph-seeking

group had formed around the ever-smiling Lisa. She looked toward Susan. "You go ahead. I'll be along in just a few minutes."

"Well, let's go look at some groceries, shall we?" Susan gestured toward the other side of the store, looking every bit as elegant in her plain attire as she did in her stylish clothes back home.

The group moved away from Lisa Lee and her admiring fans. Just as they turned down the main aisle of the grocery section, an Amish couple came walking out of an adjoining aisle, directly in their path. They were both young, early twenties if that, and the woman carried a small child in her arms. She looked toward Susan, and Julie, and Thomas, cut her eyes toward the cameras. Her face grew red as she focused her attention on the floor. Her husband took her by the arm, said something softly in a language Julie did not understand, and they walked past the group to the checkout counter.

"Well, that was a bit awkward." Kendra sort of snorted. "Ray, I'm hoping you captured that moment on camera?"

The cameraman nodded. "Got it."

"Great." She nodded. "Okay, everyone, let's get on with our journey, shall we?" Kendra walked in the general direction of the groceries.

Julie knew that it wasn't her place to say anything, and that she was here to help Susan, so she shouldn't say anything. So she shuffled forward and tried to forget what had just happened. As they walked the length of the cereal aisle, her mind tumbled over and over with thoughts, and regrets, and memories of what Thomas had said just last night. "You truly see people. You notice when someone is sad, or uncomfortable, when most people would not give them a second glance." If that truly was a gift she possessed, wasn't this the time to use it? She turned and leaned against a shelf of Toasted O's. "I don't think this is a good idea."

"What? Shopping? I think you'll get used to it." Susan's voice was light, but her eyes widened in a warning to Julie.

"That's not what I was talking about."

"Hey there. What are you all talking about, so serious over here?" Lisa bounded up the aisle, all smiles. "Did I miss something?" She moved to join the group, which had all gone stone silent.

"Julie was just saying she didn't like this." Thomas put his arms around her shoulders. "She was just about to tell us what it is she doesn't like."

Julie could have throttled Thomas at that moment. He should have known she would not want to have this conversation in front of Lisa. That would make it all the more likely to come back and hurt Susan.

"What don't you like, Julie?" Lisa's voice was full of interest. "I really want to know all concerns that any of you might have."

"Amish clothes." The words barely croaked out of her closed throat.

"You knew when you came here that this would happen at some point during your stay. We were very upfront about that." Kendra looked toward Lisa and rolled her eyes. "Let's head to the produce. We need to keep on schedule."

Lisa squeezed Julie's arm. "It's only for a week. It'll be over sooner than you think."

Susan shot her a warning glance, and then the group started down the aisle. Everyone except Julie, whose feet wouldn't move.

"Here's the thing . . ." She said the words so late, and so quietly, it stunned her when everyone stopped and turned around. She didn't dare look in Susan's direction for fear of losing her nerve, but the right words evaded her. She rubbed the back of her neck, praying for help.

"You know, it really doesn't matter what *the thing* is; this is a crucial part to the show."

Julie looked up at Kendra and felt her resolve starting to slip. Maybe she shouldn't have spoken up. But what if this really was her gift, the loaves and fish she was supposed to use, and she was too much a coward to use it at a time like this?

"Yes, we did make an agreement, but at the time I didn't understand how wrong it would be." As she said it, Thomas reached over and took her hand. She wasn't certain if it was meant as an offer of support or a warning.

"What is it that bothers you?" Lisa moved closer, squinting her eyes in concentration.

"I'm sure it's nothing," Susan offered. Julie could see the panic in her eyes. Julie had backed down throughout filming for her sister-in-law, but this seemed bigger than even Susan's dreams. This was about something larger.

The word came to her.

"Respect." Julie looked Kendra in the eye with every bit of conviction in her body flowing through her. "It's one thing for us to try this experiment so the rest of the world can get an idea of what it would be like for a modern family to try to live a more Amish lifestyle. The clothes we normally wear do that just fine. But to dress exactly like them . . . it only matters when we're here, in public. And, well, you saw how that Amish couple looked at us. That was a slap in the face. Especially with all these cameras following us around, something that flies against everything they believe in."

"We're simply taking on one more aspect of their lifestyle," Kendra said dismissively.

Julie shook her head. "No. No, it most definitely is not. From what I've seen, they are a quiet people full of dignity. And this . . . well, it goes too far."

"If you're going to break our contract, then we'll be forced to —"

Lisa's upheld hand stopped Kendra from saying the rest of whatever the threat would have been. "You know, she may have a point. This whole experiment was about a modern family living simply. It's not supposed to be demeaning or disrespectful of another group of people. That's the last thing I would want to do."

"But we've already got next week's schedule planned around that."

Lisa tilted her head to the left side. "Then we'll just have to think of something else. We've got a group full of bright minds here. Let's think this through." She looked at her watch. "But we're going to have to think about it on our way through the parking lot, because I've got a plane to catch."

Thomas squeezed Julie's hand. He leaned closer and whispered, "Well done."

The realization of what she'd just done flowed through Julie's veins in a warm tide of happiness. She couldn't remember the last time she'd felt this good about anything. It didn't even bother her when Susan refused to meet her eye.

A few minutes later, they were walking through the parking lot when Lisa called the group over. "Everyone come over here. I think I've got our answer." The group assembled around her, Kendra looking as if she'd taken a bite of something sour and needed to spit it out.

"How about *rumspringa?* Why don't we give the kids a week to ease up a little bit, out of their parents' control?"

Whitney, Angie, and Brian immediately shouted their approval, and Lisa smiled at them.

"They could go into town, maybe see a movie, eat at McDonald's. I don't know, what else do Amish kids do during their running around?"

"The Amish in this part of the country do not participate in *rumspringa.*" Kendra's voice was firm. "That's their more liberal counterparts up north." She folded her arms across her chest, unwilling to concede.

Lisa shrugged. "We didn't name this series, *Almost Swartzentruber Amish*. We named it *Almost Amish*. I think we have quite a bit of latitude in which to work here. Don't you?"

Kendra shrugged. "If that's what you want us to do." Her face was red with anger. Julie suspected they would feel the brunt of that over the course of the next few days.

"That's what I want you to do. In fact, I'm declaring tomorrow a day off for everyone. Thomas has to go to the airport, right?"

"Yes," Thomas said.

"Well, why don't you all ride in the Suburban with him, give him a proper farewell at the airport? I think it would be good for everyone to take a little break. Don't you agree, Kendra?"

It was obvious from Kendra's face that she did not agree. "If that's what you want us to do."

"It is." Lisa nodded. "I only wish I didn't have to go back tonight or I'd hang around a little longer and see how it all works out." She hugged each of them. "Good-bye. I look forward to seeing you all again soon." She climbed into a Suburban, which pulled away.

"I guess I'll see you all day after tomor-

row." Kendra climbed into the other Suburban without saying another word.

CHAPTER 28

Susan swished the water back and forth in their washing machine. The lever to churn water and laundry required a fair amount of back and arm muscles, and even though it was barely 8:00 A.M., it was already hot. She leaned as far as possible from the steam rising from around the lid. The kids had gotten especially dirty this week, and the whites were refusing to give up their spots without a fight.

"You want to switch places for a while? You've got to be roasting over there." Julie was scrubbing the back porch steps, which were currently in the shade. The water wasn't hot either, making for a much cooler job.

"These clothes are pretty dirty. May require a few times through the cycle to finish them."

"All the more reason for us to switch off." Julie left her post and walked over, prepared to take Susan's place.

Susan looked at the not yet quite clean clothes. She was tired, but they still showed their stains. She just couldn't imagine Julie truly working until they were clean. 'Why bother to get them perfectly clean when they're just going to get dirty again?' She shook her head. "That's all right. I'm good for now."

"Susan, your face is bright red, you've been pumping that lever for half an hour, and I know you're burning up. Now trade places so you can cool off, at least a little."

Susan did not release the handle. "It's very important that we get these clothes super clean." Kendra had been in a huff ever since Lisa Lee sided with Julie and overruled Amish clothing week. Susan couldn't afford to do anything wrong at this point, because Kendra was looking for mistakes to high-light.

"Yes, I know that, and I promise I'll do my very best. Now get over there and take a breather."

Susan didn't want to go, but she did, simply because she couldn't think of a way to continue the argument without getting particularly rude. "Okay, I'll switch for just a few minutes."

As if on cue, the door to the shack

squeaked open. "Susan, can I speak with you a minute?" Kendra, as usual, looked crisp and clean and cool.

"Sure." Susan followed her, the shack's cool air hitting her like a wave of relief. She took in a few deep breaths, savoring the feel of cool air in her lungs.

Kendra closed the door behind her and then leaned against it. "I need to speak with you about a situation that has come to our attention." The downward curve of her mouth mirrored the irritation in her voice.

"What situation?"

"I'm more than confident that when you first came here we explained the rules to you. In particular, there was to be no fraternizing with the staff."

Susan held her breath and fought to think through her response. It had never occurred to her that there would be a problem when she and Gary went for a walk down to the creek yesterday. "My understanding was that we were not to talk to the crew, but that the locals involved with the show were okay for us to talk to." And that's all they had done was talk.

"That is true."

"So what's the problem, then?" Maybe there were rumors flying around about them. Something Susan had never considered. But why should she care what the crew thought about Gary and her spending time together?

"The problem is your daughter."

"Excuse me?"

"This is the problem." Kendra held up a remote and pointed it at a small video screen. A dark image sprang to life, showing a car parked out in the driveway in front of the house. It was the same car that had been parked in the driveway from 10:00 P.M. to 6:00 A.M. every night since they'd arrived. Susan knew it always held a low-level production assistant who was charged with "security" overnight. Since the car was always parked closer to the production equipment than the family's house, Susan had a pretty good idea what it was they were trying to protect.

She had been looking at the same screen for about ten seconds or so when she saw movement coming from the right side of the screen — the farmhouse side. A shadowy figure approached the car. At first, the shadow approached the driver's side, leaned forward at the window and seemed to carry on a conversation with the person inside the car. "Are you telling me that this is my daughter we're watching?"

"Yes, I am."

"I don't see how that could possibly be true. The security car doesn't move into place until ten o'clock. With the early-to-bed and early-to-rise schedule we've been keeping since we've been here, the girls are in bed at that time."

"That's what we'd like to think, isn't it?"

The shadow straightened, walked around to the passenger side of the car, and opened the door. As the door opened, the interior light came on. Angie never turned her face in the direction of the camera, but her smooth brown hair and favorite pink sleeveless shirt left no doubt about who it was.

Every ounce of Susan's energy seemed to drain from her body, starting with her head and working its way slowly out her toes. Sheer willpower kept her standing in place. Her daughter had deceived her. And she'd done it blatantly. And it was going to cost them everything.

She leaned forward, trying to see who was in the driver's side of the car. Just that quick, the door shut and the light went out. She waited, thinking surely now the car would start and they would be off into the world of the great unknown. It didn't. It simply sat there, unmoving, and too dark for the camera to see inside.

Kendra pressed the remote and set it on

the table. "I don't see any argument that this is anything other than against the rules. Do you?"

Susan shook her head, too numb to think of an answer. "When did this take place?"

"Last night."

"I see." Susan was more than certain she did not want to know the answer to the next question, just as she was more than certain she must ask it. "Who was in the car?"

"Chris Baugh. He's one of the production assistants."

"The one with the black hair." Susan closed her eyes and tried to stay focused. "How long was she out there?"

"Not that long, actually. About half an hour or so."

"Half an hour." The implications of what might have happened during that time began to flip through Susan's mind, bringing with them a gut-deep, quickly building fury. Susan started for the door. "I'm going to the schoolhouse and talking to Angie. Right now."

"There's no need for that. She's on the way and should be here any moment."

She had no sooner spoken the words than the sound of an approaching Suburban broke the silence. Susan opened the door and watched as her daughter climbed from the backseat, looking totally bewildered. She looked toward Susan. "Mom, what's going on?"

"Angie, could you come in here, please?" Kendra motioned toward the production shed. "We need to talk."

Angie looked from Kendra to Susan, then nodded and walked inside. She plopped down in a chair, and crossed her arms. "What's up?"

"What's up? Are you seriously going to sit there and —"

Kendra put a restraining arm on Susan's shoulder. "Why don't you let me start. You can go outside with any unfinished mother-daughter business when I'm done."

Absolutely not. Angie needed to answer to her mother right now, and her mother was not going to wait to become part of *unfinished business.* "No. I need to —"

"When I'm finished." Kendra's voice was calm and in control. "You've got a lifetime to work out your differences regarding this issue. I, however, have to decide within the next half hour what kind of action to take, including whether or not this show will even go on."

Those words sent enough chill through Susan to at least tamp her anger marginally. She glared at Angie, who was watching the scene as her face got whiter and whiter.

"Angie" — Kendra took a backward step and then sat on the desktop behind her — "it has come to my attention that there may have been some contact between you and one of our crew. Can you tell me what's going on?"

Angie looked toward Kendra, but her focus was on her knees rather than her face. She shrugged. "I . . . don't know what you're talking about."

"Angie, don't you dare sit there and lie —"

Kendra extended her arm in the direction of Susan. "Please, I need you to use some restraint so that we can get to the truth at the bottom of this." She looked back toward Angie, her expression so carefully neutral that no one who saw her right now would have any idea this was anything more than a casual conversation. "Now, Angie, I will tell you that we do know better than this. In fact, we have a fair amount of evidence to the contrary, so why don't you just tell us the truth?"

Tears welled up in Angie's eyes and spilled down her face. She used the heel of her hand to wipe both cheeks before she looked back up. First at Susan, then at Kendra. "So what if we've talked? It's not like we're sabotaging the show or anything."

"When have you talked?" Kendra leaned forward, resting her hands on the edge of the desk and swinging her legs beneath her. She looked as though she might lunge forward and pounce at any moment.

Angie shrugged and looked down. "It's just me, really. I mean, Chris drives us to youth group every Wednesday. To me it feels rude just to sit there and pretend like the guy is not even in the wagon with us."

"I see. And have there been any other times that the two of you have had time together to talk, or have interaction of any kind?"

Once again Angie cast a glance toward Susan. Susan guessed that she was trying to gauge from her expression just how much they knew. Unfortunately, Susan did not have Kendra's uncanny ability to put on a neutral face, so it had to be more than apparent they knew there was more to the story.

Angie looked at her feet. "I've gone outside and talked to him at night, when he's acting as our night watchman."

"Has this happened more than once?" Kendra's feet began to swing faster.

"Just twice. I had trouble falling asleep a few nights ago, so I looked out the window.

The car was out there, and I knew he was probably bored to tears. He's supposed to be staying awake all night to protect us, so I thought it might help him stay awake for a while, and maybe I could come back in and fall asleep."

Kendra's feet went still as she waited for more.

"I did the same thing last night." Angie's voice was so low it was difficult to hear. "But it was never Chris's idea; it was all mine. He told me I shouldn't do that because it could get me into trouble." She rubbed the back of her right hand with her left. "I guess he was right." She looked up then, her eyes full of fresh tears. "But honestly, if you're going to get mad at someone, get mad at me. It was all my doing, not his."

Susan's breathing was getting shallow. She couldn't stay silent any longer. "You've never done anything like this in all your life, and now we come here, and all of a sudden you're sneaking out at night to hang out with some boy. And not just any boy, but one who looks as wild as they come. Angie, this is not at all acceptable. You are going to have some serious consequences to pay for this."

Angie looked down at her hands folded in

her lap and never responded, by word or movement. She simply remained still.

Susan looked at Kendra. "Am I to assume this boy will be relieved of his job effective immediately?"

"No!" Angie jumped to her feet, fists clenched at each side. "Did you not hear what I just said? *I'm* the one who talked to him; *I'm* the one who decided to go out there and see him. He didn't know I was coming out there until I showed up. This is supposed to be our *rumspringa* week, remember?"

"It doesn't matter. He knows he's not supposed to be talking to you, so his actions are still his responsibility."

"What was he supposed to do? Tell me to shut up and leave him alone? I think you would call that rude, Mother."

Angie's eyes flashed in a way that Susan had never seen before. In truth, it scared her. Had this boy gained so much control over her in such little time that she was willing to act this way?

"All right, all right. Let's calm down," Kendra said. "I'll bring Chris in here and talk to him and try to hear his side of things. I'll make further decisions based on what I find out." She slid off the desk to a standing position, a grin quirking the left side of her mouth. "I can guarantee, no matter what else happens, Chris will no longer be driving the three of you to youth group during the week." She walked over to the door and grasped the knob but did not yet turn it. "Or working night security duty. That leaves his options somewhat limited."

"But it's not his fault. I told you it was me."

"Then your recklessness has cost him his job. I hope it was worth it."

Susan regretted the words the instant they left her mouth. But they needed to be said. She hated the pain this was causing her daughter, but the sooner Angie learned that these kinds of irresponsible decisions could affect not only herself, but others, the better.

Angie covered her face with her hands, her shoulders heaving with quiet sobbing. After a brief period of time, she drew in a deep breath, wiped her eyes and looked up. "Can I go now?"

"Our conversation is finished," said Kendra. "But, Susan, I need to talk to you for just another minute." She opened the door and Angie fled through it, never looking back.

"I really need to go talk to her. We can finish this conversation when I get back."

"Um, not really a good idea. See, here's the thing." Kendra drew her back inside and closed the door. "It was intentional that we had this conversation in here. Emotional drama usually makes for good reality television, but we're a different kind of show, and having your daughter sneaking around with a nineteen-year-old member of the crew is not something we want on the Lisa Lee show — as much as I'd like to, because it would send our ratings through the roof." A covetous gleam came to her eye and she paused for a long second. "But we have to live with the limits that we've been given: I lose some rating points, and you need to spend a little time cooling off before you deal with this further. Go for a nice long walk with your daughter. We don't want any of this footage to accidentally make its way into the week's highlights. You see, there's more to it than just avoiding any hint of scandal. We need to be careful of your viewer approval ratings, too."

A cold chill raced through Susan. "What do you mean?"

"We polled viewers, and after these early segments a good portion are undecided about their opinion of you." She opened a file, looked at a graph, which Susan could not quite see clearly from her angle, then closed the file again. "In fact, a majority seem to prefer your sister-in-law. For you to have a major rift with your daughter right now . . . that could be disastrous for all our future plans."

Susan stared at Kendra, willing her feet to remain beneath her. How could this be? Julie couldn't accomplish anything on her own without Susan prodding her. She let the words soak in for just a moment, then began to let reason sink back in. "It seems to me that the Amish are known for having well-disciplined children. Shouldn't it make sense that I could be seen as a disciplinarian in this case?"

Kendra nodded once slowly, then said, "There's some truth to what you're saying. But I guess there's a balance, too. The comment that seems to come up about you more and more is the expression, 'helicopter mom.' You're familiar with it?"

"Yes." Susan was more than familiar with the phrase. "But there's a difference between wanting what is best for your child and hovering over and controlling her every move."

"Our viewers seem to think differently. And as I said, this is *not* a part of this story that we want portrayed right now."

"All right, then." Susan took a deep

breath. "I'll just go speak with Angie now. I'm guessing that our *walk* might take awhile, a long while."

"You can't do that right now because she's no longer here."

Susan stepped outside of the shack and looked around. There was no one in sight. "What? Where is she?"

"You'll need to wait until school gets out. I instructed Art to take her back to her classes immediately after she walked out of here. I know how important her education is to you." Kendra quirked her left eyebrow, daring her to respond to that.

Focus. Stay calm. "Yes, her education is very important to me, but right now, I am going to speak with my daughter."

"Have a nice walk out to the schoolhouse." Kendra shut the door to her office, effectively ending the conversation.

Julie hung the clothes on the line, glancing toward the shack, again. Something was going on over there, and she couldn't help but worry. Between Kendra summoning Susan, Angie arriving in the car and leaving just as quickly in the same car, something absolutely had to be wrong.

Just as she was hanging the last of the shirts on the line, she heard Susan's voice.

And Kendra's. She couldn't hear what they were saying, but they sounded angry. She turned in time to see Kendra shut the office door in Susan's face.

Susan pivoted on her heel and started down the driveway, toward the back of the property. Julie ran after her.

"Susan, wait." Susan didn't turn, but she did slow down just a little. Julie jogged up to her side. "What's the matter?"

Susan's face was flushed with anger, her lips pressed so tight they had gone white. "I've got to go talk to Angie."

Julie reached out and grabbed her arm and pulled her to a stop. "Susan, take a breath and calm down. Tell me what's going on."

"Apparently there are lots of things going on. For instance, my daughter has been cheating on the rules we were given when we came here. That same daughter has been downright deceitful, sneaking out of the farmhouse after we've all gone to bed at night."

Julie almost cried with relief that this wasn't something more serious. Sneaking out of the house was wrong, and she didn't blame Susan for being upset about it, but she had seen that one coming from a mile away. "I'm assuming she was sneaking out to see Chris?"

Susan's jaw dropped open. "Did Whitney tell you? Have you known this was going on all along?"

"No, of course not. I just guessed. It's been more than obvious since our first day here that the two of them have chemistry between them. I guess I just hoped they could wait till the end of filming before talking."

"You knew that my daughter was seeing that . . . gothic thug, and you never told me?"

"Susan, I didn't *know* any more than you did. I just saw the way they looked at each other."

"Well, I'm hoping that boy is going to be fired, and Angie is going to wish that's all I was going to do to her."

"Susan, you're mad. I would be, too. But let them finish up their day at school. Come work out some of your frustrations on the weeds in the garden — you know it relaxes you. By the time she gets home, you will have calmed down enough to talk to her."

Susan pulled her arm away. "I need to deal with this out here."

"I don't think —"

"I was *told* to deal with this in private. Kendra doesn't want any of this captured by the cameras. She doesn't want the word to spread around."

"Oh. Well, how about this? Let's go back to the house, work on today's chore list" — which was so huge they couldn't finish it if they had a week, much less a few hours — "and when it's almost time for school to be out, we'll walk that way together. I'll get Brian and Whitney, and you can walk with Angie. No one will think anything of it; they'll just think we're mothers checking in on our kids."

Susan let out a long breath and almost seemed like she might collapse. "You're probably right. It's better in many ways if we just bide our time."

Julie needed to do what she could to defuse the situation in the next little while. If not, she sensed an explosion on the horizon.

CHAPTER 29

A fine coat of dust covered the weathered sides of the schoolhouse. Even from a distance, the windows seemed nearly opaque. The entire place looked as old and worn and tired as Susan felt. It was times like these when she most felt James's absence. Not having a husband to back her up was one of the many ways that life had gotten so much harder in the last few years. Angie's deception, however, felt a little too familiar. One little lie, allowed to flourish, would only grow bigger and lead to more malignant lies. Susan was not going to allow that to happen in her daughter.

"Now remember, this is one of those times that can determine your future relationship right here." Julie made this statement as if she were so much wiser and more experienced than Susan.

"Thanks *so much* for the advice."

"I mean it, Susan. You've got to make her

see how much you dislike *what she did,* but that you still love her to pieces. She's got to understand that."

Susan's anger boiled up again, but this time it took a different object. "You know, maybe you should rethink your way of parenting. This being all concerned about never hurting their feelings, never letting them know that they've completely blown it — well, all that does is raise a bunch of soft kids who think they can do anything and get away with it."

It didn't feel good, but it needed to be said. She expected Julie to look away, maybe even cry, but that didn't happen. For a second she thought Julie might even yell at her. But that didn't happen, either.

"Not do anything wrong and get away with it," Julie said carefully. "Do anything wrong and yet still be loved by her mother — who may be furious, and rightfully so. I'm not even saying not to punish, severely. But you can't take it too far."

"I've never gone easy on Angie, and she has a track record of success to show for that."

"Some things are more important than success."

Susan knew she needed to stop this conversation now before it got ugly. She chose to be the bigger person and let Julie end with the last word. A wrongheaded word, of course, but Susan was too concerned about Angie right now to start dealing with Julie's issues, too.

Susan went up the stairs to the building; its door was already standing open to let cool air pass through. She hurried inside, ready to tell Angie it was time for a little walk. It took her eyes a moment to adjust to the low light, and somewhere during that adjustment she came to the realization that the room was empty. She turned back toward Julie, who was just now catching up. "Surely we didn't miss them on the way back?"

"No" — Julie looked around — "their things are still here. They're likely down by the creek again."

Susan pivoted and hurried out the door, her anger only increasing with the thoughts that the education here was so lacking. She found them sitting quietly in the shade, each with a couple of books in front of them, looking conspicuously busy with their studies. "Working on some math, Angie?"

"Mmm-hmm." She didn't look up.

"We need to take a little walk."

Angie looked up, first at Susan, then at Charlotte. "Mom, we're in class."

"My fault. I was enjoying our outdoor setting so much I forgot to check my watch." Charlotte made a show of looking at her wrist. "Y'all go on now, and have a nice day. I'll carry your books back to school; you go on with your mothers. We'll pick up tomorrow where we left off." She said the last part of it while looking directly at Angie.

Angie nodded, and even offered a grim smile in the direction of her teacher before turning toward Susan. Her mouth set in a hard line as she walked past her and didn't look back. Susan turned and quickly caught up with her daughter, but she chose not to say anything until they were far out of earshot of the rest of the group. Then she said, "Now, I want to know how long this has been going on, and I want to know what else you've been up to that they simply haven't caught you at yet."

"There's nothing *going on,* and there's nothing else. I told you everything."

"What kind of lies has that boy been telling you that persuaded you to risk everything to sneak out and be with him like that?"

"He hasn't told me any lies."

"Ha. So he'd like you to believe."

"And we didn't do anything wrong." She looked up defiantly into Susan's face. Susan simply stared back long enough that Angie broke the gaze and shrugged. "Other than sneaking out like that, but I can't help it if there are a bunch of stupid rules around here. It's bad enough we're having to live in an oven, wear weird clothes, and be separated from our friends — but we're not even allowed to talk to other people? That's ridiculous."

"You are allowed to talk to other people — your friends at church, for instance; you're just not allowed to talk to members of the crew."

"Chris is my friend from church, so I guess I *am* allowed to talk to him after all."

"Don't you dare insult me by lying to me right now."

"I'm not lying."

"That boy is nineteen years old. You go to the high school youth group at church. For everyone's sake I hope he's not part of that group. Lying like that will only get you into deeper trouble, and believe me you're already in trouble enough."

"Fine." She crossed her arms and increased her pace, never looking toward Susan at all.

"When we get back to the house, I want you to go upstairs to your room and write a three-page apology to Kendra and to me for taking part in this. As far as I'm concerned, this incident is not over, but since you're obviously not ready to come clean yet, you can just stay in your room, except for when you're doing chores, until you're ready to talk."

"Fine."

They didn't speak another word all the way home. Angie ran up the front steps and inside the house. The screen door slapped the doorframe behind her, just seconds before Susan could hear her footsteps running up the stairs, followed by the door to her room shutting. Angie had the common sense not to slam it, although Susan was more than certain she had wanted to do so.

Kendra came to the back door and motioned her outside. "I wanted to let you know that I spent quite a bit of time talking with Chris this afternoon."

"And?"

"He admitted that it was all his fault, that it had all been his idea."

"Well, of course it was. I could have told you that without putting you to the trouble of asking him. I'm just glad to know he is confessing the truth and assume you will take measures accordingly."

"I didn't fire him, if that's what you mean."

"Why not? He admitted the truth."

"See, that's where we disagree. I think he's saying what he thinks he needs to say to keep your daughter out of trouble and your family on the show."

"Angie has always been honest and up-standing to a fault. The blame lies squarely on that boy."

"Well, if that's the case, then your honest and upstanding daughter shouldn't give us anything more to worry about, now should she?" Kendra turned and walked back into the shack. Susan was more than a little certain there was a smile of victory on her face.

"What is Aunt Susan in such a lather about?" Whitney asked, watching Angie and Susan walk away. She folded the blanket the kids had been sitting on during their lesson.

"Whitney, you need to show respect when you talk about your aunt." Julie started toward the pile of Angie's books. "I've got empty hands. I'll get those things."

Brian straightened out his arm in her direction, palm facing her. "Halt. We men do the heavy lifting for our womenfolk when they've been summoned away by the pow-ers that be." He squatted down and put his books on top of Angie's. When he stood back up, his arms were fully extended. "Now go on back and cook me some supper, woman."

Charlotte laughed. "Sorry, Mrs. Charlton. I think I'm going to have to take the blame for that. I've been trying to get Brian interested in reading fiction, so I turned him on to westerns."

"And I much appreciate your efforts toward the betterment of my education, ma'am." Brian nodded toward Charlotte. "You need me to carry your books, little lady?"

"I've got it Brian, thank yo — oh no. We left our water bottles cooling in the creek. I better go down and get them."

"Not to worry, little lady. I'll just go assist ya." Brian said this in an almost perfect John Wayne imitation as he set the books back on the ground, then offered his left elbow to his teacher.

Julie laughed outright. "Brian, this little adventure has done wonders for your sense of humor."

"Yeah, yeah." He grinned, then turned to Charlotte. "We got us some water bottles to wrangle. Don't wait up."

"Good grief." Whitney adjusted her books into her right hand and started walking toward the schoolhouse. "What's Aunt Susan so *angry* about?" She looked at Julie and grinned. "That better?"

"It is more respectful, yes. And I don't think it's my place to go into a private matter between Susan and Angie."

"But you do know?"

"I know enough. I'm guessing you probably have a good idea what it might be, too."

"Aunt Susan's this berserk because Angie has actually acknowledged a member of the opposite sex? I mean, I know Angie's shy and all, but she is seventeen years old. Surely she can't find it that offensive."

"I think it's more the *way* it happened. There are rules that we are supposed to be abiding by, and that includes not talking to people on the crew. Besides, there's a bit more to it than that."

"Oh, man, tell me they didn't bust her for sn — uh, I mean, for uh . . ."

"Yes, Whitney, they did. Why didn't you tell me she was doing that?"

"I knew it would put you in the position of either having to lie to Aunt Susan or ratting me out for ratting Angie out."

"What if something had happened to her?"

"Chris?" She snorted. "He wouldn't do anything to her. Trust me."

"I wish I could be as confident of that as

you are."

"You would be if you'd been around him for five minutes when he was actually allowed to speak. Or sing. Trust me, he's a good guy."

They walked into the school building, where Whitney put her books in her desk. Julie did the same with Angie's; then they walked back outside. "Angie's scooter is still here. You want to ride it home, or shall we just walk ours together?"

"Shouldn't we wait for Brian?"

Whitney looked toward the creek. "He's probably hoping we leave. That kid's got a huge crush."

"So I've noticed." Julie picked up Angie's scooter. "I'm thinking I want one of these when we get back home."

"Mom, I'm thinking it's a necessity." They laughed.

Whitney dawdled along, in no apparent hurry. "I suppose we want to give Aunt Susan and Angie enough time to get home ahead of us, huh?"

"Probably a good idea."

"So are they super mad at her about the whole Chris thing?"

Julie shrugged. "I don't know. To be honest, I think Kendra is looking for a fight because of me, but I just felt what we were doing was wrong."

"I'm glad you did that." Whitney pulled at her long skirt. "Maybe next time you should push a little harder, though. All right?"

"I'll do my best." Julie put one foot on the scooter. "Oh, by the way, we're not supposed to talk about this anywhere inside or near the house. They don't want the hidden cameras picking up anything."

"Ew. I keep forgetting about the hidden cameras and stuff." Whitney reached down and lifted the scooter back into position. "I can't even begin to imagine what they may have captured at this point."

Julie laughed. "Isn't it the truth?"

CHAPTER 30

Susan ironed her shirt for the third time. The wrinkles just didn't want to come out. This butane-fired iron just didn't seem to be cutting it today. "I'm going to get a cup of water and try dampening this a little."

Julie looked up from her quilt squares. "You know what I think would help you more than anything?"

Susan poured some water into a cup, not bothering to respond. Julie would tell her anyway.

"I think what would be most beneficial would be for you to stand up and walk outside. Sit down somewhere all by yourself and read that paper that's burning a hole in your skirt pocket."

Susan sprinkled water on the placket and pressed the iron hard into the fabric. "I don't know what you're talking about."

"Don't give me that. Angie spent all yesterday evening upstairs in her room, she handed you some folded-up papers on her way out the door today, never bothering to look at you. You, on the other hand, never looked at the papers. It's obviously something that's eating you up inside, so why don't you take five minutes."

"I don't have five minutes."

Julie didn't say anything, just stayed put for what seemed like forever. Finally, she walked across the room, grabbed Susan's right hand, effectively stopping her from ironing anymore. "How about I finish this up, and you go do what you need to do?"

"What I need to do is to get my chores done." Julie just looked at her, waiting. "Fine, I'll go outside and work in the garden."

"Suit yourself."

Susan let the screen door slam behind her. She started down the back steps, but as she did so, she put her hand into her pocket and felt the paper. Three sheets of paper, just like she'd asked, were folded neatly inside her pocket. When she reached the bottom of the steps, instead of turning left toward the garden, she turned right and walked around the side of the house. There she leaned against the wall, took a deep breath, and pulled the papers from her pocket.

Dear Kendra and Mom,

I am very sorry that I broke the rule about talking to crew members. I know that was something we weren't supposed to do, but I did it anyway.

As for the visits to the car when Chris was on watch, as I've previously stated, that was my fault. I was having trouble sleeping, and I was worried about something that Chris understands very well. It just made sense to go talk to him about it.

"Say what?" Susan banged the back of her head against the farmhouse. Angie must have just put that part in to goad her. She started to fold the paper back up, but in spite of her intentions, unfolded it again.

I am sorry that I was selfish enough to risk his job because I wanted to talk to someone. At home, I could have talked to my friends, called someone, at least sent an email. Maybe a real Amish girl might drive her buggy down the road to visit her friend, but we don't have that here. We are not living in a true Amish community. We are isolated. I don't think this is a fair expectation.

I understand that Chris took the blame for me going out there, which is obviously ridiculous. How could that possibly be true? Do you think he snuck into my room and kidnapped me? I am responsible for my own choices, and it was my choice to go outside and talk to him. The fact that he tried to do that makes me all the more happy that I've gotten to know such an unselfish person during my time here.

Susan finished the letter, which basically reiterated the same themes, then folded up the paper, her anger beginning to cool just a little. Part of Angie's argument bothered her just a little more than she cared for. Was it possible that this was true? And what could Angie possibly believe that Chris understood more than she did? This would be something they would talk about tonight

— if they somehow managed to survive this day.

Now it was time to get back to work.

Julie couldn't help but smile as she watched the kids in their World Championship Checkers event. Team Girly-Girly was currently down two games to one, but they were making a hard charge that seemed to have Team Boy nervous. Brian sat studying the board, not saying a single word. Slowly, he slid his black piece forward, moaning as he did so.

Whitney showed not even a trace of humility as she double-jumped him, then said, "King us."

"There's no reason to king you; the game's over. I don't have any checkers left."

Julie laughed at her son as he scowled at his duo of opponents, and couldn't help but think this was what it was all about. This kind of thing was the reason they came here. When did her kids ever have time to play checkers in their real life?

"Just because you don't have any checkers left still doesn't mean that we don't want to be treated like queens. Right, Angie?"

"That's right." All evening long, Angie had said all the right things, made the right strategic moves, but there was no smile in her eyes. Julie wondered if she ought to try to talk to her about what was going on, since Susan obviously was done talking about it. It wasn't really her business, she supposed, but then there was that gift thing again. Maybe she noticed things like this so she could talk to her niece when she needed some grown-up advice — from a grown-up that wouldn't ground her.

"Attention, everyone, attention." Kendra had let herself in the kitchen door as always and came walking into the living room as if she, too, lived here. "Mail call." She held several envelopes high above her head.

"Woot!" Whitney stood up and hurried toward her. "Got anything for me?"

"I'm sure I do. But these" — Kendra lowered her hand — "are for your mother."

"Great." Julie walked over and got the stack of a half dozen letters. "Thanks." She thumbed through the stack, seeing return addresses from Thomas, a couple of friends, a neighbor, and her Bible study leader.

"Susan, we've got several for you. Whitney, Brian, Angie, here you go."

Julie watched everyone take their mail. Whitney immediately ripped open an envelope and pulled out a stack of photos. Angie sorted through her cards. One in particular seemed to bring a smile to her face. She opened it as carefully as Julie's grandmother used to open Christmas presents — so she could keep the wrapping.

With everyone happily involved in their own reading, Julie opened the envelope on top of her stack. It was from her neighbor Rhonda, a particularly chatty widow who lived alone except for her dog, Petey. Most of the neighborhood avoided her because once she started talking, it was hard to get away. She often began a conversation by asking, "Have I ever told you about . . ." Even if the victim answered yes, Rhonda would immediately launch into the story. "Oh, good, because it really was so funny that time that . . ." and she'd tell the whole story from beginning to end, not omitting a single detail.

The neighborhood just isn't the same without you and your kids. No one else around here will take the time for a little friendly neighborhood conversation like you do. And I miss Whitney and her friends batting the volleyball around in the front yard. They make a lot of noise, but it's happy noise and I like it. Petey especially misses Brian and the games of fetch. Thomas seems to be getting along well enough, but I'm sure he'll be glad when you're home, too.

Can't wait to see you,
Rhonda and Petey

Julie looked up to see how everyone else was progressing. Susan was reading what looked like a multi-page letter. She was shaking her head and biting her lips together. She flipped the page over and Julie could see that it was a typewritten form. Likely from the PTA. Susan was undoubtedly thinking about all the things she was going to have to straighten out when she got home.

Whitney was laughing and wiping tears at the same time. Brian showed no expression whatsoever, but he did nod his head occasionally. Angie still had the first letter in her hand, but she was staring out the window. She shook her head slowly from side to side. She reached up to twist a lock of hair, but didn't move otherwise. Julie wondered what kind of upsetting news she'd received and hoped that the next letter in the stack would have something that would cheer her up a bit.

She went back to the next letter in her stack, but kept glancing up toward Angie. At some point, Angie folded up the letter and returned it to its envelope. "I've got a headache, so I'm going to turn in early. Good night, everyone." She walked up the stairs toward her room. Julie was pretty certain Angie hadn't bothered to open any of the rest of the letters.

Long after Angie had gone to bed, Julie sat downstairs worrying about her. Likely she was overreacting. It was just a teenager-versus-mother spat, and it would all blow over in a day or two. But if that were the case, what happened with the letters? Something was wrong. She could feel it.

Whitney and Brian were currently arguing over a game of Scrabble while Susan was busy working up a new recipe for the following week.

Julie stood up and made a show of stretching. "I'm pretty tired. I think I'll go lie in bed and read awhile."

"Sweet dreams," Susan said without even looking up.

" 'Night, Mom."

"Good night."

Julie climbed the stairs slowly, taking care to be quiet. She didn't know why. It wasn't like she thought she was going to sneak up on anything. Once she peeked in the door and saw that her niece was resting, she could relax and chide herself for being such a worrier.

She knocked softly, not wanting to wake Angie if she was asleep, but then again, she didn't want to just barge in if she was awake. She listened briefly for a response and didn't hear one, so she turned the knob slowly and opened the door. The heat of the room hit her as soon as she opened the door. It took a moment for her eyes to adjust to the darkness. When they did, she looked toward Angie's bed and found it empty, completely untouched. The window, however, was open, which explained the warmth of the room.

Julie walked down the hall to the bathroom, only to find it empty. She returned to the bedroom, some irrational hope telling her that she somehow had overlooked Angie the last time.

The room was still just as empty.

Julie looked out the window. The security car was just pulling up, its headlights cutting through the night. Julie turned to cross the room, but as she did, she noticed the trash can in the room held some ripped-up paper. She reached in and picked up the envelope. It was from James Reynolds.

The letter had been ripped in half only, so it was easy enough to reconstruct. Julie carried it over to the lamp and held the two pieces together.

```
Hi, Honey,
  I have some really great news
for you. You know how you've
always hated being an only
child? Well, you're not going
to be one for much longer. I'm
sure by now you've guessed it.
Serina is expecting a baby! We
are so happy about it, and I
know you are, too. Well, I
wanted to be the first to tell
you.
                 Love you lots,
                           Dad
```

Oh boy.

Julie walked down the stairs and went to sit beside Susan. Susan barely looked up from what she was doing. "I thought you went to bed."

"We've got a problem." She whispered quietly, hoping the microphones wouldn't pick it up.

"Really, what?" Susan still didn't look up.

"Susan, we've got a *problem*."

This time Susan looked up. "What is it?"

Julie held out the two pieces of paper. "See for yourself."

Susan read it, her lips going white as she pressed them together so hard. "I need to go talk to Angie."

Julie reached out and grabbed her by the arm. "Susan, you can't. She's not there."

CHAPTER 31

Susan ran up the stairs to the room Angie and Whitney shared, certain that Julie was wrong. Angie had just been in the bathroom, or maybe she'd been behind the closet door looking for something to wear tomorrow. She jerked open the door, certain she would find out it had all been a mistake.

Angie's pastel quilt was tucked around the edges, unwrinkled and untouched. Susan walked over to the closet, pulled open the door, and found two rows of long skirts and simple blouses, a couple pairs of shoes, but no other sign of her daughter. The search of the upstairs bathroom proved just as fruitless.

"Angie!" Susan called down the upstairs hallway. "Angela Leigh Reynolds, you answer me right now!"

Nothing but silence.

Susan ran to the window and looked out, knowing full well where her daughter was.

Sure enough, the "security" car was parked out front. Security. Ha, what a laugh. As she ran down the stairs two at a time, she vowed to herself to make certain that young man was not only fired, he was sent back to the other side of the country as quickly as possible.

"What's wrong, Aunt Susan?" Whitney's voice trailed behind her, but Susan didn't bother to even acknowledge it. She ran through the kitchen, across the screened porch, and was almost to the car by the time the screen door slapped shut behind her. She jerked open the door. "Just what do you —"

"Huh?" The young woman behind the wheel blinked up at Susan. "What's wrong?"

Susan glared down at her. "How long have you been out here?"

"Just a couple of minutes. Why, what's wrong?"

"Have you seen my —"

Susan thought about what Kendra had said about the crew finding out about the whole Angie-Chris thing. She simply looked at the girl and said, "We thought we heard the sound of people walking around out here. Did you see anyone? Hear anything?"

"No. I haven't seen anyone at all."

Of course she hadn't, because Angie was

long gone. "Never mind, then."

By now, Julie and the kids had come outside and were heading toward her. Susan walked toward them, more specifically, toward Whitney. "Where are they?" she managed to whisper through clenched teeth.

"Who is 'they'?" Whitney looked around, appearing to be confused.

Susan knew better. "Don't give me that. I know you know about that boy from the production crew. She's not here, she's obviously somewhere with him. Where are they?"

Whitney held up both hands, palms facing the sky. "I have no idea."

"He helps take care of the animals and the barn," Brian offered. "Maybe she went down there." It was the first useful information of the night.

Julie said, "Brian, Whitney, why don't the two of you go down to the observatory and see if she's down there? I'm going to the barn with Susan."

The kids took off jogging toward the tree line while Julie and Susan hurried toward the barn. Susan pulled one of the flashlights off the shelf and shone it all around. "Angie. Angie."

There was no answer. Soon, the sound of the kids' footsteps came racing toward them. "The observatory is empty," Whitney huffed. "But we ran into Jeff, one of the other production assistants. We asked him if he knew where Chris was. He told us that he'd driven into town about a half hour ago."

Susan looked at Julie. "I'm going to have to tell the crew. I'm not going to let her leave like this and not go after her. I don't care if it does cost me this job." She started toward the shack, but Julie grabbed her arm and jerked her back.

"Wait."

"No, Julie! My daughter is out there. I can't just —"

"I have a better idea," Julie said, her voice low and firm. She held tight to Susan's arm. "Get Gary to take you. He lives in that little cottage just over the hill. He wouldn't tell anyone."

Gary.

He was her best hope for a solution to this problem. She knew Julie was right. But the thought of asking for his help, of admitting to him how out of control she was of her own daughter, embarrassed her. No, humiliated her. But what other choice did she have? If being humiliated was what it took to salvage the wreck of the current situation, then so be it.

"Do you want me to go with you?" Julie asked.

Susan considered for a moment before answering. "No. I think it's best if I go alone. Can I ask a favor of all of you? Would you please go back into the house and act like nothing is going on? I don't want the crew to get wind of this if I can help it."

"Sure. We'll do whatever you need us to do to help. Won't we?" Julie looked at her kids, who were already nodding.

"You got it, Aunt Susan. Come on, Team Little Boy — I'll take you on in a rematch."

"Without the other half of Team Girly-Girl here, you don't stand a chance." The two of them were shoving each other playfully up the steps.

Julie reached over and hugged her. "I'll do anything I can to help you. Just know I'll be praying that you'll find her, and that you'll know just what to say."

"Thanks." Susan started toward Gary's house, already formulating in her mind the things she would tell Angie when she caught up with her. She started pondering privileges that she might take away, but there were so few of them in this place already that none came readily to mind.

She approached the little cabin, thankful to see that the lights were still on. The combination of fear for her daughter and embarrassment at her failures seemed to hit her with full force as she walked up the steps to the front porch. By the time she reached up to knock, she couldn't see her hand because of the tears flooding her eyes. This only increased her mortification, but this was no time for pride. She knocked and waited.

She heard the approaching footsteps and wiped her eyes with the heels of her hands. The effort was futile; the torrent simply replaced anything she'd wiped aside.

Gary opened the door and immediately stepped out on the porch beside her, his hand on her left shoulder, his face very near hers. "Susan, what's wrong?"

Susan tried hard to swallow sobs that shook her whole body, but she'd lost almost every ounce of fight. It took what little was left simply to say two words: "Angie's gone."

"Gone where?"

Susan took a great pull of air and stilled herself. "Into town, I think. With that Chris kid."

"Does Kendra know?"

Susan shook her head. "No."

"My truck is around back. We can use that."

"Th-thank you." She followed him, hating

herself for the weakling that she'd become.

The truck was old, and even in the dark it looked rusty. The passenger door squeaked as he opened it for her. He held out his hand and helped her inside; then in a flash he was in the driver's seat and starting the engine. "We'll go out the back way so that no one sees you in the truck."

She nodded and wiped her face again. By now, she was beginning to regain some semblance of control. "I'm sorry to be babbling like this. I don't usually do things like that."

"I know." He reached over and squeezed her hand. "I know." He left his hand on hers for another second, then returned both hands to the wheel. "Do you have any idea where they might be?"

"One of the guys on the crew told Whitney that Chris had taken the car, saying he was going into town for a while. That's all I know."

"So you're not even sure that she's with him?"

"I'm sure." She paused long enough to gather her thoughts into a somewhat coherent answer. "She got a letter from home that upset her. The next thing I knew, she'd crawled out her window. I'm sure she was looking for someone to talk to." As she made the statement, it stung all the more. Teenager or not, what could possibly possess her to pick some weird teenage boy to talk to about something like this?

"Well, town isn't all that big. We'll drive down the main strip and see if we see any sign of them. Chris drives an old black Jeep. Help me keep an eye out for it."

Gary's truck lumbered over the country lanes, and Susan watched the side of the road, just in case Angie was hitchhiking. Soon enough they'd reach the four-lane that comprised the major part of the city area. Several strip malls lined the street, and in almost all the parking lots, kids could be seen sitting on the hoods of cars, on the tailgates of trucks, and otherwise just loitering around. So many kids wasting so much time.

"They could be anywhere." She shook her head, realizing the futility of even attempting to come after her. "How are we ever going to find them?"

"You could just go home and wait for her to show back up, but I know that's not exactly your style."

"You can say that again." Susan looked at every car they passed as desperation began to get the best of her. "For all we know, they might even be back at the house right now.

It's not like we have phones to get in touch with each other. Not until this moment have I fully understood the importance of modern conveniences."

"At least you're not out searching with a horse and buggy."

Susan would have laughed at this at some other time, in some other circumstances, but tonight, nothing was funny. "It's crazy for us to be wasting our time out here. Maybe I should go back, tell Kendra everything. I'm sure they could use their resources to find them."

"I guess this turned out to be a real *rumspringa* for you, huh?"

"*Rumspringa.* That's right! What else was it they were talking about doing this week? Going to the movies? McDonald's?"

"I'm with you." Gary turned the truck into the parking lot of the local movie theater. It was mostly full, and they drove up and down the four rows searching for the black Jeep. There was nothing.

"McDonald's is just down the road, and it's on our way back to the house. We can check there and then head back if that's what you think we should do."

"It's definitely not what I want to do, but I don't know that there's a better choice."

They turned into the McDonald's parking

lot, then circled around the back to look at the other side. As they rounded the back corner, Susan continued to survey every single parked vehicle. There was a particularly large pickup truck, jacked way off of its oversized wheels. She was just shaking her head at the absurdity of it when she saw what was parked on the other side of it.

A black Jeep with California plates.

"Stop!" She jerked open the door and jumped from the truck before Gary could bring it to a full stop. She didn't have time to wait for things like that. She needed answers. Now.

Julie's favorite rocking chair — usually a place of comfort and peace — jerked and squeaked as her legs refused to be still. No amount of effort could calm her nerves enough to stop them from pistoning up and down. She focused on the fabric in her lap, trying her hardest to make straight stitches. She found this all but impossible under the circumstances.

"King me." Brian's voice lacked its usual in-your-face tone when he was beating Whitney at a game of checkers. They were both doing the same thing she was, going through the motions.

Whitney put a black checker on Brian's

new king without a single bit of smack talk. She glanced up at Julie, shook her head once, then looked back down. Julie tried to focus on her quilt again.

"Knock, knock." Kendra breezed into the room and looked around. "My, my, aren't you all up late tonight? Where are Susan and Angie?"

Julie glanced toward the kids and found Whitney's gaze firmly planted on the game board. Brian did look at her, studying her like he would one of his astronomy books.

"To tell you the truth" — Julie looked from the kids to Kendra — "I'm not sure where they are."

"What do you mean?"

"They, uh, they needed to have a private conversation, so they've gone out somewhere. I have no idea where they are." Julie had carefully worded what she said so that nothing was actually untrue, but if taken for what it implied, it would hopefully steer Kendra away from what was happening.

"All right." She walked to the edge of the living room as if verifying that Susan and Angie truly weren't there. Once she'd established this to her satisfaction, she said, "Well, that's okay. It was you I wanted to speak with anyway. Privately, if you don't mind."

Oh no. The crew must have seen enough to figure out what was going on. Julie didn't want to be the one to break the news that would wreck everything. "Okay." She stood slowly and followed Kendra from the room. When she reached the doorway to the kitchen, she chanced a glance backward.

Whitney and Brian were both staring after her. Whitney opened her eyes wide for just a split second, conveying her panic. Julie turned around and followed Kendra outside.

"Let's go talk in the shack, if you don't mind."

Julie didn't respond, she just followed, her mind frantically searching for ways to defuse this situation. Nothing short of lying came to mind. The important thing was going to be to limit the amount of information given and not volunteer anything Kendra didn't already know. She likely didn't know Gary was involved, and there was no reason to get him in trouble for being willing to help. She walked into the office and took a seat, vowing to keep as silent as possible.

"So I'm guessing that you must be quite curious about how these episodes are being received by our viewers."

Julie just stared, the words having almost no meaning. *Episodes?*

She shook her head, relieved to talk about something other than what she'd expected. "I really am interested. It's Susan's deal, as far as all that goes, but I can't help but wonder how it's all working."

"We've been polling our audiences, and we've gotten some pretty interesting results."

"Really? Like what?"

"The ratings for this series have been the highest we've seen in a long time."

"That's great news!" And it truly was. Success in this show would give Susan one less thing to worry about, and at this point she had plenty. "I know Susan will be really thrilled to hear this."

Stupid. Why did she bring Susan's name up in the conversation? Now Kendra was going to want to go find her and share the news.

"Y-es," Kendra said, though her voice was hesitant. She glanced down at a graph on her desk. "Yes and no. See, the thing is, everyone is enjoying watching the simple life and your families as you struggle to live it. But the interesting thing that we've found is, the viewers appear to be more sympathetic to you than to Susan. By quite a lot."

"I don't understand."

"We didn't really, either, so we called in

more polls. It seems that most women identify more with someone like you. Someone who struggles with the day-to-day life of being a mother and housekeeper, especially in such trying circumstances. They seem to think Susan is a bit too perfect and a bit too cold."

"Oh." Julie wasn't certain what she was supposed to do with this information, but Kendra was looking at her expectantly. "So I'm not clear on why you're telling me this. Am I supposed to help soften Susan or something? I'm not really sure how to do that."

"Julie, we went into this knowing that this series had the potential to become a regular feature on the Lisa Lee show. We've been looking at all this data, and we believe that it will work. But here's the thing, I want you to be our star, not Susan."

"What?" The full weight of the burden of a missing niece, and Susan's career dreams being perhaps taken away pressed against Julie so hard that she couldn't breathe. "No, this is Susan's dream. She *needs* this."

"And we need to do what is best for our show. And what works best for a television show is connecting viewers with people whom they care about. That equals ratings."

"I can't believe Lisa would consider doing

this. I thought she genuinely liked Susan."

"I'm sure she does, and I haven't even broached the subject with her yet. I wanted to get you on board first."

"I'm on board for helping Susan get her ratings up. Listen, I am not a cook, I am not a home manager. The people of America certainly don't want to watch the chaos of my normal life."

"The women of America like a woman who struggles with the same things they do. They like to see her overcome, of course, which could be part of your continuing series."

"No." Julie shook her head firmly. "No. I would never take Susan's dream from her and make it mine. Never."

"You don't have to give a final answer now; in fact, I won't accept that right now. I want you to spend some time thinking about it."

"There's no reason. That's something I would never do. Now, if you'll excuse me, I'm going back to my family." Julie hurried from the building. She made it only until she closed the door behind her before she had to run to the bushes and empty her stomach.

CHAPTER 32

Susan jerked open the door so suddenly, a man with an armload of Happy Meals stumbled through it. He reached forward just in time to catch a loose box before it hit the ground.

"I'm so sorry. Are you all right?"

"No harm done. You want to slow it —"

Susan hurried inside, leaving the man and his admonition behind. There wasn't time for it right now.

It took a few seconds to get her bearings, but then she saw them. They were sitting on opposite sides of a corner booth, leaning in toward each other, holding hands across the table. Chris released Angie's right hand just long enough to wipe tears from her cheek with the back of his fingers; then he grasped onto her hand again.

The sight of her daughter so upset momentarily tempered her fury, but not completely, and not for long. If Angie was upset,

359

then she should have come to Susan to talk about it. Sneaking off with this . . . person, was not the answer. She marched up to the booth. "Angie Reynolds, you are coming back to the house with me right now."

Angie jerked back in her seat and looked up. "Mom! How did you find us here?"

"It doesn't matter. You're leaving with me right now."

Chris nodded. "You should go." The ruffian had the nerve to pull Angie's hand up to his lips and kiss it before he let her go. "I'll be praying for you."

"I'm sure you will." Susan couldn't believe the nerve of that boy, acting like he had any sort of real spiritual beliefs just to get on Angie's good side, or perhaps out of trouble with Susan. Either way, she wasn't buying it. "Come on, Angie. We're leaving right now."

Angie stood up slowly, her eyes trained on Chris the entire time. She walked to his side of the booth, leaned down, and hugged him. "Thank you." She let him go and stood up, her tears falling harder now. "I'm sorry." She more or less whispered the words, but she wasn't talking to Susan; she was still talking to Chris.

Susan waited until they were outside before she said, "Let me get this straight, you run off in the middle of the night with a boy you were forbidden to see, and you tell *him* you're sorry? What about the mother who has spent the last hour frantically searching for you? Why aren't you sorry about that?"

"I am sorry, Mom, but I needed someone I could talk to. Chris is the only one who understands."

"That boy would tell you anything to make you think he's truly interested in you, Angie. All you have to do is take one look at him to know his interests in anyone are far from noble."

"Maybe if you spent some time caring about the inside rather than the outside of everything!" Across the parking lot, a family of four turned to watch them. Susan tried not to imagine the smug look on the wife's face.

"Don't you dare talk to me that way." By now, Susan was shaking with rage. "We're going to get in that truck and not say a single word in front of Gary. But as soon as we get back to the farm, we are going to have a very long talk."

"Fine." Angie walked past Susan toward the truck. Gary was leaning against the tailgate, obviously making a point not to look in their direction.

As Angie approached, she did say, "Good evening, Gary."

"Evening to you, too." He raced around and opened the passenger-side door. Angie climbed in and slid across.

He held the door for Susan. "Thank you so much for bringing me out to find her. Can I ask one more favor?"

"Shoot."

"Don't tell anyone about this. I'm not asking you to lie. If someone asks, tell them the truth, but if it doesn't get brought up, will you please help keep it quiet?"

"I'll help in any way I can."

CHAPTER 33

Susan stumbled down to the kitchen the next morning and immediately lit the wood in the stove. Today's coffee would have to be extra strong, considering the fact that she and Angie had been up until well past midnight. But, in the end, the talk had been good . . . perhaps even better than that. There were many issues that had been needing a good discussion.

Susan poured the water into the percolator, then added extra grounds into the top basket. She sank down at the kitchen table, knowing it would be awhile before everything heated sufficiently. It was mornings like these that she most missed the modern conveniences like automatic-grind coffeepots with automatic brew settings.

"Knock, knock."

Kendra walked in the door, looking every bit as fresh at 5:00 A.M. as she usually did at her normal arrival time of nine or so.

"What are you doing here so early?"

"I understand we had some excitement last night." Her smile was huge, her blue eyes sparkled with enthusiasm.

Susan, quite suddenly, felt a deep sense of dread push down on her with a force hard enough that she couldn't even force a smile. "What do you mean?"

"Oh, come now. Let's not pretend that we both don't know the obvious. But I've got to tell you, I'm bringing the best news I've brought since you've been here."

"Really? What's that?"

"Two things, really. First of all, Chris will not be returning to work today. It has become more than apparent that his staying here is not going to work."

"But, wait —"

"Just like you wanted before, right? Second, and best of all, this whole episode is exactly what we needed to happen for all of America to see you at your best. The conversation you had with your daughter last night, it was . . . compelling, amazing, heartwarming. All of America is going to love you. We've already got the snippets ready to start running today. I expect the highest ratings we've ever had on this Friday's show."

"The conversation I had with my daughter

last night?" How had she been so stupid? She'd been so caught up in the moment, the cameras had never entered her mind.

Kendra nodded. "The one at this very table." She stroked her hand across the oak top as if petting a dog.

"How do you even know about that?" The cameras were there all the time, but for someone to have already seen the footage of last night, to have even checked the footage for the middle of the night, someone must have known to look. There could be only one way. Gary must have come right home and called Kendra, told her to get the cameras going because this was going to make for some good stuff. The sense of betrayal she felt went clear through to her spine.

"Come now, I told you on that very first day that there are hidden cameras all around the public portions of the farmhouse. You've always known they were there. They're on 24/7. I was very upfront about that."

"You can't use that footage. That was highly personal."

"Of course we can, and emotional, authentic footage is the best possible kind of footage. The viewers will eat it up. When one of the night crew noticed late-night lights and went to the monitor, that was the best thing that ever happened to your career, because I have to tell you, it was looking iffy at best until just now."

Susan put her hands on each side of her head and leaned against the table. "No."

"I probably shouldn't have come in here so early in the morning before you're awake enough to see this for the gift that it is. It's just that I was in the editing trailer and I saw the lamps come on in the kitchen, and I just had to come and tell you. You know what? You come talk to me after you've had your coffee. I'll even break the rules just this once and show you the clip." She stood from the kitchen table and walked out the back door, humming the Lisa Lee theme song under her breath.

CHAPTER 34

Julie tiptoed down the stairs. She got up a little early, thinking she would make some coffee for Susan, and hopefully get a chance to talk to her about how things went last night with Angie.

As she neared the kitchen, she felt the heat from the stove and smelled the coffee. She entered the room to find Susan with her head resting on her arms on the kitchen table. Asleep?

Julie didn't want to wake her, so she stopped walking, considering her next move. The coffee was percolating on the stove, and given the strong smell, it likely had been for a while. She quietly poured two cups, then went to sit across the table from Susan.

"Good morning." Susan said the words without lifting her head.

"Is it?" Julie slid one of the mugs across the table. "Your coffee's ready."

"Thanks." She still didn't lift her head.

"Susan, why don't you go back to bed? I can handle what needs doing around here today."

Susan sat up then, rubbed her forehead with her left hand, and shook her head. "No. That's okay. Thank you, though." She took a sip of her coffee. "And thank you for last night. For figuring out what was going on, I mean."

Julie reached across the table and squeezed her hand. "How are things?"

"Dandy. Just dandy." She gestured toward the walls. "I feel the need for a walk."

"What?"

"Join me?" She stood up, coffee cup in hand, and started toward the back porch without waiting for an answer.

Julie grabbed her own mug and followed Susan out to the screened-in porch. They both sat on the bench and began lacing up their work boots. "We're going to be quite the stylish ladies, walking through the place in our boots and pj's."

"Doesn't matter." Susan stood and walked out the door. Julie rushed after her, but didn't say anything, choosing to wait instead for Susan to speak when she was ready. She waited until they were past the barn. "They caught it all on film."

Julie thought about the events of last night. "All . . . as in escape, search, everything? How is that possible?"

"Well, most everything. It seems that they noticed lights on in the kitchen really late last night, so they pulled up those monitors, just in time to realize that Angie and I were having a serious talk. They recorded the whole thing."

"I thought Kendra didn't want any of this to accidentally end up on the show."

"She didn't." Susan took a sip of her coffee. "Until now. She says it is the most compelling footage they've gotten all season."

"Oh, Susan. Surely you told her she can't use it?"

"I told her. She reminded me about a little thing called the contract. They can use whatever they darn well want to."

"Oh, sweetie." Julie put her arm around Susan's shoulder. "I'm so sorry."

They walked in silence for some time, until they reached the observatory. Susan stopped and turned back toward the house. "The thing is, it was the best talk we've had in a long time. Since the divorce really. But we talked about some really personal things — about James, about Chris. For them to air it for all of America to see . . . you know how shy she is . . . this will be humiliating for her."

"Then you've got to stop them."

"I just told you, there is a contract. I can't."

"Maybe not, but don't you let it happen without putting every single ounce of your being against it. At least Angie will know that you gave everything you had."

"I never thought I'd hear these words come out of my mouth, but I don't know what else to do."

"You walk out, if that's what it takes."

"My contract forbids that, too."

"Susan, you're in a battle for your daughter's well-being. This is one of those times when you give up everything if that's what it takes."

"But what kind of example would I be setting? Walking away from a project I promised to see through to the end?"

"You'd be setting the best possible example. Showing her there are some areas where you won't compromise, no matter what it costs you."

"I don't know." Susan was wiping tears from her eyes. "I'm going to sit by the creek for a while. Think. Pray. Will you cover for me?"

"Take as long as you need." Julie walked

toward the house, her heart heavy. Everything had gone so wrong.

Susan sat just above the creek bank. Dew on the early-morning grass soaked through her pajamas, but what did it matter? She extended her legs in front of her, knees slightly bent so she could rest her elbows on them when she leaned forward, then put a hand over each ear.

It was ruined. Everything was ruined.

God, I just don't get it. I was certain You had called me here to this. It seemed to be a clear answer to prayers. This job was giving me the means to provide for Angie and me, plus the opportunity to expand Lydia's Legacy to even more women. But everything is wrong. I'm going to lose this job, go home in disgrace as a complete failure, and my daughter will still have to suffer the consequences. Why didn't I think about those cameras last night? What kind of an idiot am I?

As much as she tried to shut them out, the memories of two years ago joined in the fray of her swirling thoughts. The nights that James worked late. She hadn't thought a thing about it initially. Of course he worked late — he was an engineer in the aerospace industry, and there were things that needed to be done. All that talk about the big project they were working on.

She remembered walking down the aisle of the grocery store, her neatly printed grocery list in one hand while she squeezed an apricot with the other. One of the store employees was cutting up peaches and handing out slices for people to try, causing the area to have a fresh, fruity smell.

"Susan, how are you doing?" Annamarie Rickman, wife of one of James's colleagues, appeared, picking up a peach sample and waving it at Susan in greeting before she popped it in her mouth.

"I'm well. Busy as usual." Susan twisted the bag of apricots closed, set it in her cart, and prepared to move on.

"I hate to admit it, but I'm almost glad the AmTex contract fell through. It's been awfully nice having Jerry home for dinner these past couple of weeks, and Tommy's had him out throwing the football every single night."

Susan's foot stopped moving midstep. The AmTex deal had fallen through? The same deal that had kept James working late, even on weekends? She gripped her cart a little tighter and looked at Annamarie. "Yes, it's always nice having them home, isn't it?"

That single moment, eating a slice of peach sample, had started the slow demolition of the perfect little life Susan had always imagined she was living. But at least then she'd still had herself to depend on, as well as the deep-rooted belief that she was strong enough to make it through this and come out the other end better and stronger. Now there was a different truth staring her in the face.

Little by little, the realization began to creep in.

Everything Susan had been so confident about, all those things she'd done so much better than other people, were all illusions. All it had accomplished was building a bigger platform for her failure.

They would need to put the house on the market right away after returning home. In spite of the sluggish economy and real estate market, she felt sure it'd sell. Their neighborhood was in the best school district. Young parents paid extra to live in that area so their kids could start getting ahead early. It was the same reason she and James had chosen it all those years ago filled with dreams of what a wonderful life they would all have. How had it all fallen apart?

"Hello, there. Okay if I join you?"

Susan barely glanced over her shoulder to see Gary walking toward her. He was wearing his usual jeans and dark T-shirt. He came to sit beside her on the grass. "I saw Julie. She didn't tell me much, but she told me you were up here and that you are very upset. What can I do to help you?"

Susan shook her head. "There's nothing. At this point, it's all over." She turned to look at him now, realizing what she must look like — very little sleep, no makeup; she hadn't even brushed her hair. Not that it mattered anyway. "I want to ask you a question, and I want the absolute truth."

"You got it."

"Did you say or do anything so that Kendra, or any of the crew, would know what happened last night?"

"Of course not."

"Kendra said someone saw the lights on. I just wanted to make sure. . . ."

"All I can tell you is that after I drove you two back to my cabin, I didn't see or talk with anyone until I spoke to Julie a few minutes ago." He reached down and plucked a blade of grass, twirling it between his thumb and middle finger with enough speed to make the end whip out helicopter style. "Well, that's not technically true, I suppose." He dropped the grass blade, then turned his full gaze directly on Susan. "I saw you and Angie after, because I followed you."

"Followed us?"

"I walked far enough behind the two of you that you could talk without me over-hearing, but close enough that I could see you reach the farmhouse safely. I know there are security guards around, but I thought it was better to play it safe."

Wow. Whatever Susan had expected to hear, that was not it. She couldn't take the intensity of his gaze any longer and turned away.

Down at the water's edge a couple of birds sang greetings back and forth to each other, perhaps commenting on the pleasant sound of the water gurgling past, or the nice flavor of this morning's breakfast, or maybe planning an outing later in the afternoon. Life was so simple for animals. "I'm leaving to-day."

"I see." He plucked another blade of grass. "What happened?"

She told him the story, the part of it he didn't already know. She shrugged. "I thought coming here was going to make everything okay, but instead it's ruined everything."

"I don't know that I'd say that. Sounds to me like you might have found the thing that is most important. Maybe that is all the success you needed here." He looked out toward the creek and nodded. "I'd like to come visit you sometime, if that's all right with you."

"I'd like that." She knew it was just talk, would likely never come to pass, but it frightened her just how much she meant those words. "I've . . . got to go." She stood up and started back toward the house.

Chapter 35

Julie sat at the kitchen table, daydreaming about moving here, or at least to a little farm somewhere. No phone, no Internet. How much nicer would life be then? But if Susan decided to stand up to Kendra, it could vanish at any second.

The sound of the kids pounding down the stairs interrupted her thoughts and turned her attention back to reality. Whitney led the charge as they walked through the kitchen on their way to the barn, apparently oblivious to Julie even sitting there. Whitney called back toward her brother, "You are crazy. I did the chickens yesterday. It's my turn to feed the goats."

Brian grabbed his boots and started hopping into one. "You did do the chickens yesterday, but I had to feed them two days in a row last week because you were running late, remember? I'm taking my repayment today. You're on chicken duty."

"Come on, I never said I would pay you back for that."

"All right, then. Let's just pretend I'm running late today. You can do both jobs."

"Yeah, yeah. I'll feed your stinking chickens." She stood up and bounded out the door, her blond ringlets bouncing behind her. Julie watched them go, thinking how happy they seemed here, too. The argument over feeding chickens had all been in good humor. At home, the kids were so busy running their different directions that their interactions were usually shorter and much terser.

Julie walked over to the stove and stirred the oatmeal, then sliced some of yesterday's bread and put it in the oven for toast. She poured milk in all the glasses and set the table. Before long, the kids came clamoring back. Whitney took a big gulp of milk. "So, Mom, today is mid-terms, then we've got a week off school. I'm thinking, maybe we drive into town for ice cream to celebrate. What do you think?"

"Well, I'm not really sure."

"What's there not to be sure about? It's supposed to be *rumspringa,* right? How about just the kids go into town? That should work, right?"

"Whitney, we'll talk about it when you get

back from school."

Angie sat at the table, stirring her oatmeal without taking a bite. "Where's Mom?"

"She went for a walk."

Angie nodded and turned her attention back to her bowl. She looked up at Julie, then back down.

Julie didn't think it was her place to tell Angie about the recording, so she remained quiet during breakfast. When they'd finished, she said, "Okay, kids, time to take off for school."

They each carried bowls and cups over to the sink. On the way out the door, Angie turned. "Will you tell Mom . . ." She paused, then stood with her hand on the doorframe. "Tell her I said, 'Thank you.' "

Julie nodded. "Don't worry. I'll tell her."

"Good." Angie turned and hurried out to catch up with the other kids.

As Susan approached the door of the shack, she considered opening it and saying, "Knock, knock" — see how Kendra liked it. But she wouldn't do that. Neither would she bother to knock. She opened the door and walked in.

The room was empty.

So much for her grand showdown. She turned and started to the farmhouse when she noticed Julie doing a load of laundry, so she changed course.

Julie didn't miss a beat as she pulled the lever back and forth, but she did look up and smile. "I'm going to miss this place."

"Why is it you like it so much?" Even without the current looming disaster, conditions here were primitive enough that Susan had been counting the days back to the real world.

"It's like everything I do here is for a reason. Washing the clothes is hard, but I understand the necessity for it. Cooking in the wood stove is hard, and hot, but my family needs to eat." The water made swooshing sounds, as if saying, *has a reason, has a reason.* "When I get to the real world, there are so many things that consume my time, and most of them I just don't think are necessary."

Susan nodded, supposing that she understood to some degree. "I think most of the things you do are for a reason."

"Maybe it's just not my reason. Like for instance, school events. In elementary school we spent hours planning and preparing for Back to School Night so that the parents can get to know their children's teacher. Obviously important. But there's also the Back to School Picnic a couple of weeks later, so the parents can get to know each other. Again something that is important. And so is Thomas's staff party, and since Whitney is on the volleyball team it's only fair that I am team mother, and since Brian is in the science club, of course I should host their back-to-school party. It goes on and on. They're all important, and it amounts to a huge amount of work that overlaps each other, and instead of being intentional about my day, I end up reacting to the urgent. I don't have time for my kids when they need to talk — and they don't even have time to talk because they're so busy."

"You know, as much as I hate to admit that Rosemary has anything worthwhile to say, maybe she does have a point. Maybe we all need to focus our time a little more closely with where our talents and interests are."

"What would that be for me, Susan? Starting a quilting club?" She shook her head and looked out into the distance.

Susan put her hand over Julie's on the handle and stopped her from pulling it. She looked her sister-in-law dead in the eye. "I'm glad I could come here and do this, just so I could fully realize what I've got in you. I can't imagine the ways that we all take you for granted in the real world."

Julie reached up and wiped away a single tear from her left cheek. "Thank you."

A black Suburban pulled up the driveway and came to a stop outside the shack. Kendra and a couple other crew members emerged from the backseat. Susan took a deep breath and moved to meet her. "Kendra, we need to talk."

"Okay."

The cameraman held his camera on his shoulder, ready to capture every last bit of the drama. Susan let that serve to motivate her. If she was going to go down in flames for all of America to see, then she'd best make it good. "I know that you captured a very personal conversation between my daughter and me last night. I also understand that per my contract you are allowed to use it for your show, even if I don't want you to do so."

"That's correct."

"What's legal is legal, and I can't argue that. But what's right is right, and I will fight for that. Last night was a breakthrough moment in my family. To have it broadcast would be more than embarrassing for my daughter. While I acknowledge you fully have the right to do it, I want you to understand that, contract or not, we will walk off this show. I'm prepared to pack my bags right now and leave."

"You know that we can sue you for this."

"And I expect that you will. But I would rather be bankrupt than to live in a home with a daughter who knows that her mother didn't stand up at a time like this. I will do the right thing by her no matter what it costs me, and there is no negotiating that. Period."

"I see." Kendra looked at the cameraman, barely able to suppress a grin. "Well, thank you for your thoughts. Just go about your day as usual until I find out what the executive producers want us to do. I hate for our season to end this way. I hope you'll reconsider while I'm working out the details."

"I won't." Susan turned and walked back over to help Julie with the laundry.

CHAPTER 36

The last of the laundry fluttered on the line. Julie looked toward the shack for the thousandth time, waiting for Kendra to walk out and tell them it was over. She did come and go a lot through the course of the morning, but she never so much as glanced in their direction.

"Shall we go pick a couple of tomatoes for lunch?" Susan sounded so tired. Defeated even.

"So what's your thinking on talking to the kids?" Julie waited until they were well away from the house and any potential cameras. "Wait until we get the final word from Kendra and tell them it's time to pack up, or should we give them a little forewarning?"

Susan reached down and plucked a tomato from the vine, then stood up and wiped her forehead. "It's funny. Two years ago, I thought I knew all the answers about everything. I knew the right way to do everything. Now, here I stand, in the middle of a vegetable garden in the middle of nowhere, and I have no idea what I'm supposed to do about much of anything. Including my own child — and I certainly thought I had all the answers there." She bent down to pick another tomato. "What do you think we should do?"

Julie looked in the direction of the house, then toward the school. "Maybe we should wait. I keep praying that there will be a breakthrough and we'll actually get to stay."

Susan nodded. "So do I."

"You know, today is mid-terms. Why don't we go put these in the kitchen and take a walk over that way? We can maybe catch them at lunchtime and find out how it is going."

"Funny that you're the one suggesting that we walk to the school instead of me, isn't it?" Susan shook her head. "You want to go see how the kids feel about their test, and I've always wanted to go and see if the teacher is doing a good enough job. I think I need to work on being more people-focused and less task-focused. I should be more like you."

Julie laughed outright. "Oh, Susan, you are having a hard day, aren't you?" She laughed a little more, even wiping a tear. "I think we can all agree that we don't want a world full of Julies running around. Nothing would ever get accomplished." Julie sighed. "You have so many gifts. I wish I could have just a few of them."

"Well, let's take our various gifts and go see what's happening at the school, shall we?" Susan linked her arm through Julie's, and they walked into the house.

They'd made it only as far as the barn, though, when they heard the sound of the kids' voices. Sure enough, teenagers on scooters crested the hill. Julie reached her hand up high to wave.

"Mom, Aunt Susan, we have lots to tell you." Whitney pumped faster and was the first to arrive. She came to a skidding stop, sending a cloud of dust toward Julie and Susan. "Oh, sorry." She shrugged, but hardly missed a beat. "You're not going to believe this one."

"What?" Julie and Susan asked the question in unison.

"We're going into Nashville for the evening!"

"Say what?"

Brian arrived, breathless from the chase. "That's right. The whole family."

Whitney nodded her agreement. "We can wear our own clothes and everything. We get to go to the mall, out for a nice dinner, the whole bit. Gary is taking us in one of the Suburbans. And there won't be any cameras, just us, having fun."

"Who told you this?" Did this mean they were leaving? Julie looked toward Susan, who looked even more confused than Julie felt.

Angie was the last to arrive. She looked anxiously toward her mother. "Gary came to the school and told us. He said that the two of you are coming, too."

"What about your exams?" Susan asked.

"We finished them already. We all did great, don't you worry," Whitney said. "And we had some good news at the schoolhouse today, too, but I'll let the appropriate person share that at the appropriate time."

The following silence from the teenage crowd, including lack of eye contact, made Julie wonder if Whitney hadn't spoken a bit prematurely about something that wasn't ready to be shared. Angie studied her handlebars, and Brian scratched his chin with his shoulder.

"So, anyway . . ." Whitney looked around. "Everyone go get dressed in your favorite civvies. We're heading into the big city for the night."

Gary came walking down the hill about

then. "I gather that I am a little late to be the one to deliver the news."

"Just a bit." Susan looked at him, suspicion on her face. "What's going on?"

He shrugged. "Kendra told me she thought you all needed a night off. She asked me if I would be willing to take you to Nashville for the evening. I've already made dinner reservations" — he looked at the girls — "at a restaurant in the mall."

"Yes!" Whitney pumped her fist. "Civilization."

Gary smiled toward Susan. "And I've got a special surprise event for after that, which I expect will be both exciting and eye-opening for the family." He looked around the group. "So we'll leave as soon as you are all ready. I'll be at the car. Just come on out when you're ready."

"Hurry, everybody, hurry." Whitney ran toward the house, not bothering to look back. Angie and Brian were not far behind.

Susan looked at Gary. "So are we going to the airport after, or what?"

He shrugged. "I think they are still working all that out. Hence, the night out while they work on the details."

"If Kendra thinks that this little evening out will bribe me out of the way I feel, she's dead wrong."

"She knows that." He reached out and took her hand. "I think this may be her way of extending an olive branch. Why don't you just take the gift that's been offered and see what might happen next?"

Susan looked down at their linked hands, then smiled toward Julie. "I guess we better hurry and get ready."

CHAPTER 37

Susan followed the boisterous teenagers outside to the car. The girls were wearing their favorite outfits. Brian was wearing a T-shirt with a picture of Albert Einstein across the front. Julie wore her usual bermuda shorts and polo shirt. Susan had stared into her closet for what seemed to be a half hour of agonizing over how she wanted to look before choosing a floral sundress she hoped would be flattering.

Gary opened the front and back passenger-side doors. "Wow, you all make the transition to the modern world in a nice way."

"Why, thank you." Whitney practically danced her way into the backseat. Angie followed with a bit less fervor, but was still obviously happy about getting out. Brian climbed in with his usual deadpan demeanor, leaving Susan to wonder if he really cared one way or the other.

Susan started to climb in beside him, but Julie put out her hand to stop her. "I'll sit with Brian." She effectively pulled Susan out of the way and climbed in, leaving Susan with no choice but to sit up front.

"Looks like I'm the pilot and you're the navigator." Gary closed the door on the backseat and held out a hand to help Susan climb up into the passenger's seat.

"Too bad for us, then, because I don't know anything about navigating this part of the country."

Gary kept his hand on the door and leaned against it. "Well, we might just have ourselves a problem, then." He leaned a little closer and spoke quietly enough that he wouldn't be heard. "If I'm going to get lost, I'm glad to be in such lovely company."

Susan felt her face heat. She managed to say something to the effect of "We'll just see if you say that when we end up in Kansas."

Gary laughed outright as he closed the door. He climbed into the driver's seat and used his best announcer voice. "Attention, passengers. I need to go over the rules for the evening." The car grew dead quiet, although Susan was pretty certain she heard Whitney groan. "The rules are as follows" — he turned his head to face the passengers in the back — "there are no rules."

"Woo-hoo!" Whitney led the hoots and hollers from the backseat.

Gary turned the key in the ignition. "And off we go, into the wild unknown."

Several hours later, Gary, Susan, and Julie stood at the entrance to Sue Ellen's Grill, looking for any sign of the kids. They had, immediately upon arrival, disappeared into the center of the mall, with little more than a "see you later." Reservations were at 6:30 P.M. It was now 6:25.

"Do you think they'll show up?" Gary leaned against the wall, arms crossed, an amused look on his face.

"If it were just the girls, I'd say we might never see them again, but they've got Brian with them. In spite of the fact that the kid's a beanpole, I've never known him to miss a meal. They'll be here." Julie nodded toward the mall's center. "It feels really strange, doesn't it? All the lights, the people" — she gestured at Susan — "our own clothes."

"Yes, amazingly so." Susan looked out toward the activity. There was a young mother pushing a couple of children in a stroller. She was tall and thin with hair and makeup meant to kill. Her shorts were just that. Short. And the tank top she wore left nothing to the imagination, including the color of her bra. Susan realized that two months ago, she would have seen this woman and never thought much about it. Now, after the weeks away and modest dress, it was much more blatant.

"Susan, have you noticed today, while we've been out among the people, that this feels, I don't know . . . almost shocking."

Susan nodded. "I was just thinking the same thing."

"It's amazing what you can get used to, isn't it?" Gary said. "I've seen it more times than I care to recall. And it doesn't take long until it's not shocking anymore. Just becomes the new normal."

"Too true, too true." Susan looked back toward the woman, who had disappeared into a store. While she was looking, though, she saw the top of a blond wavy head of hair. "Here come the kids."

All three came scampering up full of smiles, but Brian never stopped. He just headed right past them all and into the restaurant, claiming that he could eat a horse and possibly a pig and a goat, as well.

Everyone else followed. As they waited to be seated, Whitney suddenly squealed. "Look, everyone, that's us!" She pointed to the television over the bar.

Sure enough, they were showing previews of the Lisa Lee show. As a group, they all moved closer so they could hear better.

The background announcer was saying, "Mother and daughter have a life-changing encounter." It showed a fairly dark scene of Susan and Angie sitting at the kitchen table, but there was no audio.

"They filmed that? Are you kidding me?" Angie's hand was over her mouth, her head shaking from side to side.

Then the screen cut to a clip of Susan, wild hair, still in her pajamas, standing outside the house. "What's legal is legal, and I can't argue that. But what's right is right, and I will fight for that. Last night was a breakthrough moment in my family. To have it broadcast would be more than embarrassing for my daughter. While I acknowledge you fully have the right to do it, I want you to understand that, contract or not, we will walk off this show. I'm prepared to pack my bags right now and leave."

"You know that we can sue you for this." Kendra's smirk looked every bit as ominous on the big screen as it did in real life.

"And I expect you will. But I would rather be bankrupt than to live in a home with a daughter who knows that her mother didn't stand up at a time like this. I will do the right thing by her no matter what it costs me, and there is no negotiating that. Period."

Then the announcer's voice was back. "Tune in Friday, to see if all is still well with our *Almost Amish* family, or if they have really flown the coop."

The group all stood huddled together in silence until the sounds of Angie's quiet sobs broke through. Susan put her arm around her daughter. "I'm so sorry, sweetie. I was just so upset that night, it never really even occurred to me about the hidden cameras."

"Why didn't you tell me?"

"I wanted to wait until it was all settled, one way or the other, before I said anything."

Angie buried her face on Susan's shoulder, slowly shaking her head. She finally pulled back and looked at Susan. "You really did that for me? Told them you would leave? Won't it ruin your career?"

"You're more important to me than any hope of a career."

"So . . . are we leaving, then?"

When would Whitney ever learn some tact? Susan didn't bother to look over at her, but she kept focused on Angie. "Are we leaving, Mom?"

Susan shrugged. "I think so. We're supposed to talk tomorrow morning before making any sort of final decision, but judging from that snippet, I'm gathering Kendra hasn't backed down, and I'm certainly not going to."

"Oh, Mom, I love you so much." Angie squeezed her tighter than she ever had. In this one moment, Susan came to believe that it had all been worth it.

Julie put her arm around Susan, whose arm was already around Angie. Whitney put her arm around Angie on the other side and then Brian, and soon they were all locked up in a group hug. She couldn't help but smile when Gary joined in between her and Brian. It was one of those rare precious moments that a mother would want to remember for the rest of her life.

"Your table is ready." The hostess motioned for the group to follow her as she led them through the restaurant to the far back room. She looked at Gary. "I thought you might enjoy a table back here where it's a little quieter."

"We appreciate that. Thank you." He quickly turned his attention to pulling out chairs for Julie and Susan.

"You're more than welcome, Mr. *Macko.*"

Something about the way she said his name caught Julie's attention.

As everyone took a seat, she watched as their hostess handed out menus. Although she spoke to everyone as she did so, Julie's gut told her the hostess's attention was focused only on Gary. She wondered if they somehow knew each other. "The specials are listed on the outside of the menu. Mary Jane will be your waitress, but in the meantime, my name is Alice. Please feel free to let me know if you need anything." She smiled especially big toward Gary, then walked from the room.

Whitney said, "It was nice of that lady to give us the back room. She must have seen that we needed to talk."

"Or else she was afraid that if she didn't get us out of there soon, we might break into rounds of 'Kumbaya.'" Angie smiled for the first time in a couple of days.

Whitney snorted. "Good one, Ang. Well, whatever the reason, I'm glad for it, because you guys have been holding out on us. When were you planning on telling us about this? When we were on the plane home?"

"We wanted to wait until things were official. There wasn't any reason to get you all upset if Kendra was going to change her mind."

"Hello, my name is Mary Jane, and I'm here to be your waitress. Would everyone like to order drinks while you're looking at the menu?" Mary Jane smiled broadly all around the table, but again, Julie noticed she kept glancing toward Gary. If he did indeed know either one of these girls, he gave no indication of it. *Strange.*

After Mary Jane left to get their drinks, Susan filled the kids in on what had transpired.

"Way to stand up to the establishment, Aunt Susan." Whitney nodded her approval, then turned her attention to Gary. "So what's your take on all this? Did Kendra send you on this mission hoping you could soften us all up and convince us to stay on the show?"

Gary laughed. "You know what I like about you, Whitney? You are straight and to the point."

"Something that your answer isn't. Are you trying to duck the question?" She actually quirked an eyebrow at him. Julie couldn't help but laugh at her daughter's audacity.

"Touché. But, no, as a matter of fact, I am not on a secret mission. I got wind of what was going on and volunteered for this assignment. Mostly because, if it is going to be your last night here, I wanted to spend some time with all of you. Because I'm really going to miss you if you go."

His gaze turned ever so briefly on Susan; then he looked all around the table. "Personally, I expect Kendra to back down. She knows she has a good thing going here, and there are some people of influence who would not want the show to end this way."

Julie thought about how much Lisa Lee had seemed to enjoy spending time with all of them. Perhaps he was right. She hoped so.

"Here are your drinks. Let's see, I know sweet tea goes right here." She set the glass in front of Gary. "Who had the unsweetened tea?" Julie, Susan, and Angie all raised their hands. She set the glasses before them. "I'm guessing the two root beers go right over here." She set the glasses in front of Whitney and Brian.

"Before you order, I was just talking to the chef. We have a couple of off-menu specials tonight if you would like to hear them." She smiled directly at Gary. "First off we have . . ."

She went on to list the specials, all of which sounded delicious. Gary nodded politely with each dish mentioned, but he also shifted in his seat and glanced at Susan repeatedly.

"All right, I'll start with the ladies." Mary Jane took everyone's order, smiled once more at Gary, and walked away, leaving Julie to wonder if there was more to this story, or if she'd simply noticed something that wasn't there.

"So, Aunt Susan, now that we're bringing all this out into the open, can I ask a question?"

Susan looked at Whitney, wondering what was left to ask at this point. Still flush with her interaction with Angie, she was prepared to be patient. "Sure."

"What is it you dislike so much about Chris?"

What? Susan knew her mouth was hanging open, but she couldn't seem to close it. This was by no means the question she'd expected.

"Whitney Kate Charlton, that is none of your business." Julie glared at her daughter. "You know better than to ask something like that."

Whitney shrugged, her face showing not a hint of remorse. "Sorry, but I'm just curious. I think he's terrific, and I can't understand why Aunt Susan doesn't." She turned back toward Susan then. "Is it his funky haircut? He's artistic, you know. Those kinds of people tend to be a bit more expressive in their appearance."

"Whitney, stop this right now." Julie reached her hand across and smacked it on the table in front of Whitney. *As if that's going to get her attention.* Nothing would shut Whitney down when she got in one of these moods.

Whitney shrugged and looked down at her root beer. She mumbled something that Susan couldn't quite make out, then looked up at Angie.

Perhaps it would be best to just get everything out in the open. "As long as we're talking about all these things, I suppose it's only fair that I answer that question. First off, the rules were that you were not supposed to talk with the crew. So for Angie to even speak to him was breaking a rule. Secondly" — Susan held up two fingers — "Angie never came to me and told me she was interested in Chris and asked for my blessing or even my opinion; she simply snuck out of the house to go meet him. Of course, my third experience with the young man in question involved sneaking away from the property altogether. I hardly find that a résumé for the kind of young man I would approve for my daughter. However —"

"But, Mom, I —"

"I wasn't finished." Susan looked at Angie and waited until Angie made a circular gesture with her hand for her to go ahead. "However" — she nodded toward Angie — "through the course of our conversation last night, I came to understand that perhaps he is more upstanding than I'd assumed."

"Thank you." Angie nodded.

"That said, it really doesn't matter, because Kendra found out about last night and kicked him off the job."

Somehow this news didn't bring the reaction of despair Susan expected from the younger crowd. In fact, Whitney actually laughed. "Is that what she told you? That she sent him away because of Angie?" She shook her head. "He was leaving today anyway, because he's got another job lined up somewhere. We've known that since the first time he took us to youth group."

"Really?" Susan marveled once again at the half truths Kendra was prepared to tell.

"But . . . if that were not the case, would you still be opposed?"

"I don't think Chris is the appropriate boy for Angie."

"Be-cau-use?" Whitney leaned forward, waiting for the response.

"Angie is a hardworking, clean-cut Christian girl. I know these quiet, moody boys, the rebels if you will, often turn the corner and become upstanding citizens, but that's mostly in romance novels. It rarely happens in real life." She held up her hand to fend off the argument she knew Whitney would launch. "I know you all are convinced how wonderful he is, but I'm saying that I see a boy who is putting out signals that he is looking for trouble."

Angie shook her head slowly as she stirred her tea. She didn't say anything, but her silence didn't necessarily mean she would follow her mother's wishes. The last few weeks had proven that.

"So I believe I heard someone say that there is some good news to announce tonight. I'm thinking right about now would be a good time for some good news." Gary laced his fingers together, then rested his chin on the back of them, face turned toward the kids' end of the table.

Whitney and Brian both looked at Angie, whose face had gone bright pink. Angie looked toward Susan and licked her lips. "Well, yes, I uh . . . got this thing in the mail today . . ." She reached down and pulled a folded piece of paper out of her purse. She held it up, still folded. "It seems that I am a finalist in a writing contest."

"A what?" Susan reached for the paper, and Angie handed it to her.

"You submit the first twenty pages of your novel and a synopsis. All entries are judged by several experienced judges, and the top twenty percent move on to be semifinalists. Then three published authors read and rank the semifinalist entries, and the top three become the finalists."

"And you're a . . . finalist?"

"That's right."

"Which means you've already been a semi-finalist?"

"Yes."

"Since when?"

"Early April."

Susan looked at her daughter, wondering where the joke was in all this. "If you've known since April that you were a semifinal-ist, why have I never even heard of this contest until this very minute?"

Angie shrugged and looked at her tea. "I knew you would be mad at me for spending so much time doing this, when I should have been working on my precalculus."

Susan stopped long enough to consider that one. She had to admit, Angie had a point. She would have been mad.

"So is that what you've been working on in class since you've been here? The notebook that you always put away every time we walk into the room?" Julie was leaning forward, all smiles.

Angie grinned up at her. "Yeah. Charlotte's been helping me tighten up my plot."

"But why is she helping you now? You must have entered this thing months ago, right?"

"Yes, but the judges for the final rounds are editors and agents. In the rare event that I should actually win my category, they may request the full manuscript. It's not completed yet, but I want to have it as close as possible, just in case."

Susan put her hand over her heart, almost to prove to herself it was still beating. "I'm at a complete loss here. I had no idea."

"Are you mad?" Angie's head was ducked, but she looked at Susan through the top of her eyelashes.

"Well, I'm shocked. And stunned. Floored? Probably. But mad? No, honey, I'm thrilled. Truly, truly thrilled. I just had no idea you were even interested in writing. Why have you never said anything to me about it?"

"You always get mad at me for wasting

time when you find me reading a novel not assigned for homework. I assumed that writing one would be considered even more of a waste of time."

In that moment, the hammer fell. The reality of things Susan had never acknowledged or even understood before. She had lost all clue of who her daughter was. Her vision blurred, but she blinked hard and fast. She was not going to cry right here, in front of everyone. "Honey, I am so sorry. I had no idea. I've been so wrapped up in my own plans for your life that I've completely forgotten to listen to you, haven't I?"

Whitney made a dismissive gesture with her hand. "Don't worry about it, Aunt Susan. We're teenagers. No one ever listens to us." She tilted her head to the side. "I think it's a denial thing, because it's embarrassing to grown-ups that we're so much smarter than they are."

The entire table burst into laughter except for Whitney. She looked around and said, "What? What did I say?"

After dinner, Gary leaned toward Susan and whispered, "Can we talk privately for a second?"

"Sure." They walked to the back part of the room, where no one was sitting at the tables. She turned to him. "What is it?"

"Well, here's the thing. The 'entertainment' " — he put air quotes around the word — "I had planned for this evening . . ." He looked back toward the table. "Well, it was to go see this Christian rock band that is performing in town tonight."

"That sounds great. It's probably the one kind of rock music I can stand, and the kids will love it."

"Well, when I made these plans I didn't understand the full extent of what has been going on with your family. You see . . . the lead singer is Chris. I don't want to do anything that would seem like I'm taking sides against you."

"Chris? As in production-assistant Chris?"

"The very one."

"He's in a Christian rock band?"

"An up-and-coming Christian rock band. In fact, that's his new job. Rumor is they've just landed a recording contract."

Susan looked back at Angie. "She never told me any of this."

"I'm sure she doesn't know about the contract. He's a very humble person and probably would consider it bragging. And . . . well, she wouldn't have told you anyway. Seems like 'rock star' probably isn't an approved career in your mind. Plus, she's a teenager. They don't tell you everything, especially when boys are involved. Trust me, I've been there."

"How old are your kids?"

"Twenty-seven and twenty-four."

"Both out of college?"

"Yep. My oldest daughter went to the University of Tennessee; my youngest just got her master's from Vanderbilt."

"Oh, that's wonderful," Susan said. "I hope I can keep it together long enough to get Angie to that point. You must be really proud."

"Oh, I am. I think she is amazing. You know her, too."

"I do?"

"Charlotte. The kids' tutor."

Susan froze. Instantly, she thought of every moment she'd made disparaging comments about Char in front of him over the last few weeks. And how could a small-town Tennessee farmer afford to pay Vanderbilt tuition? He must have sacrificed so much.

She sighed. She had lived too long in the world only as she wanted to see it. "As of this very moment, I vow to no longer operate on preconceived notions of people. And I think the best place to start is tonight, by going to see Chris's band."

"Good for you." He nodded, then started back toward the group.

Susan cocked her head. "How did Angie convince you to set this up?"

"She didn't." He stopped. "She doesn't know a thing about it."

CHAPTER 38

Early the next morning, Susan put wood in the stove, wondering if this would be her last time. Good riddance to that. But everything else? So much had happened in the past twenty-four hours that she wasn't sure how she'd feel once the final decision was made. She walked over to the dish drain and picked up the coffeepot, but as she did, the lid slipped off and went clattering across the kitchen floor.

"Knock, knock."

Susan jumped at the voice. She looked up at Kendra. "I didn't hear you come in."

"I'm not surprised, given the racket you were making with the coffeepot." There was nothing in Kendra's expression that hinted at what kind of news she brought.

Susan had no intention of playing games, so she put the lid on the counter and simply said, "Well?"

"Why don't you get dressed and come

over to the shack. We're going to film our conversation."

"No." Susan let the one-word answer find its mark.

Kendra simply looked at her for a long time, as if determined not to speak first. "You mind telling me why not?"

"Why are you filming the conversation? So you can give it to your lawyers?" She gestured at the walls and ceilings. "We are being filmed right now, so what's the point of going over there? So you can make one last episode out of it? Like I said, I am no longer a part of this show if you are intent on showing that footage of my conversation with my daughter. I need you to tell me now whether or not we should pack our bags."

Kendra put her hands on the edge of the counter behind her and leaned back. "Listen, I want you to save all this passion for the on-screen interview, so I don't want to tell you everything now. But I believe that you will be more than happy with our conversation once we get over there. There will be no lawyers involved; I can promise you that. Now, can you get dressed and come over as quickly as possible, please? We want to air this footage as soon as possible. Like three hours ago."

Had Kendra actually used the word

'please'? Susan didn't think she'd ever heard that word from her before. It could be a trick, but what did she have to lose at this point? "All right. I'll be there as soon as I can."

"Good." Kendra turned and walked out.

Susan couldn't help but smile as she hurried up the stairs. Still, she didn't want to get too overly confident, because she still didn't know what the terms might be, and Kendra had proven to be less than reliable. But there was hope, and that was something she was more than grateful for. Even if it meant cooking on a wood stove for the rest of the time.

When she sat down in the chair, the stylist took extra care making certain her hair was just right and her makeup perfect. Instead of taking her usual spot behind the camera, Kendra came to sit on an arm chair that had been newly installed adjacent to the couch. She nodded toward the camera, then turned toward Susan. "So . . . we've had a bit of a conflict this week, haven't we?"

"Yes." Susan didn't want to say more, still uncertain how that might go.

"Would you mind explaining, in your own words, what it was all about?"

"Well" — Susan looked toward the camera, her heart pounding — "my daughter and I had a disagreement this week, a big one. I'm certain all parents of teenagers have experienced this to some degree or another. When it all came to a head, we sat at the kitchen table and had a very long, very meaningful talk — the kind of talk where you don't hold anything back." Susan shifted in her seat, trying to think a few steps ahead to what she should and shouldn't say.

"We were both so upset during the conflict that we failed to think about the cameras that are in the farmhouse, so we talked about some deeply personal things that we would not want anyone else to know, and we certainly wouldn't want all of America to know." She cast a pointed glance toward Kendra. "The next morning we became aware that not only had the episode been filmed, but it was going to be the prime footage for the next episode."

"And how did you respond to that?"

"I was furious, of course. Aside from the embarrassment it would cause to me and especially my daughter, everything that we had worked through the night before, all the gains that we'd made, were going to be ruined."

"And you threatened to leave the show if

we used it, correct?"

This was beginning to feel more like a setup than an episode, but Susan couldn't quite make herself hold back. "It wasn't a threat; it was a fact."

Kendra nodded. "You were hoping that this show might help you build your career as an author of cookbooks and lifestyle books."

"I certainly was hoping that it would at least make the public aware of what I've done, what I'm doing."

"You'd sign with a major publisher and there had been plans about you hosting regular segments on the Lisa Lee show."

"Yes, that was the hope."

"What would giving that up mean to you and your family?"

"It means I'll have to sell my house. I'll have to find a job that will at least make the rent for us and figure out something else to do with my life."

"And you are willing to give all that up over one disagreement with the producers?"

"I am willing to give all that up to protect my daughter in any way I can."

Kendra looked at the cameraman. "Perfect. Cut. That's exactly what we need."

Cold dread filled Susan. What had just happened? "I think it's time you explain to me what this is all about."

"Here's the thing. Over the last twenty-four hours we've been running an ad showing you threatening to walk out because of something we were going to show about your daughter."

"Yes, I know." Susan didn't offer any more information than that, and continued to look Kendra evenly in the eye.

"Well, the feedback has been amazing and instantaneous. Your approval rating has gone through the roof. We've received thousands of texts and calls all supporting you. The Facebook page has never received that much traffic. It's like they all needed to see the side of you that was doing what was best for your daughter."

"I always do what is best for my daughter."

"That may be true, but to our viewers some of that comes across as being overly pushy toward, and on behalf of, your daughter. This" — Kendra gestured toward her — "this was going to cost you and your daughter many things, the kind of things that you are usually fighting to gain. And yet you were willing to give it up to protect something you felt was more important. This one was from the heart. America loves it."

"All those other things are from the heart, too." Susan stood up to go.

"Maybe that's the way you see it, but the people you are steamrolling in the process and the people watching them get steamrolled don't necessarily see it that way."

"I do not . . ." Susan stopped. She wouldn't defend herself. Instead, she was going to spend some time thinking about what she'd just been told. "About the footage?"

Kendra waved dismissively. "It's gone. Done. We don't need it when we've got something better to show."

Susan walked back to the farmhouse, and with each step she began to question her entire reason for being. Everything she thought she'd known about herself had proven wrong.

She'd always thought she was one of the best wives around, but James's leaving called that into question. She had told herself it wasn't her doing, it was his, and she knew that was true in a lot of ways. Regardless of whether or not she'd been a less than perfect wife, cheating was not an acceptable response.

In the aftermath she had comforted herself with the fact that at least she was the best possible mother. Now she knew that she had totally missed almost everything about Angie that was important, because she was too busy pushing her own agenda. What else was she missing?

She began to think about the one area of her life that had yet to feel the shake-up. She was pretty certain something was missing there, too. A small idea began to grow in the back of her mind. She would get through the morning breakfast and then make an excuse to get away from everyone for a while. This one was going to require some time alone in prayer.

The kitchen door flew open. "Well? What happened?" Julie's forehead wrinkled in concentration.

"Long story. Short version: we are staying."

Teenaged cheers erupted from behind Julie. *"Woo-hoo!"*

Susan sat down to remove her boots, but called out loudly enough to be heard in the kitchen. "Which means, barn chores. Now."

The kids piled out onto the porch and sat beside her. "Good job, Aunt Susan." Whitney laced up her boots. "I knew you could handle 'em."

"I never had a doubt." Brian nodded slowly as he made this pronouncement.

Angie reached over and hugged her. "I love you, Mom." She stood then, and followed her cousins out the door for the morning chores.

They were staying.

It should have been a relief, but that's not what Julie felt. She didn't feel surprised at all, and it worried her. She realized she'd never let herself think about leaving. Even with the imminent threat, she hadn't planned on going home for one second. It would've been too hard to take.

Thankfully, for now at least, she could keep pretending.

Back in the kitchen after Susan's announcement, the families had gathered for breakfast and it seemed like a good time to plan the day.

"There's no school today," Julie said, "so the three of you get to hang out with your mothers today."

"That sounds" — Whitney pulled her elbow out to the side, made a fist, pumped her arm back and forth like a jaunty pirate — "just *grand.* Nothing we'd rather do than spend every waking moment with our dear old moms, right guys?"

Angie giggled but didn't say anything. Brian mumbled, "Oh boy," and took another bite of cinnamon bread.

"But actually, Mother dearest, we have already thought up a plan for what we might want to do this week, if it's all right with everyone, that is."

"And what would that be?"

"Well, you know how Angie has read a bunch of Amish fiction? She says they all talk about the women getting together to help each other out with things, you know, like quilting, for instance."

"So you want to have a quilting bee?" Julie couldn't help the smile that spread across her face at this small victory.

"Not quilting, per se, because none of us really enjoys it all that much." Okay, not quite victorious. "And we all pretty much stink at it except for you. But she said there is something called an applesauce frolic. Apparently this is when women all get together and spend the day making applesauce."

"And you want to spend the day making applesauce?"

Whitney shook her head. "Not so much. None of us are all that excited about applesauce, either."

"Then what is it, exactly, that you are wanting to do?"

Whitney twisted her arms together, placed them on the table, and leaned forward, an angelic smile on her face. "We thought maybe we'd have a pie and cookie frolic."

"A pie and cookie frolic?"

"Yeah, and instead of inviting all the women of the community, we can invite all the kids from the youth group. They're all curious about what we're doing here. And if I remember correctly, Kendra told us on the first day that we could have friends over here. Isn't that true?"

"I'm shocked that you actually heard her."

"Much less that you can remember that far back." Brian shoved another forkful of eggs into his mouth, dodging his sister's elbow in the process.

"I don't know. What do you think, Susan?" Julie didn't really need to ask what Susan thought, because she knew exactly what she'd say.

No.

Too un-Amish. Too hectic. And certainly too unhealthy. Having a whole party built around making and eating pies and cookies . . . well, that wasn't going to work for her. The sheer bulk of butter and sugar involved would send her over the edge.

Susan, who had been at the kitchen sink scrubbing things since she returned from her interview with Kendra, glanced up from her task. She simply looked at the kids for a moment, thinking through her answer. "I don't see why not." She paused a moment. "Yes. Why don't we do that? When do you have in mind?"

Angie looked up with her mouth slightly open. Julie was certain she must look much the same way.

If Whitney noticed anything unusual, she gave no sign of it; she simply pressed forward with her plan. "How about next week? We can invite them all tomorrow night at youth group. That'll give everyone time to plan accordingly. Maybe next Friday night?"

"Sounds good to me." Susan turned back to her task of washing dishes, but there was a smile on her face.

It sounded good to Julie, too. A bunch of kids coming over to make pies and cookies, to spend time together when it would not involve texting, or video games, or television. This is what the simple life was all about.

"Let's make up some invitations. We'll hand them out tomorrow night." Whitney had turned her attention back to the teenagers.

Julie loved hearing the excitement in her voice. It was a sound that was rarely heard during the school year, between copious amounts of homework and long volleyball practices.

Julie realized she wasn't the only one who

needed this kind of life. Whether they realized it or would admit it, her kids did, too. Now Julie just needed to find a way to keep it. For all of them.

CHAPTER 39

Julie savored a moment in the living room, watching the kids design invitations. The girls were giggling and laughing, with Brian rolling his eyes almost as often. Still, he had a grin on his face that let Julie know he was glad to be included in this bit of "women's work."

"We need to find something more interesting and manly for the guys to do. We're not going to stand around and bake pies and cookies; that much is sure."

"You could have a barn raising." Angie stared up at him with just enough dare in her eyes that all three of them burst out laughing.

"Maybe not quite *that* manly. Although . . ." He rubbed his chin. "We could help Gary start working on that old fence he wants to fix up around the horse corral. A fence raising, if you will."

"That's a good idea, Brian." Angie nodded her approval, but turned back to the card she was creating without ever seeing the glow of approval spread across Brian's cheeks.

"Where is Aunt Susan, again?" Whitney continued coloring a rainbow across the front of an invitation as she asked the question.

"She went down to the creek looking for a particular kind of herb she thought she'd seen growing wild down there."

Julie was more than certain there were no wild herbs growing at the creek. Susan had needed some time alone, and that was the most plausible excuse she could come up with. The last few days had been hard on her. Julie wished she could do something to help, but didn't know what.

There was no reason to sit here wishing for something; she needed to get up and take action. "I'm going out to the garden to see what I can find for our lunch."

The kids all sort of mumbled their acknowledgment without looking up from the task at hand. Julie sat on the back porch and slid her feet into her gardening boots. As she tightened the laces, she couldn't help but compare the convenience of the rubber clogs she wore in her garden at home. They may call it the "simple life," but they couldn't be more wrong. Never would she again think of *simple* as a synonym for *convenient*. "Simple" was so much more.

"Hello, there." Susan bounded up the stairs. "I've had the most amazing idea."

"Yeah?" Julie looked over at her, relieved to see the excitement on her face. "Please tell."

"Lydia's Legacy is done."

"What? But, Susan, that is your life, your call. I think you need to take some serious time and think about a decision like this. All your cooking and hospitality books were a part of that ministry."

"I know. And now they will be a part of the new one. I'm thinking I'll call it Body-Builders, although I'm going to have to do a Google search and make certain that someone hasn't already taken that name. It's pretty catchy, isn't it?"

"BodyBuilders? Like exercise and stuff?"

"No. The Body of Christ, the Church. It will be all about building up each of the parts of the body so that we all grow stronger in our own areas, as well as share what we know in different areas. Lydia's Legacy was too focused on only one area — hospitality. This is going to be so amazing. I'm going to sit down right now and sketch it all out."

"That's great." Julie stood up and started for the door. "I'm going to make a quick trip out to the garden."

"Do you need me to come help you?"

"Nah, that's okay, I've got it handled."

Julie sank a little with each step she took toward the garden. How was it that there were people like Susan who could bounce back from adversity so quickly, make something positive from the bad so easily. She already excelled at so many things while Julie barely seemed to be able to take a step in a forward direction. She sighed, trying to tamp her regret. Because she was indeed thankful that Susan had seemingly found something new she was excited about. She deserved happiness.

Julie walked down the row of cucumbers and stopped to pick a couple. She added them to the basket, then moved over to the leaf lettuce and pulled some leaves from the side of one of the plants. "Stop feeling sorry for yourself. You've got a great life." It was true, and she knew that.

After gathering some tomatoes and onions, she started back toward the farmhouse. This time each step she took reminded her of what waited when she returned home. The busyness, the pressure, the pressure to put more pressure on her kids. The more she thought about it, the more she realized that there was nothing there for her. Except Thomas. But even he piled on the pressure to handle events at his office, to push the kids harder.

She climbed the stairs into the kitchen, trying to force herself out of her melancholy mood. She needed to enjoy the time here that she had left. She took the vegetables over to the sink and rinsed them, then placed them in the strainer to dry.

"Mom, come check out the invitations." Whitney's voice called to her from the living room.

Julie walked to the next room. "Let's see."

Whitney held up a card, a smile of satisfaction on her face. There were stick figures around an oven, and one of the stick figures wearing a skirt was holding what appeared to be a steaming pie. "It's beautiful, isn't it?" She looked at the card, then back toward Julie, a huge grin on her face.

"It's wonderful."

"Check this out." Brian held up a card he'd made, obviously using a straight edge and a ruler. It depicted a meticulously aligned double-railed fence. In the next-to-the-last section, the top rail was broken off one side and touched the ground at what Julie knew must be a forty-five-degree angle

— Brain's work was always precise. "Cool, huh?"

"Totally." It was so wonderful to see her kids enjoying the simplicity of making their own invitations. She thought of the real world, where the invitations were store-bought, or more likely, emailed. "Let me see what you've got, Angie."

Angie held up an incredible scene. She had used nothing but pencil, but with shading and shadows she'd created something almost more realistic than most paintings. It depicted a long table, plates and utensils at each seat, while pies and cookies lined the center. "That's incredible." The words simply flowed from an overwhelmed Julie. Immediately upon saying them, she realized that her adoration for Angie's superior artwork might be hurtful to her kids. She looked around to see their reactions.

Whitney simply nodded. "Yeah, Angie is our resident *artiste*." Brian nodded, but was already at work with a straight edge on another card.

"So how are you going to do the invitations? Are you going to vote on which person's to use, or what?"

"Nah." Whitney shook her head. "We're each making a stack, and we'll take them with us to youth group and hand them out."

Julie wondered if it bothered Whitney that Angie's pictures were so much better than hers, but it didn't seem to. "Are you going to target Brian's invitations to the boys?"

"We thought about that, and then we decided we'd just do it randomly. The pies might be more tempting to some of the guys than a fence raising, and some of the girls might be more interested in knowing that the boys are going to be there fixing fences than they are in baking." Whitney smiled. "I think I will try to target some of the shyer girls with my invitations. They'll see my complete lack of skill and realize that we like people just the way they are around here."

Julie stood amazed at the wisdom that sometimes came from her sixteen-year-old, flighty, seemingly carefree daughter. "That's a good idea."

"Hey, guys, how's it going?" Susan came down the stairs, carrying a clipboard in her right arm. She walked over to the group. "Looks like the invitation making is in full swing."

"Aunt Susan, can I mail an invitation to Chris?"

Julie wasn't certain who showed the most shock at this question, Susan or Angie. Either way, it was time to shut her down.

"Whitney, you know he's not allowed to —"

"He's not on the crew anymore, so it's not illegal to talk to him. Besides, he was the leader of the youth group worship band. All the other kids know him."

Angie hadn't moved a muscle since Whitney started this line of questioning. In fact, Julie wondered if she'd remembered to breathe.

"Well . . ." Susan looked at Angie. "Would you like that, Angie?"

"Yes." There could be no doubt of the hope in her voice.

Susan nodded. "I suppose that would be all right. If you can find his address."

"No problem." Whitney went back to work without further comment. So did Angie, but a smile lit up her entire face.

Susan gestured toward Julie. "Come here and look at what I've done and tell me what you think."

Julie followed her over to the kitchen table. As Susan started setting out her sketches, Julie leaned forward. "Good for you — about the Chris thing, I mean."

"Hey . . ." She shrugged. "Watching him in action the other night, I was more than impressed. Besides, I've learned I need to rethink a few things. Now seems like a good time to start. And speaking of rethinking . . ." She laid out several drawings of a human skeleton, arms outstretched, with various bones labeled.

Susan pointed toward the skull, which was labeled "Christ". "This one was easy, of course, because it's biblical." Then she pointed at the backbone. At the top, near the shoulders she had written "Pastors / Leaders". "The spine is the nerve center of the church, of course, and the pastors and leaders are there because they sort of control the direction that the rest of the body moves. Down here, though" — she pointed at the backbone about halfway down — "are the directors of the various ministries in the church. If the spine is broken down here, it doesn't necessarily shut down the whole body, but it can shut down particular parts of the body. Then here are the lay people who help with all the ministries. They are the legs we stand on, so to speak. And the arms are those with the gift of service; they are always reaching out to help whomever.

"The whole point of this new group will be to support each other in our various ministries, rather than trying to make everyone conform to the skull, or the spine. We'll simply encourage the fingers to be the best fingers possible, the toes to be good toes, and we'll make sure everyone under-stands that he or she is important."

Julie nodded. "Sounds good." Julie sup-posed she was somewhere in the mass of the legs. Not really doing anything special but just doing what she could to help. The body needed its legs, so she was happy about that. Or so she tried to tell herself. "I think I could use a group like that."

"I'm thinking a lot of people could."

CHAPTER 40

The black Suburban rolled up the farmhouse drive, spewing a cloud of dust behind it. Whitney and Brian were running beside the back door long before the vehicle came to a stop. "Dad! Dad!"

"Be careful. Get away from the car until it stops." Even as she said it, Julie knew the admonition would do no good.

When the door opened, they flew into his arms. Thomas put an arm around each of them and hugged tightly. "Wow, it's just been two weeks, but I've missed you guys!"

Brian pulled away and motioned with his head toward the barns. "Come check out our kids."

"You have kids? I didn't even know you were married." He kept his arm around Whitney until she, too, backed away.

"Ha, ha. Very funny. He means baby goats, Dad. Well, they're not so much babies anymore, because we're not having to bottle feed them anymore, but they're still little and really cute."

"Sounds terrific. Let me hug your mother first, though. I don't want her to think that goats are more important to me than she is." Thomas put both arms around Julie and pulled her close. "I've missed you."

"Gross, Dad. Can we move it along now?"

Whitney pulled at his arm, but he didn't loosen his grip. "No, we cannot."

Julie sank into his hug, reveling in his strength and support. "I've missed you, too."

He kissed the top of her head. "I guess I'm about to go see me some kids."

"Excellent! Let's get moving." Whitney took three giant steps toward the barn, then stopped and planted her feet. "Wait, where's Angie? She'll want to come with us. And Aunt Susan, too."

"I'll go find them." Brian ran toward the house, but before he reached it, the screen door screeched open and Susan and Angie emerged.

"Welcome back, Thomas." Susan waved and smiled as she hurried toward them.

Angie jogged across the distance and flung her arms around him. "Hi, Uncle Thomas."

As they walked toward the barn, the children talked nonstop about what they had been doing and what they had learned to do, and gave him the updates of family olympics. "It sounds like you all have had an amazing summer."

"You haven't seen anything yet. Wait until tomorrow's pie frolic and fence raising."

The heat of the kitchen was unbearable, but given the giggles, the sound of which must have carried for miles, Susan thought the teenagers had somehow failed to notice. The smell of baked goods, some burned, some perfect, filled the air between the house and the barn.

"We've got a new pie. Who is game for a piece?" Whitney bounded down the back stairs toward the group of mostly teenage boys involved in the fence raising. They all set down their hammers and saws and hurried over to the plate Whitney held above her head. "One at a time, one at a time."

Two lone figures remained fence side, not bothering to come for this latest sample. Angie and Chris stood side by side. Chris was actually working on a length of fence, Angie standing close beside him holding nails. They both smiled almost constantly.

"You know" — Gary came up beside Susan, a sliver of apple pie wrapped in a napkin in his hand — "I'm happy enough that you let the kids invite Chris just because

435

I think he's a great kid, and I think he and your daughter really are growing to care about each other. But, to be completely honest, even if none of that were true, the look on Kendra's face when she saw him . . ." He began to chuckle and soon Susan joined him. A moment later, they were leaning on each other's shoulders, laughing all-out.

She pulled back and nodded. "You're right. That alone would have been worth it." She looked toward the shack and giggled a little more.

He wiped his forehead with the back of his sleeve. "Susan, I need to tell you. . . ."

Her heart all of sudden lurched.

"I've . . . got to leave. Tomorrow. It looks like I might not make it back before the end of the summer. But I didn't want to leave without saying that being here with you has made this summer so worth it. To me."

"Where are you going?"

He stared off in the distance. "Long story."

The sound of hammering and saws started up again as the boys finished their treats. Susan looked at Gary, and the feelings of abandonment she'd just gotten over all came flooding back. "They need your help over there. I guess it's best that we say good-bye now."

"Susan, wait, I really want to see you after this is all over."

"Sure. The next time you're in California, give me a call."

Like that was ever going to happen. She turned and hurried into the house, not wanting to show the emotion that was overcoming her. All along she'd been telling herself she wasn't interested, and yet, with just one good-bye, that proved to be a lie. And now it was over without even really ever having started.

As the last of the kids left, Julie collapsed in a chair. "Whew. That was quite the shindig."

"The house still smells good." Thomas made an appreciative sniff of the air. "In spite of a couple of burned pies."

"Nobody's perfect." Whitney dropped to the floor, a chocolate-chip cookie in her hand. "So, Angie, in those Amish books you read, do they talk about how hot the house gets during those cooking frolics? We've got air-conditioning here, and I'm still soaked with sweat."

Angie, her face still a little dreamy, shook her head. "Nobody wants to read about sweat. They read those books to escape for a little while into a simpler lifestyle. One

they wish they could lead."

Whitney twisted her hair around her finger and looked up at the ceiling as if in thought. "Seems to me, we're the ones who make our own lives overly complicated. We've got lots more choices than Amish people do — if we choose to do thirty things, then we shouldn't be whining about how busy it is."

Whitney's words sank right through to Julie. There was so much truth in them.

Then the story of Stephen came back to her. Even the apostles couldn't do everything, no matter if it was a good thing, a thing that truly needed to be done. What she needed to do was find out what it was she was *supposed* to do, and do it with all her strength. She just didn't know what that was.

As they climbed into bed that night, Thomas said, "I'm really amazed at the difference in you and the kids after this summer. You all seem so much happier and more content."

Julie shrugged. "We've been out of the pressure cooker for a while."

"You're like a different person." He put his hand on her cheek. "I was a large part of the heat in that cooker, I know, and I think we need to figure all that out. I want to hold on to what you have found here, if we can. We need to sit down and perhaps look at our goals for the coming year, and readjust accordingly."

"I was thinking the same thing earlier tonight. We need to pick out the things that are most important to us and focus more on them."

He nodded. "Maybe we should make a mission statement for our family and ourselves. Try to stay more on task in the future."

Julie nodded, having no idea what her mission statement might entail, other than taking care of her family. But how did something as vague as that protect her from exactly the same situation she'd already been in?

She didn't know the answer, but she went to bed praying that God would show her.

CHAPTER 41

The final weeks passed without major event — good or bad. Susan somehow managed to push her way through them, put on a happy face, and do what she'd come here to do. Angie would be able to complete high school in the home she'd grown up in — that had been secured — and she had further solidified her plans for the new BodyBuilders. Those were the things that were most important.

She padded down the stairs for the final morning. Clanking sounds were coming from the kitchen, letting her know that Julie was already up and about. Time to celebrate their successful completion. "Good morning." She rounded the corner, already smiling.

" 'Morning." Julie quickly turned away, busying herself at the stove. She had turned fast, too fast.

Susan walked closer. "You okay?"

"Fine." Julie didn't look at her; she just sniffled.

"What's wrong?"

Julie shrugged and turned toward her, blinking fast. "I don't want to go back."

Susan stopped herself from her impulsive response, *you're kidding me.* "Julie, you are one of the smartest women I know, but there's a new word I want to teach you, and you need to add it to your vocabulary effective immediately."

"Really? What?"

"No." Susan paused long enough for it to sink in a little. "You can't allow people to pressure you into filling your schedule so full that you don't have time to do what you do best. Pick one or two projects you are really passionate about, and let someone else step up to the plate to handle the others."

"It sounds like a cop-out to me."

"No, it's not; it's common sense." She knew that Julie wasn't convinced. "Have I shown you my newest sketches for Body-Builders?"

"No."

Susan hurried upstairs, then back again. She pulled out the sketch showing the skeleton but with some of the muscles and organs inside.

"I see where Angie gets her artistic talent. This looks like it's straight out of a science book."

"Hardly." Susan shook her head, seeing a million flaws. "But here's the point. We don't just need the skeleton — structural people — in our lives. The body won't live without its vital organs, either. I think that has become the problem with so many of the things we do as women. We need the heart." She drew a circle around it. "No one really sees the heart; it's buried beneath layers of bones and muscle. Think about the heart's job. It shoots blood in a million different directions all over the body. Still, no one ever says, 'Gee, the heart is really good at helping the brain,' or 'look at how well the heart helps the left leg balance the body while the right leg is injured.' No, it is behind the scenes. And that . . . is you. You are the heart of almost anything we do. And I think we've spent far too long giving praise to the brain and the left leg without ever acknowledging the heart behind it all."

"You are overstating. I'm just a little worker bee behind the scenes."

"No. That's not true. You take some time and pray about it. You'll see that I'm right."

The thud of footsteps on the back porch caused them both to turn. By the time Ken-

dra had pushed open the kitchen door with
her typical "Knock, knock," Julie had wiped
her eyes and busied herself at the coffeepot.

"Good morning, ladies. I have a little treat
for the families today."

"Really? What?" Susan asked.

"We were thinking that as your last activity here on the ranch, we would set up a
television in the living room and let you
watch all your episodes. I think you will find
it eye-opening and entertaining."

"Or embarrassing." Julie sort of laughed
as she said it.

"Endearing," Kendra said. "That's what
this whole thing has been. As soon as the
kids are done with their morning barn
chores we'll get started."

"Sounds great." Although in truth, Susan
wasn't so certain that it did. She'd come
here as the woman who thought she knew
everything about parenting and domestic
life, and was leaving here realizing just how
far she had to go. Something about watching the demise played out on television
made her wonder if she wanted to watch.
She thought perhaps Julie's word might
have summed it up best.

Embarrassing.

Julie and Susan sat in the rocking chairs,

the kids gathered around them on the floor, as Kendra pointed the remote at the television monitor and pressed play. Of course, standing all around them was the camera crew, prepared to capture every expression, every sentence, in case they said or did something interesting during this viewing.

The opening scene showed Lisa Lee in her studio kitchen, gathering all the ingredients for shoo-fly pie. She was standing behind the counter, talking about the nuances involved in the recipe, and how even seasoned cooks had trouble making this one just right — at least just right for someone who knew what they were supposed to taste like.

She smiled at the camera and said, "So we're going to have our *Almost Amish* family try their hand at making this. We've thrown in a few twists, just to make it a bit more interesting." She grinned over to someone just off-camera. "Today, for instance, we're going to show their first attempt at cooking on their new wood stove, and we're going to have Julie be the one to cook. She's not a fan of cooking or the spotlight, but let's see what happens." The scene went to a clip of Julie sitting in the interview room that first day.

"Get a grip, Julie." She watched her hands

tremble on the screen. "Stop being so melodramatic. It will be fine."

The audience giggled; then the camera returned to Lisa Lee. "We've let Susan try to coach her for the last day or so, with some rather . . . interesting results. Take a look."

The camera went to a snippet of Julie working on her pie crust, then looking out the window when the girls called her to come outside. It then cut to a wide-angle shot of Julie and the kids working the clothes wringer and laughing, with an obviously annoyed Susan approaching from behind. "Why aren't you working on the pie?"

Julie and Susan argued on-screen a bit before ending with Julie saying, "It's not about pies, or even clean curtains. It's about slowing down enough to really spend time with the family. Now, get over here and start enjoying it."

Everyone in the living room laughed at the memory of their first days there. Susan shook her head. "I had no idea I sounded so grumpy."

Julie reached over and squeezed her arm. "I'm sure it was the editing."

The scene then switched to Lisa Lee in the studio, laughing along with the rest of

445

the studio audience at the clip they'd just seen. "To make things even more complicated, we put a couple of different kinds of molasses in the pantry. Of course, we put the *correct* one behind the less favorable one. Not only that, but we had the production assistant do something we call 'Greeking the labels,' which means covering up any kind of brand name. Julie went to select her ingredients about an hour ago. Let's see which one she got."

The camera showed Julie picking out the flour and sugar, and reaching for the front bottle of molasses. The scene flipped back to Lisa Lee. "Uh-oh. Wrong choice." Everyone giggled. "All right, now I'm going to get us started on making a shoo-fly pie, and we'll check back in on our Tennessee progress in a little while."

By the time it got to the end of the episode, Julie had laughed so hard, she had tears pouring down her face. "It's bad enough to have me cooking, but to set me up like that . . . no wonder."

On they went to the next episode and the next. Over and over the pattern seemed to emerge of Julie noticing someone who needed help, or encouragement, or someone to talk to. As much as she knew that editing condensed everything, she began to understand for the first time that Susan maybe did have a point. She did notice things that no one else did. She noticed those things in her regular life, too, but she was often so busy she couldn't take the time to stop and cheer someone up or praise someone.

For the first time in a long time she saw that she maybe did have a gift. And for the first time, she knew what she had to do. She had to make sure she had the time to use the gift, make sure she was available to help the people right in front of her needing help.

CHAPTER 42

Julie stood outside her California home and stared. It had been three months since she'd seen it last, and she found it amazing what a new appreciation she had for the place. "It feels good to be home."

"It's good to have you home," Thomas said, coming up beside her." You know what I found out when you were all gone? That a neat, organized, and quiet house isn't nearly as wonderful as I'd imagined it to be."

Julie laughed. "Well, one of the things I learned while I was gone was not to overextend myself so much. So I think we all know better than to think my house will ever be neat and organized to Reynolds family standards. But it's going to be filled with love. I'm going to make sure to set time aside to take care of my most important people — my family."

"Well, good luck with that. Wait until you see the pile of phone messages you have waiting for you. And I can't begin to imagine what your email in-box is going to look like."

"No worries. Susan had me practicing the word 'no' all the way home on the plane."

Whitney laughed. "But *she* didn't take that word so well when you gave her that for an answer, did she?"

"No, she didn't." Julie smiled at the memory.

"You told Susan no? About what?"

"She's starting a new group at church to replace Lydia's Legacy. Instead of trying to teach everyone about how to be a gourmet cook and hostess extraordinaire, it's going to be a group of women with different gifts who get together to support each other. Help each other learn how to do things better that they don't do well, but also to let women know that it's okay if you lack a gift someone else has in bucket loads."

"What did she want you to do?"

"She wanted me to be the assistant administrator. You know, handle the enrollment, make sure that the groups have all their supplies each week, things like that."

"Sounds like something you'd be great at."

"Maybe. But I don't think it's where I want to be. I don't want to be running around fixing the details. I think I'm supposed to be available to talk to people during the class, see if anyone is feeling left out, whatever. And, at my suggestion" — she looked toward Whitney and smiled — "we're going to do a special quilting project. It will be a good chance for the women to sit around and talk to each other, and we can give the quilts to charity. That is something I can get excited about."

Thomas smiled and kissed her on the cheek.

"And by the way, I've invited Susan and Angie over for dinner tomorrow night. And I've also invited another friend, too, although I'm not certain they'll make it."

"Someone mysterious?"

"You might say that."

Susan leaned back on one of Julie's lounge chairs, sipping an iced tea and eating a bite of chips and salsa. The lounge was wiped clean, but she felt it could use a good scrubbing. She pushed the thought aside. That was just who her sister-in-law was — distracted, messy, and the biggest, most beautiful heart she'd ever met. The kids were screaming and splashing in the pool, enjoying the best of southern California life.

Thomas looked over the top of the grill. "Doorbell just rang."

"Oh, Susan, will you get that for me? I need to finish mixing up my guacamole."

"Sure." Susan walked through the house to the front door, prepared to tell the neighborhood kids that it wasn't open swim right now. She pulled open the door. "It's not —" She had to grip the doorknob to hold herself upright. "What . . . what are you doing here?"

Gary smiled as he extended a bouquet of flowers. "Uh, would you rather that I not be here?"

"No!" Susan said the words with a bit too much force. "Please forgive my lack of manners. Come in, and please tell me how it is you came about being here right now."

"Your sister-in-law invited me."

"How? You've been gone."

"I got her cell number from Kendra, and I called her yesterday and told her I would be in the area and asked if she thought you'd still be open to seeing me. I guess it was sort of a juvenile thing to do, instead of just calling you directly, but . . . well, what can I say? She invited me to dinner tonight and suggested we make it a surprise."

"How long are you in town?"

"A week. Although, I'm here on business and will be in L.A. a good bit of the time. Julie invited my business associate, too, but

I wanted to clear it with you before he comes here."

"Why would you clear it with me?"

"It's . . . uh . . . Chris."

"A business associate?"

"Long story. But he's actually got a gig playing at one of the larger churches in Thousand Oaks tonight. Do you think the kids would want to go?"

"Please come in, and we'll find out."

"Hey, Gary, good to see you." Brian was the first of the kids to notice his arrival. They barely blinked at his appearance; somehow he just fit in so well. Soon they all joined in a happy chorus of greetings.

Susan waited until they calmed down to say, "It turns out that Chris and his band are in Thousand Oaks tonight. Would you want to drive down to see them?"

Angie was out of the pool drying off within a millisecond. "When do we leave?"

The teenagers barely stayed long enough to eat before they disappeared. As the grown-ups lingered over dessert and conversation, Julie said, "I'm going to miss that farm. I hope I get back to see it sometime."

"So do I." Gary looked at Susan. "And I'm hoping Susan wants to see it again, too."

"I'd like that."

"Good. How about next weekend?"

"Are you still working there?"

"Yes. And no." He toyed with his coffee cup. "You probably should also know my last name is not Macko. It's Buchanan, just like Charlotte's."

"I don't understand."

"I am still sort of working at the farm. You might say that I . . . own the place."

"What? I thought it was some burned-out record producer in Nashville who . . ." Susan stopped talking and looked at him. "Are you kidding me?"

He shook his head. "I was ready to slow down a little, and it was just what I needed."

"I suspected it all along." Julie took a sip of her Diet Coke, looking a bit too smug.

"You did not," Susan said.

"Yep, that's my gift. Watching people. And from the beginning I noticed that Kendra gave him way too much respect for him to be a handyman. And in the restaurant in Nashville, those waitresses knew who you were. That's why they put us back in the special room."

"That's why you were using a fake last name." Susan finally began to understand exactly what had happened.

He nodded. "And that's the kind of stuff I'm ready to move away from. I'm ready to be just plain ol' Gary. Of course, if I keep

453

hanging out with this one and the path she's on, they'll be giving us special tables because of her."

"You think you could handle that?" Susan teased.

"I'd sure like to find out."

EPILOGUE

She couldn't imagine a more fulfilling day: an entire morning spent packaging beautiful hand-sewn quilts, preparing them to be delivered to a school for orphans in South Africa. Each quilt contained squares with handwritten messages from the women who had worked on them. Some held Bible verses, others, a word of encouragement. This was the second box to be shipped this year, and the notes of thanks had been overwhelming.

Julie's fingers ached from last-minute touch-up sewing; her back ached from hours spent being up late trying to get these finished in time to ship for the Christmas holidays. Julie put the last box in the shipping container and stretched out her arms and back. She looked at her watch. There was forty-five minutes before the Body-Builders meeting. Today, she was to give her report on the quilts, their impact, and hold up the two quilts that were being kept here as a silent auction — the money which would go to help the same school in South Africa.

There wasn't enough time to make it home, so she decided to treat herself and stop in at the local Starbucks. As she sat sipping her tall, nonfat, double-shot latte, she watched a couple of women walk through the door. Each held a clipboard in her hand and a stressed-out expression on her face. Julie recognized them both from the junior high PTA. They comprised the hospitality committee and had each been more than a little upset when Julie told them she would not be renewing her pledge to bring in homemade baked goods to the teachers' meeting once a month. Julie had told them she would be more than happy to buy muffins from the bakery and bring them in, but the women had been adamant: the teachers deserved home-baked goods.

"Yes, I agree that they do, but I simply won't have time for that this year." That had been her final answer.

As the women walked past her with their coffees in hand, Julie overheard one of them whisper to the other, "She doesn't have time to cook for her kids' teachers, but she has time to hang out all day in a coffee shop."

The words found their mark and stung more than a little bit. Guilt began to grow heavier and heavier upon her shoulders, until she found it hard to take the next step. Then . . . she remembered what she had already accomplished today.

She remembered the way her household was running so much more smoothly now. How they'd managed to find a few nights a week to eat homemade meals she'd actually enjoyed cooking.

She thought of Brian and Whitney, how both seemed to be smiling more. How Thomas and she had never been closer.

She remembered the hours spent two weeks ago praying with a woman who'd looked exhausted and desperate at Body-Builders.

She remembered the quilts and all they would mean to the children overseas: children whose teachers never got fresh-baked goods from parents.

That's when the thought that had been residing in pieces throughout Julie's mind finally crystallized into one cohesive and indelible truth. She stood up and walked from the coffee shop.

When she got to her car, she looked in the rearview mirror for just a moment. She saw

the face of a woman who was making a difference.

"I love my life."

She started the car and drove off.

ACKNOWLEDGMENTS

Heavenly Father — For Your grace and love beyond what I can fathom

Lee Cushman — For your love and support in all things. Hooray for us — we built a house and survived to talk about it (and are still speaking to each other!)

Caroline Cushman — You are an amazing, loving, and upbeat person — truly beautiful inside and out. I want to be like you when I grow up

Ora Parrish — I'm quite certain there has never been a more loving and supportive mother to have ever walked this planet

Leah Cushman — Your courage and love always inspire me to be a stronger and better person

Carl, Alisa, Katy, and Lisa — It is wonderful to be part of such a fun family

Gary, Carolyn, Lori, Kathleen, Brenna, Kristyn, Judy, Denice — Great friends and cheerleaders

Carrie Padgett, Mike Berrier, Shawn Grady, and Julie Carobini — Writing buddies extraordinaire

Dave Long — You are an amazing editor, motivator, and friend. I am so grateful that I get to work with you

Shana Oates — For patiently walking me through the inside world of reality television

QUESTIONS FOR CONVERSATION

1) Amish life is much more difficult than modern life in so many ways. Why do you think many modern women envy this lifestyle?

2) Name three things about modern life you would be more than happy to give up. Name three that you couldn't do without.

3) Were your parents more like Julie, who trusts her kids to find their own way; or Susan, who believes that kids need to be pushed to achieve their potential? Which kind of parent are you (or which kind do you think you will be)?

4) There is a fine line between pushing yourself (and your kids) too hard and being lax. How do you try to differentiate between the two?

5) Susan had always envisioned herself as the quintessential wife and mother. When her marriage fell apart, a large part of her self-esteem began to erode. From which of your strengths do you derive the most self-worth? What would happen if that suddenly fell apart?

6) Do you consider yourself more of a Susan, type A, in control person; or a Julie, type B, pushed around by the type A person?

7) Can you think of a God-given gift or talent that you possess but have been too busy to use?

ABOUT THE AUTHOR

Kathryn Cushman is a graduate of Samford University with a degree in pharmacy. She is the author of four previous novels including *Leaving Yesterday* and *A Promise to Remember,* which were both finalists for the Carol Award in Women's Fiction. Kathryn and her family currently live in Santa Barbara, CA.

She enjoys hearing from readers at kath ryncushman.com and on Facebook.